BRIMSTONE KISS

PHANTOM QUEEN DIARIES BOOK 10

SHAYNE SILVERS
CAMERON O'CONNELL

ARGENTO
PUBLISHING

CONTENTS

Shayne Silvers & Cameron O'Connell

Brimstone Kiss

The Phantom Queen Diaries Book 10

A TempleVerse Series

ISBN 13: 978-1-947709-38-6

© 2020, Shayne Silvers / Argento Publishing, LLC

info@shaynesilvers.com

SHAYNE AND CAMERON

Shayne Silvers, here.

Cameron O'Connell is one helluva writer, and he's worked tirelessly to merge a story into the Temple Verse that would provide a different and unique *voice*, but a complementary *tone* to my other novels. *SOME* people might say I'm hard to work with. But certainly, Cameron would never...

Hey! Pipe down over there, author monkey! Get back to your writing cave and finish the next Phantom Queen Novel!

Ahem. Now, where was I?

This is book 10 in the Phantom Queen Diaries, which is a series that ties into the existing TempleVerse with Nate Temple and Callie Penrose. This series could also be read independently if one so chose. Then again, you, the reader, will get SO much more out of my existing books (and this series) by reading them all in tandem.

But that's not up to us. It's up to you, the reader.

You tell us...

HELL HATH NO FURY LIKE A GODDESS SCORNED...

Thanks to a witchy homebrew, Quinn MacKenna—part-time goddess, full-time troublemaker—has slipped past death's door to rekindle an old flame and snuff out an old friend.

But in order to do that, Quinn will need allies, be they an alcoholic ferryman, a deadly Horseman, or some of the most feared and respected gods this side of the afterlife.

In a do or die effort to track down her old nemesis, Quinn must first expose dark truths, strike a bargain with Hades himself, and journey to a realm fraught with bloodshed and brimming with booze. The sort of place only a warrior could love—or a scrappy redhead from Boston.

Quinn quickly becomes immersed in all manner of schemes and intrigues that threaten to distract her from her goals—like starting a bar fight in Valhalla, or flying with the Valkyries, or surviving the mists of Niflheim with the power of a stolen kiss. Quinn's devil may care attitude will lead her down a brimstone path paved with good intentions, reminding her that, sometimes, you have to be willing to lose everything if you want to find anything.

Especially if that thing happens to be a mythical city littered with ancient treasures.

In the end, Quinn will have no choice but to wallow in the past or embrace her future as her toughest crucible threatens to become her greatest failure. Will she emerge victorious, or will she remain doomed to wander the beyond for all eternity?

Come hell or high water, there's only one way to find out.

DON'T FORGET! VIP's get early access to all sorts of Temple-Verse goodies, including signed copies, private giveaways, and advance notice of future projects. AND A FREE NOVELLA! Click the image or join here: www.shaynesilvers.com/l/38599

FOLLOW and LIKE:

Shayne's FACEBOOK PAGE

Cameron's FACEBOOK PAGE

We try our best to respond to all messages, so don't hesitate to drop us a line. Not interacting with readers is the biggest travesty that most authors can make. Let us fix that.

I wished I could say I went strutting towards that bright light everyone talks about when I'd died. I'd given it some thought before—how my every step would be accompanied by a chorus of angelic harmonies, how I'd tip my halo as though I'd just turned water into whiskey, how a host of cherub angels in their silk diapers would throw open Heaven's pearly gates the instant St. Peter himself crossed my name off the VIP guest list, his fellow apostles ushering me in with tears of joy running down their holy faces, and how I'd be greeted by martyrs lazing on cumulus couches and nimbostratus armchairs.

If only.

First of all, I was pretty damned sure Heaven had blacklisted me some time ago for conduct unbecoming. Secondly, I had a sneaking suspicion I'd left the Almighty's jurisdiction altogether; being a part-time goddess came with all sorts of theological conundrums I hadn't even considered yet, including a debate as to who or what had rights to my immortal soul— assuming I still had one. But then, since I wasn't really dead, I'd banked on sorting all that out later, thank God.

In any case, there was no white light. There were no heralds harking. There were no haloes, no chubby baby angels, no saints, no cloud furniture, and definitely no bottles of aged whiskey with my name splashed across their label being served by John, the Baptist Bartender—another fantasy I'd entertained.

There was, however, a creepy guy with a boat.

"Alright, it's your turn."

The boatman leaned forward, his blood-curdling words slithering through my mind as he passed me a fresh beer. The fact that he hadn't slurred a single syllable confounded me under the circumstances, but then maybe that was because he hadn't actually spoken. Much to my dismay, the creepy bastard's mouth was sewn shut with a knotted leather cord like poor Billy from *Hocus Pocus*. Not that his impairment had kept him from drinking; the ivory-skinned horror had polished off his last beer by practically dousing himself with it, leaving me feeling more than a little queasy.

Of course, that might also have been the result of the three beers I'd had to toss back to keep pace with him, or perhaps the boatman's appearance in general; he wore a burlap robe covered in spilled beer, his ebony eyes sitting like chips of obsidian in the deep hollows of his face, one fleshless, skeletal hand wound tight around the beer can. I found myself staring at the proffered drink, thinking how great it would be if I could shoot laser-beams from my eyes so I could blow the beverage to smithereens and call this whole thing off. Or, better yet, wings to fly away from here. Why hadn't *those* come with my upgrade from mere mortal to goddess? Stupid, useless godhood.

"Fine." I snatched the beer from the ferryman's hand...or tried to, at least. Instead, I nearly toppled over and ended up rocking the boat so violently that Charon—the boatman's name, supposedly—had to plant his paddle, which looked increasingly like a freaking halberd the more I drank, to keep us from tumbling into the churning river water below. The second he touched it, green runes flared to life along its length, reminding me of a canine companion I very much missed.

"You won't win," Charon insisted.

"Aye, well, I don't drink like I used to," I grouched, my eyes pinched shut while I fought to reestablish my equilibrium. Unfortunately, that just made things worse; the misty riverbank we'd reached not so long ago reeked with the stench of brimstone and copper pennies, undercut by the faint odor of cheap beer. "Besides, I wasn't the one who started this."

"Pay me, and you're free to go."

I opened my eyes to find Charon holding out an empty, grasping hand, a close-lipped smile spread across his leathery face, pulling at the seams of his skin. The bony digits of the other caressed the ice chest he sat upon, fondling its plastic exterior like a possessive lover.

"I told ye, I don't know what you're on about."

"Your coin. I can't let you off without it. Check under your tongue. Sometimes they put it there. I have no idea why."

"Aye?" Without thinking, I began probing my mouth with my fingers, wondering if Charon were right, somehow. Maybe I'd missed it...wait, no. That was absurd. I pointed an accusatory, spit-soaked finger at the ferryman. "Dammit! That's not funny."

But Charon was already laughing so hard I thought he might bust the cord binding his mouth shut. I realized he'd already cracked the beer he'd tried giving me and drank at least some of its contents, leaving a fresh stain splashed across his cheeks and chin. Crazy, alcoholic bastard.

"I don't give up," I growled. "Ye haven't won, yet."

"It's just a matter of time. And we have a whole lot more of that than I'll need." Charon poured the rest of the beer over his face like a drowning man before crumpling it between his skeletal hands, relishing the crunching sound it made. "I can keep this up for eternity."

Unfortunately, I couldn't disagree with him; Charon certainly had me over a barrel. After downing Circe's potion—effectively a homebrew designed to keep me in a perpetual coma while I sorted out this whole Underworld business—and saying farewell to my friends, I'd somehow ended up in his boat, floating downriver, unable to explain how I'd gotten there or why I didn't have a coin to pay him for his services. Something which, it turned out, was tantamount to treason here in the Underworld.

Not that Charon had been particularly understanding; the boatman had threatened to throw me overboard ages ago for wasting his time. In fact, it wasn't until I noticed his booze supply that I'd managed to reason with him. And by reason I mean challenge him to a drinking contest with one simple rule: whoever quit first had to do whatever the other wanted. In my case, that meant getting him to ferry me to wherever Max had ended up, then to find Ryan before he went and crashed the biggest after party of them all. It had only occurred to me after Charon took me up on my offer without so much as a secondary condition that I might have made a mistake.

Oh, well.

You die and you learn, I guess.

I sighed, my sluggish, vaguely nostalgic thoughts drifting back to the friends I'd left behind, to my sleeping crew and my former companions. Had James and Circe already begun their lover's dance, moving to that clumsy, beautiful choreography which governs all our steps? Were Tinkerbell and Tiger Lily thriving under Barca's care? Were Cathy and Eve still soaring the skies in Fae? And what about those I'd come to find? What were they up to in this infernal place? I shook my head, hoping to clear it, only to find Charon studying me with a raptorial gaze that made my skin crawl. Eventually, he sniffed and scratched at his head as if at a loss what to do with me.

To be honest, I felt the same way.

"What d'ye plan to do to me if I lose?" I asked, my skin crawling at the idea of being under Charon's thumb—not to mention the notion of actually *losing*, which was perhaps even worse.

"Maybe I'll have you take over for a while. I could use a vacation. The boss says dead people don't get sick days, and so neither do I." Charon snapped his bony fingers. "Or maybe I'll see what Hecate would give me for you. She really enjoys her pets."

"I'm not exactly domesticated," I muttered, mustering my drink-addled thoughts for another round. "Come on, then. Give us another."

Charon gleefully retrieved another beer and tossed it my way. This time I caught it, having sobered up at least enough to manage that. I popped the top, listened to the beer sizzle and froth, and took a long pull. I wiped at my lips with the back of my hand, swallowed, and felt his swill work its way through me.

"This stuff is the worst." I held the can up, squinting. The beer had no label, though I noticed it was decorated with a skull-and-crossbones symbol that seemed to waver in the dim red light that suffused the cavernous chamber we drifted in, almost as if the emblem were being jostled by a rippling current. The effect left me feeling dizzy.

"Yeah, well, it should have turned your soul inside out by now," Charon replied, shrugging. "I'm just waiting to see how much longer you can stand it."

"Wait, what?"

"Oh, look. We've got company." Charon flicked his eyes to the foggy

4

bank, where a cloaked figure had appeared as if by magic. "Guess we'll have to finish this some other time."

I opened my mouth to reply, then closed it, caught off guard by the newcomer's presence. There was something familiar about him, about the way he walked towards us, that I couldn't put my finger on. Indeed, it wasn't until he threw back his hood and stared at me like I was some sort of apparition, and not the other way around, that I recognized him.

"Quinn? Is that you?"

"Hemingway?" I scowled, trying to remember when I'd last seen Othello's lover in the flesh and failed. New York, maybe? God, had it been that long? "What are ye doin' here?"

"I *work* here. But what about you?" Hemingway's eyes, so much older and wiser than the handsome cast of his twenty-something features would have led me to believe, danced back and forth between Charon and me so fast I thought he might be having a seizure. "You shouldn't be here. How did you cross over?"

"If I say it's a long story, would ye leave it at that?" I asked, hoping the Horseman of Death wouldn't grill me too much about how I'd circumnavigated death's application process. Hell, I hadn't even sent in my resume, and my references needed some serious updates.

"So much for that Guide to Hell," Hemingway growled, clearly frustrated. "He had one job."

"I dare you to fire him," the ferryman chimed in with a blood-curdling wheeze of laughter, slapping at his beer-soaked knees.

"Very funny, Charon. So, why didn't you let anyone know you'd found a stowaway?"

"I would have mentioned it, eventually."

"Eventually?"

"Probably."

"Of course." Hemingway massaged the bridge of his nose. "We've had a break in. One of the old entrances. The boss wants you to check it out."

Charon muttered something surly and anatomically impossible under his breath. Or in the back of his mind? Honestly, I didn't want to give it too much thought; telepathy wasn't as appealing as Patrick Stewart had made it out to be. Either way, it was clear the boatman wasn't eager to go run an errand on behalf of whoever ran this particular branch of the Underworld.

"Was it the Eighth Sea gate, by chance?" I asked, dimly aware that the odds of Ryan *and* someone else breaking into the Underworld back to back were highly unlikely. "Ye know, the Titan realm?"

"How would you know that?" Hemingway stared daggers at me. "I think maybe it's time you give me that long story of yours."

"Sorry, can't." I waved him off. "Charon and I have a drinking contest to get back to."

"You what?" The Horseman glanced down at the beer can I held with an expression of confusion, then complete abhorrence. "Don't drink that! Are you insane?"

"It's her fourth one," Charon replied, sounding somehow smug *and* impressed at the same time.

"But that's...that's...she shouldn't have been able to do that."

"Right?" Charon said, holding his hands up as if he had no idea what was going on.

"The hell are ye two on about?" I eyed the beer can with sudden interest, holding it at arm's length as though it were a snake about to strike. "What is this stuff, some sort of poison?"

"No."

"Yes!"

The Horseman and the ferryman glared at one another, clearly at odds. Eventually, Hemingway turned his attention to me, his panicked expression dwindling until only awe remained. He cleared his throat and gestured at the beer.

"That's Charon's special brew. He makes it from the waters of the River Styx. The river you're on, now."

I blinked owlishly, processing what the Horseman said with so much difficulty it felt like I was a computer from the dial-up era. Seconds passed while I replayed his comments regarding the River Styx, after which I realized not only where I was, but also who I'd challenged to a drinking contest: Charon, the ferryman who transported souls to their respective realms as dictated by the sort of person they'd been in life. In the Greek tradition, this had included everything from paradise to perdition, including some exceedingly unpleasant locales I had no desire to visit. The River Styx, meanwhile, has its own role in mythology, not the least of which being the part it played in making Achilles a demigod badass—all except for his poor ankle, which hadn't gotten doused.

Which I guessed meant I'd been drinking Achilles' bath water.

Gross.

"That's filthy," I said, swatting at the boatman, who leaned back to avoid the blow with more grace than I'd have given him credit for. "And how d'ye know it wouldn't kill me?"

"I didn't."

"Come again?"

"It just seemed like the simplest solution," Charon replied, probing at the cord binding his lips like a child plucking at a rubber band. "You were on my boat, but you weren't dead. Figured there'd been a clerical error somewhere."

"So ye tried to poison me?!"

"Do you see what I've been dealing with?" Charon asked, turning his attention to Hemingway and rolling his glittering black eyes. "She's so *alive*."

"Yes, I see," Hemingway replied, eyes narrowed, his tone implying something far more ominous than I'd have expected given our witty repartee. "You're immortal, aren't you?"

Now it was my turn to clear my throat.

"Well, see...I guess so. I mean, I haven't exactly put it to the test or anythin'."

Frankly, I wasn't certain whether I was or not. During my daylight hours, it seemed I was nothing more than a frail human being with all the capacity I'd had before discovering my divine roots. At night, I became a shadow-wielding, flame-spewing goddess with more power in my little finger than half the minor gods I'd encountered over the years. But did that mean I was immortal? That I could take a bullet or lose a limb or swallow poison and shake it off like a scraped knee?

"Seems Charon put it to the test for you," Hemingway said, his eyes glinting with amusement. "I'm assuming you haven't told Othello, yet?"

"It's sort of a new development. I've been...out of town."

"Good," Hemingway replied. "Then you can tell me all about it on the way."

The Horseman leapt from the bank onto the boat, landing with such easy grace that the vessel barely rocked, as though he weighed far less than I'd have thought. For a brief moment, I thought I saw something else standing in the boat—a hulking, skeletal figure with a skull for a face. But it was gone between one blink and the next, little more than a flicker, leaving me with goosebumps and a case of the willies.

"Do I look like a taxi?" Charon asked, sounding nonplussed.

"She knows about the break in," Hemingway said, defensively. "Don't you think he'd want to hear what she knows sooner rather than later?"

"Well," Charon replied, scratching at his cheek as if considering, "she did drink three whole beers without exploding. I'm sure he'd like to talk to someone who could do that."

"Ye thought I would explode?!" I exclaimed, waving my hands about, thrown by the ferryman's sudden admission. "Wait, no. First, who is 'he' and where in the hell are we goin'?"

"Nice one," Charon said, chuckling. "'Where in the hell', I'll have to remember that."

"Wait, what's so funny?" I asked.

"Take the Acheron. It's wider, and the Styx always gets backed up on holiday weekends," Hemingway suggested to Charon as he settled into the boat, his sprawled limbs leaving very little room for Charon and me, ignoring my question altogether.

"I was going to take the Cocytus."

"Oh, gods, no, don't do that. All the lost souls do on the Cocytus is wail and cry."

"I know, isn't it great?"

"There's something wrong with you, I hope you know that. Anyway," Hemingway continued, turning to me, "why don't you go ahead and fill me in on what all you've been up to since we last saw each other? How's that plant of yours holding up?"

Distantly, I realized he was referring to Eve; he'd known what she was and had let her remain in my care for reasons I'd never entirely understood. If I was being honest with myself, I had to admit I knew very little about Hemingway and his fellow Horsemen of the Apocalypse. Their roles were straightforward enough—war, death, famine, and pestilence weren't exactly vague concepts—but how they chose to play them was a mystery. You'd think they'd want to make Judgment Day an international holiday, maybe get their faces thrown on whatever End of Times currency we'd wind up using, and yet they seemed pretty damned hellbent on doing the opposite. Pun intended.

"I'll answer that once one of ye answer me questions," I countered. "Where are we goin'?"

"Oh, I thought you were being funny on purpose," Charon said, sounding put off. The boatman plunged his paddle into the surging river waters and, just like that, we were off again. "Hell *is* where we're headed. An isolated part of it, anyway."

"We are?" I experienced a sudden wave of apprehension that had nothing to do with motion sickness or a budding hangover. "To see whom, exactly?"

"Management."

"His boss," Hemingway elaborated, catching sight of my expression. "Well, one of them, at any rate. Regardless, you should cheer up. We're getting you an audience with Hades, Lord of the Underworld, himself. Something which, I should add, more than a few Greek heroes would have killed for."

"Mostly died for," Charon chimed in. "Historically speaking."

"Ye lot aren't goin' to take 'no' for an answer, I take it?"

"It's either this, or I let Charon drop you off at the Mourning Fields." Hemingway shrugged, as if my decision made no difference to him. "That's where the unrequited lovers end up. Basically a bunch of lost souls complaining about never finding love for all eternity. Think about every friend you've ever had whining about their latest crush...only they go on and on and on, lamenting over the one who got away. Forever. Oh, and they spend most days watching every season of *The Bachelor* on repeat when they aren't busy screening Hallmark movies that never made it to television."

"I t'ink I would rather die. And yes, I know who I'm talkin' to."

"Like I said, it's your choice."

"Fine, let's go see Hades," I said, huffing, distantly aware of how ridiculous that statement would have sounded out of context. Me, chatting with the god of the dead? What would we even have to talk about, aside from how many people I'd put here in my time? "Wait, this isn't goin' to take long, is it? I came here to do something."

"Is that so?" Hemingway asked, arching an eyebrow. "Well, I wouldn't worry too much about that. Hades isn't the sort of god to drag his feet, although I expect he'll be fairly preoccupied when we first arrive. He's what you might call a...micromanager."

"More like a control freak," Charon corrected, snorting indelicately.

"How so?" I asked the ferryman.

"You'll see for yourself. Wouldn't want to ruin the surprise."

"Why do I feel like I'm bein' threatened all of the sudden?"

"Because," the infamous boatman replied, grinning at me in a way that would have haunted a saner person's dreams, his obsidian eyes flashing with amusement, "you aren't stupid."

2

*C*haron docked his boat along the riverbank, pinning us in place with his radiant paddle, seemingly unperturbed by the veritable horde of wraiths—dark, vaguely sinister silhouettes with faintly glowing eyes—spilling out from a sprawling granite structure that looked one part courthouse and one part bastille. In their shadowy hands, they carried papers tucked away in manilla folders as well as thick plastic binders and steel briefcases. For some reason, the entire scene reminded me of students fleeing the school after the final bell in a cult coming-of-age classic...provided the sexually repressed teenagers were played instead by terrifying shades with administrative ambitions.

"What the hell are they?" I asked, my voice a hushed whisper, my throat a little raw from having glossed over the majority of my story up to this point, leaving out only a few pertinent details—stuff I wasn't ready to tell Hemingway, for one reason or another.

"Lobbyists," Hemingway replied. "Lawyers. Accountants. Bankers. Hades recruits them all to work for him and keep this place up to code."

I cringed at the thought of dying only to end up working a nine-to-five as a glorified clerk. I mean, talk about Hell. Hemingway must have seen my face; he chuckled and stepped off the boat onto the bank, holding out his hand.

"I wouldn't pity them," he suggested. "Most worked themselves into an early grave. The ones who didn't, the ones who broke camp and made a good life for themselves, often end up elsewhere. Besides, you know what they say, busy spirits are happy spirits."

"Pretty sure that isn't how that sayin' goes," I mumbled as I reached for Hemingway, only to hesitate when I felt a desiccated hand take my arm. I turned to find Charon staring at me, his mouth puckered in what might have been either a smirk or a sneer, his skeletal fingers clinging to the meat of my bicep.

"Here, take this with you," he insisted.

The boatman passed me a shooter of oozing amber liquid, like one of those single use bottles you can buy at any liquor store. This one's label was missing, however; only the faint patina of torn paper remained to show where the glue had once sat. I turned it over in my hand, confused.

"What is it?"

"A gift. And a reminder."

I felt Hemingway stiffen as he caught sight of the shooter, though he remained silent. Indeed, he seemed content to let this—whatever it was Charon was up to—play out; the Horseman stepped away, inspecting the building with such scrutiny that he might as well have had a hand in its construction. I slipped the shooter into my pocket, warily.

"A reminder, huh?" I echoed. "Of what, exactly?"

"That our little contest remains undecided." Charon released my arm and tapped the side of his head. "Don't forget, whatever I want. That was the deal."

"Whatever *I* want, ye mean," I countered, smirking despite myself. "So, what's in the bottle? More bath water?"

"Something to remember us by," Charon replied cryptically, failing to appreciate my joke. "Now, get off my boat. I've got actual dead people to see."

Hemingway returned to help me step off the boat as Charon plucked his paddle from the water and nestled it in the crook of one shoulder. He gave us both a wave before fetching another beer from his chest and cracking it, the sound somehow loud enough to be heard above the gurgle of the River Styx. I watched him go, wondering whether I'd ever see that crazy son of a bitch again. Part of me hoped not; I wasn't sure I wanted to go up against him in a drinking contest a second time. Frankly, I doubted I'd survive it.

"Come on, death waits for no one," Hemingway insisted, tugging my hand before releasing it and marching towards the dreary building.

"And just how long have you been waitin' to use that line?" I asked, rolling my eyes.

"I have no idea what you mean."

"Uh huh. So, Hades runs this place?" I asked as we walked, forced to dodge the milling spirits as they shuffled past, seemingly oblivious to my presence. Hemingway, however, was able to pass through them without so much as a sidestep. The shades parted for him like he was radioactive or something, their eye sockets flashing a little brighter as he went by. Not that I was surprised; in this hellish place, we might as well have been on the red carpet—which meant I was following the leading man so he could introduce me to the director.

Or the director's secretary, at any rate.

"Sort of," Hemingway replied as we reached the gaping doorway, only to be accosted by a severe looking creature in a black pantsuit that covered her like a silk glove, her alabaster skin radiating mercurial power—unmistakably that of a goddess. She held a clipboard in one hand and a pen made entirely of smoke in the other, its tip so bright with heat it looked like the lit end of a cigarette. Her dark hair was worn back in a tight bun, held in place by what seemed to be a writhing rattlesnake, its sand-colored scales a perfect match for her eyes.

"You're not supposed to be here, Horseman," she said, primly. "You have work you should be doing, elsewhere."

"Hello to you too, Persephone."

I gaped, recognizing the name immediately. Persephone, also known as the Queen of the Underworld, who ruled alongside her husband, Hades. Frankly, I'd always found her mythical backstory one of the most interesting; stolen away by Hades and later tricked into remaining by his side for at least a portion of the year, she was a fascinating character whose role oscillated between victim and accomplice depending which scholars were to be believed. As far as first impressions were concerned, however, I was leaning as far away from victim as possible.

There was nothing weak about this one.

"Don't be glib, Horseman. We've had an unusually hectic day, even by our standards." The goddess flicked her gaze to me and back. "Who's this creature you've brought with you? You know we don't allow mortals all-access passes down here."

"Her name is Quinn," Hemingway replied hurriedly, as though worried I'd cut in with some smartass comment, otherwise. "She knows who accessed the gate, and has some idea why. I thought Hades would like to speak with her."

"We already know all that," Persephone said, shooing us with her pen. "We caught two of the intruders. My husband is speaking with them now." She licked her lips. "It shouldn't be long before he knows everything worth knowing."

Caught two of the intruders? Which ones? I opened my mouth, prepared to demand to see them, then hesitated. I had to consider whom I was addressing—not to mention whose turf we were on. Unfortunately, if I wanted to find out who'd been taken and what was being done to them, I had to rely on tact, not bravado.

"May I see 'em?" I asked, putting on my most innocent voice—the one I used whenever a teacher caught me out in the halls in school, or when I got caught stealing some priceless relic from a highly warded vault. "The ones ye captured, I mean."

"Why?"

Persephone's suspicion lashed out at me like a physical blow, and I felt the beat of her power against my skin. It was a slap, nothing more. A reminder of how low I—the pathetic mortal—stood in the pecking order. After all, as hierarchy went, Persephone was bound to one of the mightiest gods ever known and had been for so long there was no telling what all she'd picked up or how much power she'd amassed. And yet, the instant her energy stung me, I found myself seeing—not red as the metaphor would suggest—but white.

"Because I said so."

The words came rumbling from my throat, brimming with the threat of violence, with the promise of unleashed power. I felt the wraiths flooding around us hesitate, drawing away from me as if I'd done something far more frightening than I could imagine. Hemingway actually took a step back—not in fear, but in appraisal.

"What is she?" Persephone asked the Horseman, her curt manner unchanged. "And don't bother lying to me. Mortals don't look like that."

"Excuse me?"

"She's…" Hemingway drifted off for a moment, ignoring my outburst. "Something different."

"Ah," the goddess replied, somehow managing to put all her derision into that one sound. "Well I could hardly turn her away, then. Any chance she'll surprise him?"

"Only one way to find out."

"Wait a second," I said, palming the side of my head as my racing heartbeat slowed and the wraiths resumed drifting heedlessly past. "What are ye talkin' about, now? Surprise whom?"

"My husband is notoriously hard to shock," Persephone replied, meeting my eyes at last. "It's become a sort of game among us. Trying to rile him up."

"Are ye sure that's a good idea? Rilin' up the god of the dead?"

"Probably not. But simply because we spend eternity caring for corpses does not mean he can afford to become one. That, child, is what makes a strong marriage: discouraging your beloved's worst habits at every turn."

"I'll…keep that in mind."

"See that you do." Persephone secured her pen to the top of the clipboard, its smoldering tip still blazing. "Come along, then. Maybe having you present for the interrogation will speed this process along."

I tried to spare Hemingway a glance to be sure we weren't walking into some sort of trap, but the Horseman was already hot on Persephone's shockingly high heels. I sighed, shaking off the residual buzz from Charon's beers, and followed, determined to find out who'd been caught breaking into Hell.

We passed through the building's grim interior to the sound of clacking keys and pen scribbles, weaving between long tables occupied by dozens of wraiths at work transcribing documents or writing suicide notes or whatever it was creepy ghost folk did on their lord's behalf. I shuddered, my skin crawling at the idea of being forced to work in a place like this for all eternity.

Of course, that was nothing compared to meeting the boss. The instant we reached the door at the far end of the building, its otherwise bland sheet metal exterior swimming with our reflections, I could sense his smothering power. Indeed, there was a flavor to it. A texture, too. Glancing at my two companions, I realized I felt something similar—albeit significantly lesser—from them, as well.

From Hemingway, the fragrance of black licorice and the sensation of finely carved bone. From Persephone, pomegranate and dried flower petals. And, on the other side of the steel door, the faintest whiff of burnt ash and the feel of still water. I wasn't sure why I was able to sense these things all of a sudden, only that I could. Did it have something to do with the beer I'd drank at Charon's insistence, perhaps a side effect of the hangover? Or were my godlike powers merging into my daytime hours, as Circe had suggested they might? It could have been either, both, or neither, I decided. Hell, I wasn't even really here, except in spirit.

But then why did I have a headache?

"There's no need to treat us this way," a voice said from the other room, loud enough to be heard over the general hubbub behind us.

"Yes, especially me," a second added.

The first belonged to a woman, the second a man. I recognized both, though I wished I didn't. Helen of Troy and Narcissus—the Greek contingent of my misfit crew—caught trespassing in the Underworld by Hades himself. And now it looked like a reunion was eminent.

How serendipitous.

"Husband!" Persephone called, rapping her knuckles against the door. The snake wound in her hair began to shake, agitated, its rattle like a promise of violence. "I've brought someone to meet you. It's important."

I hated to admit it, but part of me had forgotten all about my treasonous crew in the aftermath of my bout with Frankenstein and Ryan's subsequent departure. It seemed like so much had happened since then, and yet I found myself growing angrier with every passing second as we waited for Hades to answer. They'd abandoned James and the other Neverlanders, siding with the enemy for reasons I couldn't fathom— reasons I was determined to hear for myself as soon as I got my hands on them.

The door swung open with the barest whisper, and the smell of burnt ashes grew stronger until it felt like I was choking on cinders and wood smoke. The sensation of still water crashed into me, doing what Persephone's power had done, except tenfold. Not a slap, but a slam—severe enough I wobbled on my feet, steadied only by Hemingway's hand at the small of my back.

"You get used to it," he whispered through gritted teeth, his own face betraying the slightest strain. The Horseman's eyes seemed to burn with some infernal light, but they weren't trained on me. Instead, Hemingway studied an obscenely tall figure looming within—a being I wanted very much not to look at, for some inexplicable reason.

Refusing to play the role of a coward now that I'd made it this far, I steadied myself with a long exhale and gave the god of the dead my full attention. He was, in a word, beautiful. Standing perhaps three feet taller than me in a cloak of roiling smoke that licked at his heels and curled off his broad shoulders, Hades had a thick mane of pure white hair two shades lighter than his pale, artfully crafted face. His hands were long and slender, the hands of a painter or a pianist. And yet, when he beckoned us forward with them, I learned his talents resided primarily in the manipulation of the dead; in my spirit form, I felt compelled to rush to his side, to do whatever he wished—whatever had to be done.

Fortunately, the spell, the illusion, lasted for perhaps only a couple seconds before Hades himself broke it by hacking out an uncomfortable cough that sounded vaguely like a cat being strangled—not that I would know. Embers spilled from his lips, dancing in the air as if he'd just stuck a hot poker in a fireplace. He waved at us apologetically and snatched a pair of thick-lensed glasses from the desk he stood beside.

"Apologies, something got lodged in my throat," Hades rasped, his voice not terribly dissimilar from the ferryman's, albeit lacking even the slightest inflection. "Darling, would you—"

"Yes, of course. I'll be back in a moment," Persephone interjected, slipping between Hemingway and me with a movement so sinuous and graceful I'd have accused her of being a dancer in another life. The perks of being a goddess, perhaps? I sure hoped so; my gangly ass would welcome the advantage.

"Quinn! It's you! Aren't you so glad to see me?"

I wheeled to find Narcissus bound to a steel chair, his eyelids pinned open by some sort of ocular clamp that managed to make a mockery of his stunning features, sitting back to back with a hooded figure I recognized all too well. The Greek flashed me a smile as though he didn't look like a LASIK patient about to go into the operating room. Helen, on the other hand, was simply tied up; the demigoddess glanced over her shoulder and stiffened at the sight of me. I felt my lip curl in contempt before I could stop myself, before I could even listen to their paltry excuses.

"D'ye two lead Ryan to the Gate?" I asked, my fists balled so tight I could feel my nails digging furrows into the skin of my palms.

"Don't answer her," Helen commanded.

Narcissus, who'd already begun opening his mouth, clamped it shut with an audible snap. Of course, I wasn't the only one looking for answers; Hades' power flooded the room, though it seemed to coalesce around the two Greeks, crushing them beneath its immense pressure. I saw Narcissus huddle beneath the onslaught, panting with the effort it took to breathe. Helen merely bowed her head, trembling.

"Here you are, husband."

"Thank you, my love," Hades replied, taking the glass of water Persephone had retrieved. I hadn't even noticed her return, oblivious thanks to Hades' flexing of power. The god of the dead tossed back the glass' contents and took a deep breath. "Much better. Now, let's get back to this, shall we?"

Hades approached Narcissus, towering over the seated Greek to an almost comical degree. Indeed, were it not for the circumstances, I'd have probably laughed. But whatever Hades had planned lacked a comedic element; Narcissus started to whimper as the god of the dead crept forward, moving so smoothly it was like he floated across the stone floor rather than walked. As I watched, he reached into the folds of his murky cloak and withdrew a stack of papers so thick I thought he might kill Narcissus for real with it by merely setting it atop the Greek's head and letting gravity do the rest.

Except that wasn't what Hades had in mind.

"Underworld Census Volume B, Section 3, Subsection 2, paragraph 17," Hades began after donning his glasses, turning the massive tome so that Narcissus had to look at the absurdly tiny script that littered each page. "Shall I begin with the F's, this time?"

"No, not the F's," Narcissus whispered, sounding so horrified it sent chills up my spine. "Anything but the F's."

"Florakis, family of 32. Floros, family of 9. Fotopoulos, family of 25." Hades went on, listing more and more names, followed by the total number of family members, his droning voice dragging us all down until it felt like my very soul wanted to curl up and die. Narcissus, by this point, was crying openly, tears tracking down his face.

"So...cruel," he sobbed. "Can't stand...it. So...boring."

"Answer your friend's question, and it can all be over," the god of the dead insisted, clearly referring to me despite not having so much as spared me a single look since I arrived, despite the fact we'd basically crashed his little torture session.

"Narcissus," Helen began, "don't—"

But it was too late.

"It was the only way!" Narcissus wailed, tilting his head up to stop his nose from running. "How else was I supposed to stop this from happening?!"

Before I could ask what "this" meant, Narcissus promptly turned into a freaking flower. A literal flower, its stem planted firmly in the grain of the chair he'd been sitting in a second earlier. I recognized the drooping plant immediately—a narcissus. I turned, searching for Hemingway, hoping to confirm I hadn't just hallucinated the Greek's transformation, only to find the Horseman conspicuously absent—almost as if he'd never been there at all.

But where the hell could he have gone?

I turned back to the bizarre torture scene playing out before my very eyes, acutely aware that I was essentially at the mercy of the King and Queen of the Underworld now that my chaperone had disappeared— meaning there would be no one to intervene should they decide to make my little vacation a more permanent arrangement. But I was also certain of one other thing: if Hemingway didn't show back up soon, he wouldn't be the Horseman of Death by the time I got my hands on him.

He'd just be dead.

3

*N*arcissus returned to human form mere seconds before Hemingway reappeared, looking oddly disheveled and a tad flustered around the edges. Spooked, I'd have said, if I thought anything could truly upset an agent of the Apocalypse. Ordinarily, I would have glared at the bastard and demanded to know what he'd been playing at when he'd abandoned me, but I was too wary of drawing unwanted attention to interrupt the impending interrogation; I'd largely managed to avoid notice up until now by keeping quiet and occupying the furthest corner of the office. Fortunately, the god of the dead seemed as curious as I was to know why Hemingway had fled.

"Problem, Horseman?" Hades asked, swinging his steely gaze past me to land on a frazzled Hemingway.

"Minor emergency," the Horseman replied, clearing his throat. "It's been dealt with."

"Ah," Hades said. "Back to business then. So, Narcissus, you were saying something about planning to wake Nemesis?"

"Yes! She cursed me to turn into a flower whenever I get too...excited. It's been very trying, especially for me." Tears welled up in the Greek's eyes, though from the clamps or actual sadness, I had no idea. "So, you see, when Helen came to me and proposed we wake her, I had to agree. She told me her mother would remove the curse as a reward. Helen even showed me how to control it, somewhat."

"Did she, now?" Hades asked. "Helen of Troy, was it?"

Helen flinched but said nothing.

"Remove her hood," the god of the dead commanded, gesturing at me with one long, tapering finger. "Let's see what lies beneath."

Without so much as a second thought, I did as Hades asked; I left my corner, slipping past Persephone and around the bound Narcissus to stand before the Greek I'd sailed with, the demigoddess whose advice I'd heeded, the woman who had stood firm with me beneath Typhon's vengeful gaze. I threw back her hood, revealing the face I'd seen that day in the gingerbread house—a profile so exquisite I thought I'd never seen someone so beautiful. My eyes were drawn to it in pieces, roving over the lips, the arching brows, the smooth glow of her skin, the glowing tresses of her hair.

"Enough of that," Persephone hissed, snapping her fingers.

The illusion flickered.

What lay beneath was not an unattractive face: small-boned and angular, a shrewd intelligence made the most out of what would otherwise have been relatively plain features. That being said, hers was not a face to launch a thousand ships. Maybe a dozen, at best. Which meant Triton had been right, after all; this was not Helen of Troy, but an imposter masquerading as a demigoddess. But then who was she, really? And why impersonate Zeus' daughter?

"What are you all looking at?" Narcissus asked, straining to see over his shoulder with his buggy eyes. "I want to see. Helen, dearest, what's going on back there? Tell me!"

"You're not Helen," I accused, ignoring the Greek, surprised to note I wasn't nearly as angry as I'd been standing outside. More than anything, I found I was curious. Sure, this woman had lied to and manipulated me, even abandoned my crew in their time of need, but there was something in her fiery expression that felt genuine—a descriptor I'd never have bestowed upon the Helen of Troy I knew. "Who are ye, really?"

"So, you found your way here, too," the woman replied, ignoring my question. Her voice was altered slightly. More bitter, less sibilant. She stared me up and down, lips pursed. "I suppose I shouldn't be surprised. The madman thought you might."

"Frankenstein?"

"Did you say Frankenstein?" Persephone asked, jerking at the name. "Victor Frankenstein?"

"Aye. D'ye know him?"

"He's a thief," the goddess spat.

"Yes, well, he's done quite the number on your friend," the imposter interjected, contemptuously. "I should have suspected he'd betray us the first chance he got. I just didn't realize it would be so soon."

"Ye were plannin' to backstab them, first," I reasoned. "No honor among turncoats, I take it?"

"You know nothing. I did what I had to once I realized neither you nor the boy were going to lead me to the Gate." The woman sneered up at me, her eyes narrowed in disdain. "And after all the lies I had to tell just to hitch a ride with you. What a waste."

"Ye had no idea what Atlantis was or how to find it. It was the Titan Realm you wanted to reach all along." I shook my head, playing back our past interactions, our conversations about the role of the mythical city, our navigation of the map we'd consulted, our talk of prophecy and ascension. Had it all been a lie? But why the elaborate deception? "So, ye lied to get us to take ye there. But why go to such lengths? Wait, was Oberon in on it?!"

"I don't answer to you," she replied, spitefully.

"I suggest," Hades drawled, "you answer her questions, Penelope of Ithaca."

The woman fidgeted, eyes downcast, the illusion shattered. Distantly, I noted Narcissus sputtering in disbelief, spouting reprisals. But I ignored him; I was too busy trying to adjust to the news that I'd been working with Odysseus' wife all along.

"The Fae Lord knew nothing," Penelope responded before I could demand more answers, sounding more frightened than contrite. "I found out he was looking for a guide to Atlantis and volunteered. I convinced Narcissus to follow me and do as I asked. His antics make for excellent cover."

"I don't understand," I admitted, thrown by her sudden confession. "What were ye hopin' to achieve?"

"I wanted to find my husband."

"What? D'ye mean Odysseus, or Agamemnon?" I glared at the imposter. "Because I remember ye lyin' to me about that, once before."

"Odysseus, you fool. He's gone missing." Penelope met my gaze, her expression raw. "He was always Athena's favorite. Her chosen hero. When her war began, he chose to join her cause. But when it ended, he failed to return home. Again."

I scowled, recalling Penelope's role in Homer's *Odyssey*; beset by suitors and tasked with waiting for her husband after the fall of Troy, the woman had spent decades fending off unwanted attention using nothing but her wits and an insistence on maintaining propriety. So, this time she'd decided she'd had enough of waiting. I supposed I couldn't blame her—not that I was inclined to give her a pass for lying to us.

"And ye thought he was in the Titan realm?" I watched her face, noting her shifting expression. I thought back to our last real conversation. "No, not there. The Underworld, that's where ye wanted us to go. Ye seriously think he's dead?"

"If he isn't, he will be," she swore. "But no, I couldn't be sure. Initially, I had hoped to speak with the spirits of the dead and find out. My husband spoke often of the answers they provided." Penelope's gaze flicked to Hades, who stood with his arms folded staring into the middle distance as if lost in thought. "I swear, Lord Hades, I had no idea the Frozen One would break down the Gate."

"The Frozen One?" Persephone echoed, ignoring Narcissus' sudden twitch.

"The leader of the trespassers," Hemingway explained, relaying what I'd told him of Ryan and his exploits. "Apparently he's been terrorizing the Eighth Sea for some time."

"Impossible," Persephone scoffed. "Gaia has relinquished much of her power, but in that realm her will is law. She would never allow such a thing."

"He has a devourer," Penelope interjected.

All heads turned to her as if on a string, including Hades'; the god of the dead looked practically lively with a single arched eyebrow. I, meanwhile, was left to curse my foolishness. The devourer he'd stolen from me! I'd forgotten all about the powerful artifact—the glittering jewel I'd recovered from Balor's irradiated corpse.

"How did he come by it?" Hades asked.

"I don't know. All I know is that he's been using it to get stronger. To amass power. The mad scientist is helping him, enhancing him surgically. The effect is...grotesque."

I felt my skin crawl at the thought, envisioning the horrifying, patchwork creature I'd battled back in Massachusetts. Frankenstein's monster. Was that why Ryan hadn't recognized me—why he'd changed so drastically even before our tussle in the underground laboratory? Had Frankenstein's influence been present even then? I couldn't be certain, but the idea of my old friend being operated on, being reforged into something equally malformed, made me sick to my stomach.

"What is he planning?" The god of the dead stepped close, looming over us both, the proximity of his stifling power making my joints ache. "Why does he invade this realm?"

Penelope shuddered and refused to meet the god's eyes.

"Because she lied to him," I replied, searching the woman's face, though I knew with a grim certainty that I was right. "He t'inks he can reach Atlantis from here, doesn't he?"

Something unreadable flashed across Hades' face, but the god of the dead stayed quiet. Hemingway, I noticed, was studying me more intently than the situation warranted. Had I done something unexpected? Breached some sort of Underworld etiquette? I couldn't be sure.

"My husband spoke of Atlantis once," Penelope replied, her voice oddly forlorn. "He claimed the spirits of the dead whispered of it. That they'd seen its wonders for themselves. I merely passed that bit of information along and let the Frozen One come to his own conclusions."

"What did Odysseus think of their whispers?" Hades asked.

"He thought it was a trap, a lure meant to entice the living."

"Of course," the god of the dead replied, thoughtfully. "Odysseus always was quite clever."

"Where does the Titan gate lead?" Hemingway interjected, locking eyes with the pensive Hades.

"Once it led to Tartarus. But my little brother begged me to destroy that route. He was not eager to see our father freed by his kin."

His kin, meaning the other Titans, I realized. Hades' father Kronos, who had spawned the Olympians before eating them one by one to stave off a fateful prophecy, had once ruled the progenitor gods before falling to his divine offspring. As for his little brother, Hades could only be talking about Zeus. As in *the* Zeus. Which also meant he was also referring obliquely to the prison built to contain Kronos; imprisoned by his children after war between the Olympians and the Titans, the King of the Titans was rumored to reside in a black pit found at the deepest depths of the Underworld, known as Tartarus.

"And where does it lead, now?" Hemingway asked.

"It...detours." Hades removed his glasses and began cleaning their lenses with the tail end of his smoldering cloak—though, unsurprisingly, all that did was fog them up worse than before. "By now, I expect this Frozen One will have left our jurisdiction."

"Wait, how is that possible?" I blurted out before I could stop myself. "I mean," I stammered, heart racing, "isn't the entire Underworld your jurisdiction?"

"Of course," Hades replied. "But the afterlife is a place with many names. I rule but a piece of it."

"Where's the detour lead?" Hemingway asked, impatiently.

"Helheim."

"I was afraid of that."

"Why, where's Helheim?" I glanced around the room, struck by the apprehensive expressions on everyone's face. Except Hades, of course, who seemed as implacable as ever. "What's with the long faces? What does that mean?"

"It means there is nothing I or any of my servants can do," Hades replied.

"And what about me?" I asked, aiming the question at the Horseman. "Can't I go after him?"

Hemingway opened his mouth to speak but closed it as the scent of burnt ash flooded the room and a wave of power crashed over us all. I gritted my teeth with the effort to stay standing, to turn and face the source of such overwhelming power. I found Hades studying me as if noticing me for the first time, his fingertips bridged and pressed to his lips, his calm repose at odds with the intense pressure beating against my skin.

"And who, may I ask, are you? Besides an intruder." The god of the dead held up a hand to still Hemingway, who'd jerked at the accusation. "Come now, she has spoken well enough up to this point. Let's hear her out."

I wanted to speak, but my mouth was suddenly way too dry, my skin clammy, my mind utterly blank—talk about brain dead, I thought, though the joke fell flat even in my own head. Something told me Hades wouldn't find it funny, either.

4

*T*he room was silent as the grave, which—under the circumstances —was saying something. Even Narcissus, who'd offered a running commentary that we'd all ignored up to this point, had shut his gob the moment Hades' power had coursed through the room. Everyone, it seemed, was waiting for me to answer the god's question.

Who was I?

I didn't bother spouting my credentials, nor did I waste Hades' time with a philosophical response—the first would take too long, while the second had a very real chance of landing on dead ears. Right now, I needed the Lord of the Underworld to know one thing and one thing only about me.

"I'm the only person who can stop the Frozen One. That's why I'm here. What I came to do."

"And why should we trust you to do such a thing?" Persephone asked, her suspicion plain. The snake in her hair wriggled in agitation as she stalked to her husband's side, flashing its fangs at me like a spitting cat.

"Because Gaia sent her," Hemingway answered, speaking up on my behalf. "And because she survived a drinking contest with Charon."

"Is that supposed to impress us?" Persephone asked.

"He had her drink his special brew."

"Truly?" Persephone's snake hissed as the goddess whirled to face me. "And why aren't you dead?"

But Hades held out an arm as if to halt the Q&A before it could begin in earnest. He slipped his glasses into a smoldering pocket, the smoke swallowing them up like a fog bank. The pressure I'd felt earlier ramped up again, though less oppressively than before, dancing along my skin rather than crashing against it.

"What do you sense from me, child?" Hades asked, holding his arms out wide as if in invitation.

"Ashes," I said, recalling both his unusual scent and the texture I'd associated with him from the beginning. "Ashes and still water."

Hades actually smirked.

"And from them?"

I told him, pointing first to Persephone and then to Hemingway. Both reacted to their descriptors, though only Persephone seemed appalled; Hemingway looked more intrigued than upset. Somehow, I'd done something he approved of. Indeed, something both he and Hades found interesting. The god of the dead leveled his gaze, staring down at me from his haughty perch.

"Horseman, take my chariot. Escort this one to Fólkvangr, then feel free to report to the Others. They'll want to know what has happened." Hades looked faintly sad for the briefest moment, though I had no idea why. "Be sure to tell them it's possible that the time has come. To prepare."

"The time for what?" I asked.

But it seemed Hades was done talking to me; he turned back to the prisoners, forked tongues of smoke seething along his shoulders. Penelope withered under his attention until Hades crooked a finger and lifted her chin. The woman trembled like a kicked dog.

"Your husband's name has yet to be recorded in my books," Hades said, his voice softening in an unprecedented display of tenderness. "I know what it is like to long for a reunion. But you do not belong here. I must insist you take the flower and return only when your time has come. Dear wife, would you please see to their travel arrangements?"

"Of course, husband," Persephone replied, her voice breaking. For a moment, with her lips unpursed and her eyes bright, I saw just how much the Queen of the Underworld cared for her spouse and decided to take her marriage advice a tad more seriously.

Not that marriage was ever going to happen.

"Thank you, Lord Hades." Tears brimmed in Penelope's eyes. "I swear it."

"And of course *I* swear it!" Narcissus declared, openly crying. "But, uh, Lord Hades...does that mean I won't be getting rid of this curse? Because that's really why I came..."

"I cannot help you with that."

"Well, you're useless."

The rattlesnake lunged for the Greek, who promptly returned to his floral state with a startled cry. Persephone plucked the flower from the chair and snapped her fingers, freeing Penelope from her bonds.

"He's lucky this is my favorite flower," Persephone told her, spinning the narcissus round and round as she headed for the door.

Penelope, meanwhile, made to stand but ended up stumbling into my arms, her legs seemingly unable to bear her weight. I briefly considered dropping her on her ass—it would have served her right, in my opinion. But the sudden press of her lips against my cheek, mere inches from my ear, stopped me.

"Frankenstein hopes you'll chase after them," she whispered, gripping my arm tighter than she had to. "He plans to set a trap for you. Don't fall for it. She isn't what she seems."

The wife of Odysseus straightened and stepped away, avoiding eye contact with me as she left the room at Persephone's insistence. I watched her leave, wondering whether I should call her back and demand more answers. Frankly, she was getting off unbelievably easy; if I were in Hades' shoes, I'd have made her sweat a hell of a lot longer before letting her off the sickle.

"Back to work," the Lord of the Underworld said as he headed for a desk on the far side of the room. "I trust you'll see yourselves out."

"Come on, Quinn." Hemingway waved for me to follow. "We should hurry."

"A word of advice, child," Hades added, glancing back at me over his shoulder. "Very few who find their way down here ever resurface, and time is never on your side. Don't linger any longer than you have to."

"Shit!" I exclaimed, throwing up a placating hand, struck by something he'd said. "Please, I forgot to ask. There's someone I need to find, someone who's lost. He's like me. I mean, he isn't dead, just lost. His name is Maximilliano Velez. D'ye know how I can find him?"

"It's possible." Hades pulled out the chair to his desk, its leather seams strobing with volcanic light. "But first I have to know what you would do to be reunited with this lost soul."

"Ye mean besides huntin' down and stoppin' the trespassers for ye? Shouldn't that be enough?"

"You said yourself that you came here to stop this Frozen One," Hades replied as he slipped into his chair. "Don't pretend like you're doing me a favor."

The instant the god of the dead sat, his cloak evaporated, replaced by a suit roiling with black flames, his tie and artfully folded pocket square flaring scarlet. Hades fetched a notebook from his desk and thumbed through it, his dull gaze flicking across the pages at a freakishly rapid pace. At that moment, he looked to me like Hell's most dangerous accountant.

"I'll repeat myself this once: what would you give to be reunited? Surely we can strike a deal."

"I don't know," I admitted, uncomfortable with the sudden turning of the tables. "What would ye want?"

"As it so happens, there are a pair of troublemakers causing all sorts of mischief under the supervision of a peer of mine."

Hemingway groaned, but Hades ignored him.

"If I return your lost soul to you," the god of the dead continued, "I would ask that you pay them a visit and pass along a message at your earliest inconvenience."

I wasn't sure I liked the sound of that, but—when I really thought about it—the deal seemed better than wandering the afterlife shouting Max's name to the literal heavens. If passing along the message led me to Max, then there wasn't really a choice to be made.

"And what's the message?"

"Tell them their machinations have begun to pay off, and that it's time they reveal their hand before we all end up paying the price for their hubris."

"Alright...and who exactly are these troublemakers?"

"Calvin and Makayla Temple."

5

*H*ades' chariot was made of pure gold, its luster richer and more vibrant than anything I'd ever seen before. But then maybe that had more to do with the fires that blazed damn near everywhere we looked —from the braziers mounted along the tunnel walls to the volcanic currents of the Phlegethon surging far beneath our feet—than the quality of the precious metal. The flames were reflected in the chariot's clean lines and sloped curves until it seemed to writhe in place. Or maybe it was simply that it was a study in contrasts: four pitch black horses heaved at their glinting bridles, their eyes pitted and smoking, their hooves sparking whenever they struck stone, sending embers spiraling into the smoke-filled air.

Apparently Hell was a pyromaniac's wet dream.

Who knew?

"Did it not occur to you to ask me to find your friend?" Hemingway folded his arms across his chest while we waited for the specters to finish preparing the chariot for us, exasperation written across his face. "*Before* you struck a deal with Hades, I mean?"

Actually, it had.

"Pretty sure askin' for favors all the time is the easiest way to lose a friend," I replied, eyeing the horses and wondering whether Hades would cook me for all eternity for stealing one—I'd always been fond of black accessories, and nothing says "badass" like an infernal steed. "Besides, I wouldn't want to owe Captain Apocalypse a solid."

The Horseman grumbled something under his breath and rubbed at the bridge of his nose, speaking loud enough for me to hear only once we stepped into the chariot and he'd taken up the reins from the sycophantic shade who'd escorted us.

"Listen, there are some things I need to tell you about where we're going," he began. "And I should warn you: when Hades makes a contract, even a verbal one, he considers it binding. I hope you're prepared to follow through on your end."

"As long as he sends Max along like he promised, I'm fine with those terms. Max is running out of time back in the mortal realm. I had to take the risk."

"How do you plan to help him?" Hemingway asked, whipping the reins in a practiced manner that made me question whether or not he'd driven one before. I was also left to wonder just where the Horseman intended to go; the stone ridge we'd reached after leaving Hades dropped off precipitously, its base hugged by a torrent of raging fire. Before I could ask, however, the chariot rocketed upwards, pulled by the ridiculous horsepower of four obscenely muscled steeds. In seconds, we left the barren ground and its fires behind, the hooves of each stallion burning holes in midair that lingered, leaving starbursts in my vision as we ascended.

Well, I guess that answered *that* question.

"I'll cross that burnin' bridge when I come to it," I shouted over the rush of scalding wind, clutching the side of the chariot with a literal death grip, mindful of the cavernous, stalagmite-riddled ceiling overhead. "What is it ye wanted to tell me about this place? Fólkvangr, was it? Why there, if Ryan is in Helheim?"

"That's part of what I wanted to tell you," Hemingway called back. "Helheim is a small region within Niflheim that cannot be accessed by the living. It's surrounded by a river, Gjoll, that sucks the life out of any who cross it and keeps the dead from leaving. Its sole entrance is guarded by one of the Jötunn, a giant hound named Garm, who can scent any intruder from miles away."

"How giant are we talkin'?"

"Big enough to step on you by accident and not notice."

"Yikes. Sounds like quite the security system. But if Helheim is so well protected, how's Ryan supposed to access it?"

"All the realms connect in unique ways," Hemingway explained. "And they each have their own hierarchies. Their own geography. The Norse realm is no different, Beneath Yggdrasil, the World Tree, there sits nine realms." The Horseman held up a flat hand and began ticking it lower with each name. "Asgard. Vanaheim. Alfheim. Midgard. Nidavellir. Jotunheim. Svartalfheim. Niflheim. Helheim."

"So it's sort of like how Catholics think of Heaven, Purgatory, Earth, and Hell?"

"Yes, though Purgatory sits adjacent to Earth, not above it." Hemingway waved that away. "In any case, there are paths that connect the Underworld to Helheim, just as there are roads that lead from Elysium to Heaven. But they are infrequently used and notoriously hard to access, which is why what your friend has done is so problematic. He's bypassed security."

"How much damage could he do down there?" I asked, baffled by the notion that Ryan could make any Hell-adjacent realm worse than it already was. I mean, wasn't that the point of those places? To suck in every imaginable way? "I mean, isn't Helheim bad enough without his help?"

"It is a realm of ice ruled by Loki's Jötunn daughter, Hel, where the souls of those who died from sickness or old age reside. I've never been there, myself, but it is not rumored to be a terribly cruel place. I don't know what your friend will make of it, but I expect he will upset the balance, one way or another. And, if what you've told me about his time in the Titan Realm is true, that is not something we can let resolve itself."

"Sure," I said, nodding. "But then why not just drop me off in Niflheim and let me find me way from there?"

"One does not simply walk into Niflheim," Hemingway intoned, sounding eerily like Sean Bean in *Lord of the Rings*. "By all accounts, it is a realm of mist and death—"

"Wait, ye haven't been there, either?"

"No," Hemingway admitted begrudgingly. "I am not welcome there. The Norse have their own escorts to the afterlife, and they don't take kindly to strangers."

"Ye mean the Valkyries," I said, recalling the role the winged maidens played in fetching souls in Norse mythology. I'd even met one, once; Hilde had been on loan to an FBI task force before getting kidnapped by

Rasputin's henchman and shipped off to a Russian prison. Last I'd heard, she and Agent Leo Jeffries had taken some much needed time off and booked themselves a well-deserved pleasure cruise.

"Yes." The Horseman of Death shuddered, though with anticipation or fear I couldn't be sure; he had his face turned away to study the passing landscape below—nothing but volcanic veins gushing over patches of charred rock. "Anyway, to survive Niflheim, you will first need to curry favor and be granted an Aesir blessing. Hades knew that, which is why he insisted I take you to Fólkvangr. That's the paradise where Freya, the Valkyrie benefactor, resides. It also connects to Valhalla, which I'm sure you've heard of."

"The mead hall where warriors go when they die," I asserted, grinning. Personally, I'd always thought Valhalla sounded like an afterlife tailored to me in particular; fight all day, feast and drink all night...what else could a red-blooded girl ask for?

"Half the warriors. The other half go to Fórkvangr as part of an agreement Odin struck with Freya to end the war with the Vanir." Hemingway shook his head. "But that's not important. What matters is that you find one of the Norse gods and receive their blessing to enter Niflheim. Without it, the mists will try to strangle you and the beasts that call it home will swallow you whole. You'll also need a way to enter Helheim. That I can't help you with. You'll have to ask around."

"And Hades couldn't have given me a blessin' because...?"

"It wouldn't have done you any good, seeing as how he's not one of the Aesir and has limited power outside the Underworld. Besides, Hades doesn't bless. He curses. For that matter, so do a fair number of Norse gods. So try not to piss any of them off while you're visiting."

"Alright, so let's say I get this blessin', find me way into Hel, and stop Ryan. What then? What about Max, and the deal I made to talk to Calvin and Makayla Temple?"

Saying their names out loud felt even odder than I'd expected; I found myself suffering from the same rush of conflicted emotions that I'd experienced standing in Hades' office. I mean, sure, Nate and I had made our peace, but there was plenty of animosity left over for the role his parents had played in my conception—not that I was complaining about being born, necessarily, but still. Indeed, Nate himself had decried their meddling the last time he and I spoke—assuming our time together had been more than just a fever dream brought on by a manipulative god. I still wasn't certain what to think about my time under Morpheus' influence—so much so I'd kept it to myself when relaying my story to Hemingway.

"I'll make sure Hades keeps his end of the bargain and sends Max to you," the Horseman replied, snapping me out of my thoughts. "It may take some time to arrange, though. As for the Temples...I'll ask Charon to deliver you, if you make it that far."

"I t'ink ye meant to say *when* I make it that far."

"Did I?"

"That's it, the next time I speak to Othello, I'm tellin' her to dump your gloomy ass," I fired back, smirking.

"I wouldn't push her loyalty, at the moment," Hemingway replied, glancing at me sidelong. "She's had a lot to deal with lately. The world has become a...different place since you last walked it. One you may not recognize, assuming you ever make it back to the mortal realm."

I opened my mouth to ask what on earth that cryptic comment was supposed to mean, but Hemingway interrupted me with a gesture and an outstretched arm.

"There it is."

6

*F*ólkvangr spread out before us in a flash of late afternoon light as we left the foreboding cavern and its volcanic streams behind; golden rays of sunlight washed over the chariot, bathing the sable horses in its radiant glow. The horses whinnied and fidgeted as Hemingway urged them to descend, clearly agitated to have left the darkness behind. I, on the other hand, could do little but marvel at the gorgeous spring countryside with its cragged ridges and wildflower fields, its lush forests and sprawling meadows. As I watched, we soared over trees as tall as redwoods and carved statues that stood like sentinels at either end of towering bridges fashioned by hands more deft than any mortal's. Rivers and waterfalls swarmed the landscape, causing a fair amount of fine mist to drift across the sky, and yet there were no rainbows.

Curious, that.

"This reminds me of the Otherworld," I said wistfully, reminded of that realm's richness, its vibrant wildlife.

"It should. Paradise, after all, is born from the human imagination," Hemingway replied. "The fact that natural beauty is a precondition shouldn't come as a surprise, even if mortals often fail to appreciate such beauty during their limited lifespans."

"Ye sound bitter," I noted, cocking an eyebrow. "Got somethin' against the sprawl of civilization?"

"Not at all. I've got no skin in the game anymore." Hemingway turned towards me, and again I saw a leering skull flicker behind the flesh mask that hid his true face. "But I do find it interesting how many versions of Hell are either on fire or buried beneath the ice. It seems like every mortal knows what to fear, as well as what to cherish...you'd think their world would reflect that."

"Aye, well, we mortals rarely act in our own best interest." I showcased the quickly approaching valley, aware that I could have made any number of decisions and ended up not only more content with my lot in life, but also, well, *alive*. "Case in point. Imagine what I could have done with me life if I'd gone and become a dental assistant, instead."

"A dental assistant?"

"It was me aunt's idea. She was worried I'd end up with the wrong crowd." I nudged the Horseman, waggling my eyebrows. "Guess I proved her right, huh?"

"Hah hah." Hemingway adjusted our trajectory so we leveled off not ten feet from the valley floor, the horses' hooves still singeing the air. The Horseman shook his head, his eyes haunted with some secret knowledge I could only guess at. A memory, perhaps. Or maybe visions of a future yet to pass. "Perhaps you're right. The problem is, I'm not sure how much longer civilization is going to be left unchecked."

"What d'ye mean by that?" I asked, alarmed by his fatalistic attitude. But the Horseman didn't elaborate. Instead, he pointed to a narrow pass that ran between this valley and the next.

"Through there you'll find the entrance to the base of Freya's tower. Look for the door among the trees. It will be well hidden but shouldn't be guarded."

"Why the secrecy? Couldn't ye just take me to the top and be done with it?"

"Sorry, but no. Freya...won't want to see me right now, and I wouldn't want to cross blades with her Valkyries twice in one day."

"Wait, *this* is where ye went when ye left me alone with Hades?" I asked, snatching at the Horseman's sleeve. "Why? What happened?"

"That's none of your concern."

"But—"

"I said drop it."

I flinched at his brittle tone, drawing away and releasing Hemingway's arm. For the first time since meeting the Horseman, I felt the push of his power; the scent of black licorice dominated the air and my skin prickled as though he'd run a bony digit up my spine. Granted, his energy felt like a playful slap compared to Hades' overwhelming presence, but that didn't mean he'd held back.

"Quinn, I—" Hemingway began.

But I was already leaping from the side of the chariot, my heart pounding in my chest, my cheeks flushed at the thought of being chastised for asking a simple question. I landed, rolling with the impact, and came to my feet before Hemingway could stop me—assuming he'd even considered it. I didn't bother looking back; whatever his expression, it wouldn't change the fact that he'd not only snapped at me, but refused to explain why he'd acted as he had.

No matter how many centuries—or even millennia—the Horseman had on me, I was no child to be spoken to so dismissively.

"Say hi to Othello for me," I called back over my shoulder as I began marching towards the breach between the two valleys, the plush grass cushioning my every step. For a second, I thought Hemingway might say something—offer a word of encouragement, perhaps, or at least a farewell. But what I heard instead was the snap of reins and the clomp of hooves signaling the Horseman's departure. For some reason, that hurt far worse than the slap of his power had.

It's funny...people liked to say life is too short to be miserable.

But then I guessed they'd never argued with Death.

rue to Hemingway's prediction, the tower door was remarkably difficult to find; I spent at least half an hour searching for it among the trees beyond the pass, forced to duck beneath the thick, looping vines that hung between the boughs, each as thick as my wrist. It took long enough, in fact, that I began to worry how much time I had before night fell and I was forced to succumb to the alien will of my inner goddess—assuming the same rules applied here in Fólkvangr as they did in the Titan Realm. And yet, when I turned to track the sun's descent, I realized it hadn't moved so much as an inch across the sky.

"Perpetual golden hour," I muttered, squinting as I slipped beneath the drooping boughs of yet another tree. "That's nifty."

I sighed, creeping forward with my arms outstretched, moments away from returning to the pass and reconsidering my approach when my fingertips brushed a stone surface hidden behind a patch of dense foliage tucked away in the shadow of a larger tree. I peeled away the leafy obstruction, careful not to cut myself on any thorns or bristles, only to jerk back with a curse. My whole hand stung, my fingers throbbing to the beat of my pulse, and a dim light strobed where my fingers had been, flashing first silver, then green. Frustrated and impatient, I yanked the remaining plant life aside to find a series of symbols carved into the face of the door I'd uncovered, some of which were still shimmering.

They were runes, I realized. Nordic runes. Archaic symbols used by the Norse to form a written alphabet. Only these were unlike any I'd ever seen before—angled and reflective, they reminded me more of complex diagrams than the runic carvings I'd seen up to this point. I reached out to trace one of the etchings with the index finger of my hale hand and felt the stone cool to the touch; whatever had zapped me before seemed to have either worn off or run its course. I bent close, eagerly searching for signs of a handle or lever, peering so intently that I didn't notice someone was right behind me.

"A trespasser, huh? That's new."

I turned to find an armored figure studying me from the edge of the forest, a winged helm slung under one arm and a plain wooden spear clutched in her other hand. The armor I recognized, but not the Valkyrie who wore it; I'd seen Hilde in a remarkably similar getup when we'd first met, though she'd been more of a sword and shield type of maiden. This woman had finer features than Hilde: a slimmer nose, narrower cheeks, a more pointed chin. She was edgier, too; she had one blue eye and one green, and the sides of her head were shaved, leaving a single blonde braid to trail down her back. Oh, and she'd apparently gouged what looked like a child's rendition of a lighthouse across her armored chest as some sort of hyper-aggressive fashion statement that meant absolutely nothing to me.

"Looks like Valhalla Barbie got a makeover," I said, moving away from the door with a groan.

"Funny," the Valkyrie deadpanned before brandishing her spear. "Now, tell me what you're doing trying to break into our tower before I turn you into a stick puppet."

"Easy there Joan of Bark," I insisted, raising both hands in mock surrender. "I come in peace."

"Who are you?" The Valkyrie's dual-colored eyes narrowed as I straightened and stepped out from the shadows, forcing her to squint up at me. Before I could answer, however, I found the tip of the spear hovering inches from my throat. "You aren't one of the chosen *hugr*. How did you get here?"

"D'ye not catch the 'I come in peace' part of what I said? Or are ye hard of hearin'?" I asked, feigning pity. "Ye should've just told me that from the get go. It's nothin' to be ashamed of."

"Look, I'm not in the mood to joke around. Which means I'm going to stab you unless the next four words out of your mouth give me a reason not to."

"Well, that's just dumb."

Searing pain lanced across my wrist, and the Valkyrie's spear came away dripping with my blood before I could say another word. I hissed and snatched at the slim cut that ran across my forearm, cursing up a veritable storm. I glared at the Valkyrie.

"Ye actually cut me!"

"It's just a flesh wound," she replied, nonplussed. "Three words this time. Make them count."

"Suck me dick."

This time when the Valkyrie struck, I was ready; I danced left, ducked the non-lethal strike I'd suspected was coming, and barreled forward, slamming into the smaller but much better protected spear maiden. We tumbled to the ground with me on top, forced to use what little leverage I had to keep her arms pinned over her head. After several seconds of squirming, the Valkyrie released the spear and helmet, bucking so hard it felt like I was riding the steel horse Bon Jovi never shut up about. I gritted my teeth but held on, aware that the instant her gauntleted hands were free enough to strike, my kidneys would pay a steep price for my gamble.

"Get off me, dammit!" the Valkyrie yelled, sounding more inconvenienced than anything.

"I...am so...tellin' Hilde!" I shouted as I struggled to keep her from rolling sideways and crushing me beneath her weight.

The Valkyrie froze, and I suddenly found myself grunting and squirming all by my lonesome—not the most attractive image, admittedly.

"You know Hilde?"

"If I say 'yes', are ye goin' to slice me open again?"

"Depends. When did you last see her?"

"Not sure," I admitted, my mind sluggish after having essentially pinned the Norse equivalent of an armored tank for a solid minute and change. "Time hasn't exactly been linear, lately. But I'd say the airport in Boston, after we got back from Russia."

"She's in *Boston*?"

"Well, not anymore, she..." I hesitated. "Any chance we can finish this conversation standin'?"

"Fine by me."

"D'ye promise not to stab me, this time?"

"No, but I promise to warn you before I stab you. How's that?"

I muttered a curse under my breath but rolled off the Valkyrie anyway; her armor was cutting into my skin more than her spear had. Turned out that while the medieval set looked awfully stylish—albeit a bit impractical —all those metal bits made for a very uncomfortable wrestling match. Once on my feet, I raised my wounded arm above the level of my heart, waiting for my pulse to slow and the blood to stop seeping from the laceration.

"Still can't believe ye cut me."

"I can't believe you told me to suck your dick."

"Did I, really?" I asked, surprised by the vulgarity of my anatomically impossible challenge. "Sorry about that. Sometimes me mouth says t'ings before me brain has time to process."

"I can relate," the Valkyrie replied, grinning. Which should have been odd given the fact that a couple minutes ago I'd wanted to knock out her eyeteeth, but wasn't; there was something about her I found myself drawn to. Something familiar, though I couldn't be sure what it was.

"Tell me the truth," she continued, "do you really know Hilde?"

"Aye. She saved me life once. Maybe more than once, dependin' what bits ye count," I added, recalling the time Hilde had sheltered me from the Russian firing squad back in Boston, not to mention the time she'd come crashing into a mechanic's garage to mow down several mercenaries before they could murder us all.

God, those had been the days.

"I'll have to tell Freya," the Valkyrie said, visibly relieved as she retrieved her fallen spear and helmet.

"Tell her what, exactly?"

"Hilde has been missing for years, now. Freya will want to know she's alright. She *is* alright, isn't she?"

"As good as can be expected," I replied, unwilling to share the details of Hilde's captivity in Russia lest the spear maiden get all stabby again. "But she wasn't missin'. She told me Odin loaned her out to the FBI, which..."

I drifted off, struck by the sharp look the Valkyrie gave me at the mention of Odin, AKA the Allfather, AKA the Wanderer, AKA the Raven God, AKA...well, you get the gist; basically, the one-eyed leader of the Norse gods had more handles than P. Diddy. Of course, if the Valkyrie's disapproving scowl was any indication, I was willing to bet Odin's next moniker was going to have something to do with being spitted alive.

Odin, he done it, now!

"Who sent you?" the Valkyrie asked, her suspicions returning at the mention of the god. "Was it Odin? One of the other Aesir?"

"None of the above. And, before ye ask, it wasn't one of the Vanir, either. Or the giants," I added, cutting off her next reply. "Or the elves, or the dwarves, or whatever else ye all have livin' under that World Tree of yours."

"Then who?"

"Well, I hitched a ride with the Horseman of Death."

The Valkyrie's face paled.

"But," I forged ahead, "I was actually sent here by Hades. I have a request to make of Freya."

"Did you say Hades?"

"The one and only."

The Valkyrie fell silent, biting nervously at her lip.

"So," I said, feigning nonchalance as I showcased the door that allegedly led into the tower above, "any chance you'll take me to your leader?"

"Freya just left. She'll be at Sessrumnir. That's her house," she explained, correctly deciphering my baffled expression. "Come on, it isn't far."

I fell in step with the Valkyrie, probing at my torn sleeve, tsking at the stain my blood left along the shredded leather seams. But I didn't complain. For some reason, whatever I'd said had clearly shaken the spear maiden to her core; there was no sense kicking her while she was down. No, I'd simply wait until the perfect opportunity to complain about my maltreatment at her hands—likely to Freya, herself.

Anything to get me that blessing I needed to chase after Ryan.

"Say, what's your name, by the way?"

"Kára," the Valkyrie replied, sounding distracted. "Call me Kára."

8

J couldn't be sure how long we walked to get to Freya's house, only that it was one of the most scenic experiences of my life. In fact, I was so invested in our surroundings that I forgot all about my injured wrist and inadvertently left a conspicuous trail of blood as we went. Until Kára casually pointed it out to me, that is, the way you might indicate a stain on someone else's carpet during a dinner party. According to her, those noble souls who called this place home—spirits she called the *hugr*—suffered wounds as any ordinary mortal might, only to be swiftly healed by the power of Fólkvangr itself.

"Guess I'm not that lucky," I said, raising my arm for further inspection. "Odd, though. It should have closed on its own by now. Ye didn't cut very deep."

"No, I didn't," Kára replied with a gallic shrug. Indeed, if the Valkyrie felt any guilt for her part in wounding me in the first place, she hid it well. "But you're right, it shouldn't still be bleeding like that."

"Ye t'ink there's somethin' to it? Some reason I'm not healin'? Like I normally would, I mean."

"I can't be sure. We don't get many strangers here. But I'm certain Freya will have some idea what's happening."

"Assumin' I don't bleed out before we get there," I replied, nonplussed. Oddly enough—other than the inconvenience of my sopping sleeve and the stickiness between my fingers—I felt remarkably fine despite the considerable blood loss. If not for the slight pain whenever I balled my hand into a fist, I might as well have spilled red wine down my sleeve.

"I'm sure you'll be fine," the Valkyrie drawled. She gestured with her spear, indicating a massive inselberg that dominated the horizon to the northeast. "Besides, we aren't far, now."

"Past that hill?"

"Past? No." Kára flashed me a grin that transformed her austere beauty into something warm and welcoming, her green eye glinting in the light, her blue nearly black in the shadows. "Look again."

I did as the Valkyrie suggested only to realize that what I'd mistaken for a massive hilltop was in fact the hollowed-out shell of a giant reptile—presumably the gargantuan remains of a jötunn tortoise. Not that I could blame myself for my assumption; patches of moss spread along the carapace like grass, a quarry's worth of stacked rocks sealed off the gaping holes the creature's extremities had once occupied, and a fine white mist obscured the rest, rising like smoke from a chimney to spiral high into the sky, forming clouds in the shape of charging cavalries and foreboding shield walls.

"That's her freakin' *house*?" I asked, floored by the sheer size of the place.

"One of them." Kára sniggered, then waved for me to join her with one gauntleted hand. "Where else would you expect a goddess to live?"

I refrained from revealing my own status—undocumented though I was—thinking it best to keep my divinity under wraps in case I needed it for leverage at some point in the not so distant future. Inwardly, however, I began seriously reconsidering my real estate investments. After all, even on a part time salary, shouldn't a goddess be able to afford something more on brand than a loft apartment in the heart of Boston? Maybe once this was over, Freya could pass along her agent's information. I could see it, now...me, starring in the next episode of Lifestyles of the Rich and Faemyth, swathed in a silk gown, allowing the camera crew to capture my celestial essence.

Chateau MacKenna, here we come.

"Huh. Does she ever rent it out for parties?"

"Yes, actually. Every evening, more or less. This is where the *hugr* come after training with us. Sessrumnir largely exists to give them a haven, a place to rest and recover."

"Wait, they train with ye? With the Valkyries, I mean."

"Yes. We Valkyries prepare them for what's to come, and Freya makes sure to honor their commitment as often as she can with some much appreciated facetime, and even the occasional Poetic Edda reading."

"What d'ye mean, 'what's to come?' And what commitment?" I asked, trying hard not to get distracted by the notion of what Nordic slam poetry would be like, or what you might call it. Runic rhyme? Viking verse? The spoken sword? I shook my head, refusing to get sucked down that rabbit hole.

"I mean Ragnarök," Kára replied matter-of-factly, as though referencing the Nordic equivalent of the apocalypse in casual conversation were commonplace. "When the fated time arrives, the *hugr* we train will become the vanguard of Freya's army, and we will be their captains."

"Ye seriously believe Ragnarök is goin' to come about? *The* Ragnarök. Like the cataclysmic destruction of the known universe Ragnarök?"

"That's the one. And yes, I do." Kara raised her chin a bit, turning her face towards the sun hanging motionless in the afternoon sky. "In fact, it may have already begun. Either way, time isn't on our side."

I frowned, struck by the use of that particular phrase. Hadn't Hades said something like that before sending me away with Hemingway? I decided to ignore the coincidence, more concerned with the fact that a Valkyrie thought Ragnarök—a Doomsday prophecy that quite possibly exceeded Biblical proportions in scope and breadth—was not only a legitimate threat, but impending. Unfortunately, before I could ask any follow-up questions, Kára reached for me, clasping my forearm with an iron grip that had nothing to do with the armor she wore.

"Come on, I think Freya will want to hear what you have to say sooner rather than later. I'll fly us the rest of the way."

"Fly us? In what?"

"In? Nothing. With? These."

Before I had time to react, a pair of fantastically ornate metal wings decorated in silver filigree burst from Kára's shoulder blades, unfurling with the sound of swords being unsheathed. They were thick and squat, shaped differently than Hilde's had been—an idiosyncrasy I voiced almost immediately.

"Good eye," the Valkyrie admitted, her wings flexing as if glad to finally be set free. "Hilde's specialty was her ability to maneuver in mid-air. We each have our talents, and our wings are often suited to strengths we may not even know we possess. Some even claim they match our personalities.

"And what are your wings designed for?"

Kára grinned.

"Takeoff."

Without warning, Kára exploded upwards, dragging me along by my arm, her wings beating so powerfully at our backs that we cleared the first twenty feet in the space of a heartbeat; my ears popped as we ascended, wind slapping against my face so hard it brought tears to my eyes. I tried to scream, to curse, but my voice was drowned out by the gusts and Kára's laughter.

Apparently the Valkyrie was enjoying herself.

In what might have been seconds but felt like several minutes later, she leveled off and angled for the roof of Freya's house, which was considerably closer than it had been only moments before. I, meanwhile, squirmed in her grip like a fish out of water, kicking my legs so hard it felt like I was running in mid-air.

"Stop that!" she yelled. "I've got you, so enjoy the ride."

"What the hell was that?" I barked back up at her, my shoulder throbbing with pain. "Ye couldn't have warned me?"

"Ever seen a sports car go from zero to sixty in a matter of seconds?" Kára asked, laughing again. "Well, as flyers go, I guess you could say I'm a Bugatti."

"I don't care if you're a freakin' rocket ship, ye damned canary! Next time, give me a heads up."

"And spoil all the fun? Not likely. You should have seen your face."

Kára mimicked an expression that mirrored constipation more than it did terror, then began chuckling so hard her convulsions vibrated down my arm. Realizing I wasn't going to garner any sympathy, much less an apology, I decided to ignore the Valkyrie and do what she suggested: admire the view. From this height, I could see just about as much of Fólkvangr as I had in Hades' chariot, though the stunning vistas seemed to give way to harsher terrain to the east. I pointed with my free hand, curious.

"What's over there?"

Kára was silent for a long moment.

"That's Odin's half of this realm," she answered, at last. "Valhalla. See that thing that looks like a mountain, just over there? That's his mead hall."

"Jesus, that's huge!" I exclaimed, unable to accurately account for the distant shape and its relative size.

"Well, you know how men are. Always trying to overcompensate, somehow."

"Even gods?" I teased.

"Especially gods," Kára replied, sounding strangely bitter. "If you ask me, the only men worth a damn are the ones who want nothing from you and can appreciate when you offer them something anyway."

"Speakin' from experience?"

"Something like that."

Kára descended before we could talk more, dipping incrementally towards a clear stretch of shell, its lovely starburst pattern visible now that we were so close. A lone figure in a dark feather cloak waited for us, hardly larger than my thumb from this distance, her back turned, her hair billowing in the wind. Somehow, I knew without a doubt who I was looking at long before Kára told me who she was; I could feel her muted power much as I had Hades' from behind his door. To me, it smelled like honey and reminded me of the thick, thorn-covered brambles that can so easily ensnare the inattentive—a potent combination worthy of any goddess, but especially appropriate for an all-powerful one.

Like Freya.

e met Freya at the apex of the turtle's shell, our boots clunking against the carapace with every step—not that I expected the downstairs neighbors to be terribly upset. From what I could tell, the *hugr* were throwing a party beneath our feet; the voices of men and women carried, often accompanied by laughter and even—at one point—what sounded like a bawdy song.

"What are they celebratin' down there?" I asked Kára. But the Valkyrie was too distracted to answer; she ducked her head as Freya approached, her dual-colored eyes tracking the intricate patterns beneath our feet as though they held untold mysteries, or offered answers to questions that plagued her. I repeated my question, flicking the helmet she carried under her arm.

"Huh? Oh, the usual, I expect."

"Death," Freya chimed in upon arrival, her manner somehow both gracious and imperious—like she was delighted to play host but felt she was doing us a favor all the same. "But also life. Whenever they hone their skills, the *hugr* recall the thrill of battle and are reminded of the precarious nature of mortality. Here, they are reminded what it means to revel in victory.

"Sounds like fun," I admitted. "Though I'm not sure war was meant to be this glamorous."

I swept an arm out, emphasizing the glorious view from our elevated vantage point. And it was gorgeous. In actuality, however, I took the opportunity to surreptitiously study the goddess; standing a few inches shorter than I was, Freya had the full-figured body of a woman in the prime of her life. Indeed, she reminded me of a flower in full bloom, as though at any moment she might begin to wither and die—a notion that made her all the more alluring. Her honeyed scent rode the air like a perfume, and again I sensed the barest prickle of thorny vines along my skin.

"Perhaps not," Freya replied, shrugging. "But it is my understanding that mortals believe life is most precious when it is threatened, and that beauty is most appreciated when it begins to fade. I chose this place with all that in mind."

"Is that why the sun never sets, here? Because golden hour is the last before night falls?"

"It is one reason."

"What are the others?"

"Tell me why you are here, and perhaps I'll answer you." Freya flicked her gaze to Kára, her expression softening. "I noticed you flew her to meet me, which means you thought this was important. Does it have something to do with what we discussed earlier?"

"What?" Kára looked startled but recovered quickly. "Oh, no, Lady Freya. I found this woman, who clearly isn't one of ours, trying to break into the tower."

"I wasn't tryin' to break in," I protested. "I mean I *was* plannin' to open the door, but no one said anythin' about it bein' locked."

"We argued and fought." Kára gestured for me to display my injured arm, ignoring my objection. "At one point, I nicked her."

"Not 'at one point'," I countered. "Ye cut me before we fought, ye little—"

"Anyway, it won't stop bleeding, and she says she has a request for you. I thought the combination was pressing enough to warrant an audience. I hope you agree, my lady. If not, allow me to throw her from the battlements, myself."

"I pinned ye once, canary," I growled. "Don't ye t'ink I won't do it again."

"Beginner's luck," Kára replied, lightly. "My lady? Is something wrong?"

Except Freya wasn't listening. Instead, she stepped close and took hold of my injured arm, leaning towards the flesh of my wrist as though she were a vampire about to strike. I fought to pull away, but her grip was far too strong; the goddess' lips hovered just over the oozing wound, so close I was afraid she might end up with my blood staining her mouth.

49

"How did you enter this realm?" Freya cocked her head to stare up at me, her gaze fierce and unyielding. "The living don't belong here."

Kára took a step back and flung her training spear to the ground. It skidded across the tortoise shell, clattering, as the Valkyrie reached for the sky and drew from the aether a spangled silver trident that I quickly found hovering a few inches from my throat.

"I am sorry, my lady. I did not know what she was."

"Easy there, Aquachick. Listen, alright? Yes, I'm alive. Or mostly alive, I guess. I'm not exactly clear where I sit on the spectrum. But I'm not here to cause trouble. Hades sent me." I winced as Freya's grip tightened, threatening to grind my bones to dust if she applied even a smidge more pressure. "Jesus, ease up, will ye?"

"Why did Hades send you?"

"Because Helheim has a pest control problem, and he thought ye lot could use an exterminator." I reached up to gingerly push the tip of Kára's trident a few inches farther from my jugular. "And that would be me."

"Helheim?" Freya asked, bewildered. "What's happening there?"

"I have no idea," I admitted, truthfully. "All I know is that it's been invaded by someone strong enough to subdue the Titan Realm. Someone I have to stop. And, in order to do that, I apparently need a blessin' of some sort to enter Niflheim, includin' whatever ye can give me capable of gettin' me past Helheim's security. Preferably without bein' eaten or dyin'."

"Did you know about any of this?" Freya demanded of Kára, who stared at me with open surprise. The Valkyrie shook her head so violently her braid slapped against her aptly-named breastplate.

"She didn't mention any of that to me when we met, or on the way here. But she did say she knew Hilde, which I believe is true."

"Hilde? What's she have to do with this?"

"She claims Odin was the one who sent Hilde to Midgard, by Hilde's own admission."

"Odin?" Freya's grip became a vice and my arm began to turn blue even as she whirled on me. "When did Hilde say this happened?"

"It didn't come up," I hissed, pain making my voice thready. "Look...if ye don't want to believe me, or help me, then fine. Just let me go, and I'll ask someone else. The Horseman said I needed the blessin' of an Aesir or one of the Vanir. I'm sure I can find someone willin' to help."

Of course, that was a bluff; I had no idea how many Norse gods called this particular realm home, but I seriously doubted any of them would be handing out blessings like participation trophies at a youth soccer tournament. In fact, assuming Hemingway hadn't sent me here on some wild ghost chase, I had to assume Freya was my best bet.

Which didn't bode all that well, considering I was about to be a cadaver with a missing limb.

"Kára, you know the Horseman," Freya said after a tense moment of silence, eyeing the Valkyrie. "Can you find him and confirm she's telling the truth about why she's here?"

"I..." Kára began, looking startled. "Yes, my lady. I can do that."

"Good." Freya released my arm with a sickly sweet smile. "In the meantime, I'll see to your wound, and you can tell me all about Hilde."

"What about the blessin'?" I asked, grimacing as I held my throbbing appendage to my chest. "And Helheim. Is there some way to sneak in? I don't have time to waste."

"That depends. Tell me, are you any good at sneaking into places you don't belong?"

"I'm here, aren't I?"

Freya's smile grew chilly.

"I take your point. Well, if what you say is true, I trust Kára will find out. And, if it's a blessing you want, I may have a solution that will benefit us both."

I groaned, inwardly. What was it with these gods and making deals? Why couldn't any of them just accept that I was doing them a favor by seeking out Ryan and be grateful, for Christ's sake? Rather than complain, however, I motioned for Kára to get her trident out of my face and go about her business.

"Hurry back," I insisted. "Please."

The Valkyrie jerked her chin sharply, her wings unfurling with the same surreal grace as before. She bent her knees and leapt, propelled skyward by the immense strength of her wings. I raised my good arm to shield myself from the sudden buffeting, marveling at her absurd speed as she zipped westward.

"They are impressive, aren't they?"

"Who? The Valkyries?" I turned to find Freya watching me, her gaze half-lidded, her expression unreadable. "I'd say so, sure. But then any woman who kicks ass for a livin' tends to impress me."

"Oh, but they are far more than that. Ambitious, driven, passionate...they are warriors, yes. But also caregivers. Teachers. Even lovers."

"Ye would know better than me," I replied, shrugging. "I'll give 'em this, though, they've got the rest of us beat when it comes to style."

I tapped my jacket with a curled middle finger, imitating the gesture Hilde had shown me to transform my top into something both warmer and heavier than my current outfit provided. Despite how long it'd been since I last wore the standard-issue Valkyrie wear, I still knew most of the signs by heart. I had really, really liked my customizable Valkyrie wear.

Too bad I'd short-circuited them.

"Where did you learn to do that?" Freya asked, her eyes suddenly as wide as saucer plates.

"From Hilde."

"She shared *seiðr* magic with you?"

"Is that what you call this?" I asked, tucking my thumb and sweeping my other fingers into a makeshift blade—the sign Hilde had made when she wanted to produce a sword out of mid-air, from what I recalled. Freya made to grab my hand before I could finish, but I was too fast for her this time; I danced backwards, narrowly avoiding her grasp, and prepared myself for a fight—whatever I had or hadn't done, I had no intention of being at her mercy a second time.

I wasn't sure my poor arm could take it.

"That was not for her to show you," Freya hissed, displaying a hint of true discomfort since we'd met. "Come with me, now. I want to know everything."

"And what if I don't feel like sharin', all the sudden?" I growled, hackles rising.

"I'm afraid I must insist."

Freya's power came at me all at once; the sensation of vines wrapped tight around me, their invisible thorns piercing my skin, making me cry out. In seconds, all that honey began to flood my senses, spilling into my throat and lungs until I could hardly draw enough breath to scream. I writhed against her power, my flesh bound and feverish. Hers was an insidious, vibrant strength that offered more pain the longer I resisted.

"Submit, and this will end."

Submit? Me? If I could have laughed, I would have. Instead, the word triggered something within me, some reservoir of power I hadn't realized lay dormant within. It came rising to the surface, filling me with a warmth that reminded me vaguely of the gut-bubbling buzz I'd experienced in Charon's boat. I let that warmth become heat, fed it until the honeyed scent burnt away and the vines began to char. They fell away in a sudden flash of white light.

"What are you?" Freya asked, breathlessly, her face strained, her lips curled in a frown that threatened to disrupt the beautiful illusion she represented.

"Ye know," I said, struggling to control my own breathing, "I'm gettin' really tired of answerin' that fuckin' question."

10

*F*reya raised a fist liberally coated in a dark green salve that reminded me of the dankest weed I'd ever caught a whiff of and began sliding it up and down the linen bandage she'd prepared for my wounded arm. I, meanwhile, pinched my nose before the rank funk gave me a migraine...or got me too high to function.

"Are ye sure that's necessary?" I asked, my voice nasally and echoing in the round antechamber Freya had escorted me to after our brief contest of power. "It stinks."

"The smell will fade," Freya assured me. "Fólkvangr knows you are alive and refuses to let you heal, so I must trick her into believing you belong."

"I thought this realm was yours. Shouldn't ye be able to tell it...her...to heal me and be done with it?"

"Don't be silly. Nature is not something to be bossed around, especially not by us. We gods answer to her, not the other way around. Anyone who believes otherwise is a fool."

"How very...enlightened." I grimaced as Freya began applying the foul-smelling wrap, winding it around my wrist and forearm. It was cool and slick against my skin, though soon a hot, prickling sensation ran up my arm. I shook my head as I processed Freya's words, reminded of my inner goddess and her innate belief in divine superiority—her detached, entitled view of the world. "I take it ye don't feel the same way about mortals. Or is it free will you're contemptuous of?"

"You mean because I tried to force you to do as I wished?" Freya shook her head. "Hierarchies are an integral part of nature. Dominance creates order from chaos. Besides, if you were too weak to stand against me, then why would I bother sending you to Niflheim with my blessing? You would simply have died."

"Does that mean ye intend to give me your blessin'?" I asked, eagerly.

"Did you even hear what I just said?"

"Of course I did. But I also meant what I said before. Time is of the essence."

"More than you know," Freya replied, cryptically. The goddess rose and went to a mahogany bowl full of water to wash the muck from her hands. "And I am considering it. First, I want to hear back from Kára. But, assuming you did not lie to me, there is something I would have you do in exchange for this blessing you want so badly."

"Of course there is," I groused. "And what's that?"

"I have a task for you that only a stranger to this realm can achieve. Given your predilection for sneaking, and having seen your unique power —however you came by it—for myself, I believe you are more than capable. The question is, are you willing to make the trade?"

I mulled her question over for a moment, distantly aware that she'd given me an opening to explain how I'd come by whatever power I'd used to chase hers away. The trouble was, I hadn't the faintest idea; it hadn't felt like my inner goddess coming to my rescue. In fact, the all-consuming heat I'd experienced defied explanation. Should a goddess of night be able to channel such warm energy? I realized I didn't know. There was no user's manual for this sort of thing, no *How to Be a Goddess For Dummies* to brush up on.

"Alright, I'm listenin'," I replied, waving for her to continue. "What's the job?"

"I need you to go somewhere neither I nor my Valkyries can go without drawing unwanted attention. I need you to be my spy."

"Okay...and where would that be?"

"Valhalla."

*P*erhaps an hour or so later, I found myself sitting on a bench full of hairy men, pretending to be one of them as I tossed back a flagon full of uncommonly strong ale, wary of the precariously balanced helmet that sat cockeyed on my head; Freya's Valkyries hadn't been able to find one that fit before I'd left Fólkvangr behind courtesy of a rainbow-tinged Gateway. Fortunately, the majority of Odin's chosen warriors— exclusively men, I was loathe to notice—seemed far too inebriated to pay attention to the tall, fair-skinned redhead in their midst. Of course, the animal skins the Valkyries had draped over my shoulders and tied about my waist to make me appear broader than I was didn't hurt.

"Another!"

The cry came from a different table but was quickly echoed by a second, then a third, as pewter flagons hit wood with cacophonous thuds. In moments, a slew of fair-haired serving maids came wading between the benches, refilling mugs and flashing beatific smiles that would have sickened me if they hadn't been so damned genuine—if these women were upset with their lot in the afterlife, they certainly didn't show it.

"Would you have more?"

I turned to find a freckled maid with hazel eyes that looked nearly yellow in the torchlight poised over my shoulder, her fingers playing with my braided hair—another of Freya's thoughtful additions. I cleared my throat, thrust it down an octave, and accepted her offer. As I passed over the mug, I leaned back so as not to be overheard, inviting the maid to come closer.

"Something else I can do for you?"

"Magni and Modi. I wish to speak to 'em. Where are they?"

"The Allfather's grandsons?" An inquisitive look passed across the serving maid's face but was quickly supplanted by a coquettish smile. "Why bother with them? Wouldn't you rather finish your drink and come lie by the fire with me?"

The fire. Yikes. I glanced past the serving woman, eyeing the mound of bouncing, writhing bodies that "lay by the fire" in an orgasmic pile. In hindsight, I supposed I had either forgotten all about the third "f" Valhalla was known for or simply repressed it. It seemed I'd arrived in time to skip the fighting and join the feasting, which left...well, tossing down a bearskin rug and going at it like there was no tomorrow. Of course, I knew nothing would give away my cover faster than a game of show-and-smell.

Besides, I had a job to do.

"Later, perhaps." I took a judicious sip of my ale. "I need to find the brothers. Can ye point 'em out to me, or not?"

The maid huffed but did as I asked, gesturing across the improbably large mead hall towards two hulking figures sitting in the shadows of a distant corner, nursing their beers in private. The one on the right—based on Freya's description—was Modi; unfortunately top-heavy, he had the look of a lifer on parole: nothing but swollen shoulder muscles and an impossibly thick neck to go with a lion's mane of blonde hair. His companion, Magni, lacked his half-brother's hefty bulk but made up for it with flair; whorling tattoos covered every exposed inch of him, including his face and shaved head, their blue ink standing in stark relief against his thick red beard and beady brown eyes. I frowned, wondering why the two sat so far removed from the festivities; according to Freya, the brothers lived for a good fight and a better feast.

"I wish you would reconsider," the maid insisted, sliding a hand along the smooth curve of my jaw, her nails gliding along my skin. "And not just for your sake. There are not many as pretty as you among Odin's chosen."

"Aye, well, they don't make 'em like me around here," I replied as I drew her hand away, patting it. Part of me, admittedly, was flattered. Of course, a much larger part wanted to know how she kept her nails from chipping in a place like this. Instead, I asked the more pressing question. "Why aren't the brothers joinin' in with the rest of ye? I mean, us?"

"They mourn their father's passing. Thor was beloved by many. But surely you knew that already."

"Actually, I heard he was a dick," I muttered, slipping from the bench to stand alongside the maid, who stared up at me in open surprise. "What? Did I say somethin' I shouldn't have?"

"No. But...to speak of Thor in such a way...it is simply not done." The maid flicked her eyes from side to side as if preparing to cross an invisible street before raising on her tiptoes to whisper in my ear. "Do not say such things in front of Magni and Modi. They will take your head, and no one will stop them, no matter how they felt about Thor, personally." She drew away, searching my face with that coquettish smile. "If you change your mind about the fire, find me. Night will fall soon, and these vaunted warriors will begin to fade. Something tells me you won't suffer from that malady."

Now *that* made me laugh.

"Not generally, no. But I have an advantage they can't compete with," I replied, chuckling. "Anyway, t'anks for the advice." I squeezed the maid's arm, extended my goodbye, and made for the mead hall's corner booth. My marks—that's how I'd thought of them ever since Freya explained who I was meant to spy on and why—didn't so much as bat an eye as I lounged against the nearest wall some ten feet away. But then that was the point: as a fresh face among thousands, the odds of being outed the way one of Freya's Valkyries or one of her *hugr* might have been were far slimmer.

Or so the goddess had explained.

"And why d'ye want me to sneak into the mead hall?" I recalled asking after agreeing to Freya's proposition. "Is it your husband? Afraid he's up to no good?"

"Odin won't be found in Valhalla. In fact, that is why I'm sending you. My husband has other priorities at the moment. But his fellow Aesir are restless. Many believe he is not the god he once was. I believe a few have even gone so far as to propose treason, though I cannot prove it."

"Shouldn't the Allfather be able to nip that in the bud?" I'd frowned then, recalling Odin's legendary foresight at the expense of his own eye. "Surely he knows who speaks against him?"

"Ordinarily, I would say yes. But someone he cares about very much has gone missing, and he's been...distracted." Freya had looked troubled, then. "I believe his grandsons are at the heart of the conspiracy. In his absence, they became terrors—heathens reveling in their newfound freedom like hounds let loose on the livestock. But now that the Allfather has returned and brought change to our way of life, they resent his authority."

"Returned from where?"

"That's not important. What matters is that you find out whether Odin's grandsons are indeed plotting his downfall. Their names are Magni and Modi. You won't miss them, but try to be sure they don't spot you. They don't take kindly to strangers, especially not after what happened to their father."

"Who is their father?"

"Was their father. His name was Thor."

"Wait, *the* Thor? Are we talkin' about Captain Hammertime, himself?"

Freya had shot me a dirty look, then.

"Ah, right. Sorry. How'd he die?"

"Screaming. But that was the path he chose. He was always a spoiled child. Only this time, he tried to push someone around who would not be moved and suffered as a result."

"The natural order of t'ings, eh?"

"You learn fast." Freya had dipped her chin, a faint smile tugging at the corner of her lips.

"And, if I do this, I'll get your blessin'?"

"Find out what Magni and Modi are up to, and I will give you what you seek."

"And what if it's all smoke and no fire? What if they aren't plannin' to overthrow the Allfather?"

"If I'm wrong, I will be relieved. But you must be sure. Magni and Modi are not subtle creatures. You will know their hearts the moment you hear them speak."

And—in that, if in nothing else—Freya had been right.

"The question isn't when we're going to kill the one-eyed bastard, it's how," Magni said, confirming Freya's suspicions with a single sentence, his gravelly voice grinding just loud enough to be heard above the general hubbub of the hall.

"Killing him is not that easy," Modi replied, gloomily. "Or else Father would have done it long ago."

"The Allfather is not what he once was. We've seen it for ourselves. That's why he hid Mjolnir from Father. He feared having it used against him. And now that we know where it is, we can force him to bow before us."

"Then the Temple upstart will pay for what he did. Him and his pet dog."

Magni said something in a voice so low I couldn't quite make it out, something about keeping promises and...drowning puppies? I crept closer, my heart racing after hearing the brothers throw out the Temple surname, wondering what Nate had gotten himself involved in this time. Was he still Zeus' prisoner? If so, what did he have to do with Thor's death?

"At dawn, we ride," Modi asserted, pleasure radiating off him in waves. No, not pleasure. Power. He was flexing his power, sending it out into the room in little waves. But, unlike Freya and the denizens of the Underworld I'd encountered until now, his energy had a diluted feel to it that left a brackish taste in my mouth. Indeed, neither brother seemed particularly powerful—perhaps demigods, at best.

"Yes, at dawn," Magni agreed. "Now, about that source of yours, did Loki say...hey, who's that?"

I struck my most unassuming pose and froze, pretending as hard as I could that I didn't exist. Maybe Magni and his brother would dismiss me as a drunk, or—at worst—tell me to beat it...unless they thought I was eavesdropping and decided to beat *me*, instead. Fortunately, it turned out I wasn't the one who'd piqued Magni's interest.

Unfortunately, I knew exactly who had.

*a*n absurdly tall woman carved a path through rosy-cheeked warriors, shoving them aside with nothing but the sheer breadth of her finely muscled shoulders. Those who foolishly refused to budge were subsequently helped to their feet by their companions, and within seconds a hush settled on the hall as every eye began tracking the blonde. She wore a pale leather jerkin trimmed with white fur that bunched at the throat and waist, a pair of similarly decorated thigh-high boots, white leather pants, and a white wolf headdress that framed her startlingly beautiful face with its savage teeth.

"Child!" the blonde bellowed, her glacial blue eyes locking onto me from across the mead hall. "I felt you enter our realm, and now I have found you at last!"

I felt my mouth gape open of its own accord as I played back the memory of her voice—so loud then that it had threatened to cause avalanches. What the hell was *she* doing here? I glanced surreptitiously at the two brothers, cursed under my breath, and hurried to close the distance between the newcomer and myself. Once within reach, I took her by the arm and drew her aside, painfully aware that she dwarfed even me in this form. Not that I was surprised; the last time I'd seen her she'd been the size of a mountain—literally.

"Skadi," I hissed once I was sure we wouldn't be overhead, using the name she'd given me long ago, in another realm, "what are ye doin' here? And since when are ye mortal-sized?"

"I was too big to fit through the door," Skadi replied affably, bathing me in the radiance of her smile, her voice booming to the rafters as though she had no volume control to speak of. "We jötunnar learned this trick long ago."

A collective gasp rippled through the mead hall in response to Skadi's offhand comment, and I turned to find a cluster of Odin's chosen warriors had formed a loose circle around us. Even worse, Magni and Modi seemed intent on reaching the front of the line, their heads bobbing in unison above the notably shorter crowd.

"You do not seem pleased to see me, breaker of chains."

"Call me Quinn, please," I insisted, grimacing at the unfortunate nickname. "And of course I am. I wasn't sure what happened to ye after we left the Valley of the Dead."

I said "left" out loud, but inwardly I felt the more accurate term would have been fled; the realm Othello and I had invaded with the help of a treacherous vampire—not to mention the magic that had sustained it—had collapsed not long after we freed Skadi from her prison, forcing us to survive several centuries' worth of would-be thieves and ravenous monsters. In any case, it hadn't been pretty. Truthfully, I could have lived my whole life without solving the mystery of what happened to Skadi...especially if finding out meant I might die thanks to her blowing my cover.

"I returned to Thrymheim. The mountain welcomed me as it once did my father, and now I rule atop it as he did." Skadi puffed out her considerable chest and planted meaty fists on her slim hips. "But today the mountain spoke of changes."

"The mountain spoke?"

"Yes, through the thunder for which it was named. You see, since the thunder is no longer bound to serve Odin's brat, it often tells me of the world. Today, it told me of the usurper, of the one who claims to hold winter in his sway. It also told me of you and of your quest to stop him. And so I have come to give you a gift."

Unfortunately, I barely heard the latter part of what Skadi said; subversive whispers broke out at the mention of Thor—also known as Odin's brat, the god of thunder. Worse still, Magni and Modi broke through at that precise moment, their faces ruddy with rage. Modi's flaxen hair began to shine, his muscles bulging with power as he took one floor-shattering step forward.

"Who are you to enter Valhalla and speak of the Aesir with such disrespect?" Modi demanded.

"Let us go," Skadi insisted, ignoring the fair-haired brother. She planted one absurdly heavy arm across my shoulders, its weight enough to make my knees buckle. "You will like Thyrmheim. It is loud and strong, like us."

"My brother asked you a question," Magni hissed, his tattoos swirling in concentric circles that made me a little nauseous to watch.

"Do you hear something?" Skadi asked me, feigning confusion. "It sounds like the yapping of a pup. Listen."

"You dare—" Modi began.

"There it is again."

"That's it!" Modi snarled and rushed the giantess, lunging for her as though he might tackle her to the ground and begin pummeling her for such insolence.

Instead, the giantess open-palmed slapped the son of Thor into the nearest wall. Which, by the way, was some thirty feet across the room. Magni's jaw fell open as he eyed the man-shaped dent his brother's body had made in the solid wood. And, for one very brief, glimmering moment, I thought the bastard might turn tail and run.

But then his eyes fell on me.

"You! You were spying on us," Magni said, stalking forward until he was almost within reach. "What did you hear?"

"Nothin'!" I lied, holding up both hands as though I'd been caught stealing from the candy jar. "I mean, unless ye consider ye two plottin' to kill Odin as somethin'."

Magni's eyes danced across the faces around us as the eavesdroppers leaned in, clearly wondering what I'd meant. Seeing their uncertainty, the son of Thor threw out both hands and addressed the growing crowd like some sort of ringleader.

"Einherjar! Odin's chosen! We have intruders among us. Two lowly creatures who were not chosen by the Allfather, himself! What say you to that?"

As if on cue, a series of cries bubbled up from the crowd of onlookers. Some were tamer than others—shouts of "kick them out" or "make them apologize" that were quickly overtaken by harsher, more aggressive suggestions like "put their heads on pikes" or "skin them alive." Magni began pumping his arms in the air, encouraging their bloodlust. Fortunately, it didn't take a genius to see where this was going.

So, before Magni could whip them into a complete frenzy, I did what any sane person about to be torn apart by a mob would do: I kicked their leader in the testicles with everything I had, smashed a pewter mug across his head, and pushed the nearest warrior into a crowd of unsuspecting drunks.

And, with that, the bar fight was officially on.

13

*U*nfortunately, the series of blows I'd landed—while therapeutic for me—seemed to have very little effect on the bearded hulk. Magni rose to his feet with a groan, shook his head like a concussed football player, groped at his crotch, and glared at me even as his would-be mob began surging in on itself.

"What have you done?" Magni demanded.

"Isn't it obvious?" I waved a hand in the general direction of the crowd, ducking as a flagon flew past my head. "Ye got 'em all riled up. All I did was give 'em a push."

Skadi laughed as a fist fight broke out between two revelers to our right, their scuffle taking them into a table full of nearly passed out drunks. In seconds, the bench was empty as more warriors joined the fray. The giantess clapped me on the shoulder.

"Well done!"

"That's enough!" Magni bellowed, pointing at me, then Skadi. "I'll show you what it means to insult the memory of Thor in Valhalla, you filthy—"

The giantess lashed out with one foot and sent Odin's grandbaby soaring into the rafters before Magni could so much as utter another word. I winced as he collided with the ceiling, then crashed to the floor, squashing several warriors in the process. I turned to find the giantess grinning from ear to ear.

"Enjoyin' yourself?"

"I love my home," the giantess replied as she began cracking her neck and rolling her absurdly toned shoulders, "but it gets lonely. I have no one to wrestle but the bears, and they do not enjoy being pinned as much as they once did. Besides, it seems Odin's warriors have forgotten the first rule of Valhalla."

"Not to talk about Valhalla?" I ventured.

"No." Skadi beckoned a small group of onlookers who'd managed to avoid the excitement, her eyes gleaming. "The rule is never to back down from a challenge, no matter what."

"Even if that challenge could get ye killed?" I muttered, falling into a fighting stance, my pulse racing at the very real possibility of being pummeled to actual death by Odin's spirit army. After all, I hadn't healed before—there was no reason to believe I'd recover from injuries sustained in an all-out bar brawl.

Not that I regretted anything, mind you.

"Goddesses do not die," Skadi replied, knowingly, before leaping into the fray.

"What about part-timers?" I yelled after her, but she was too far gone to hear me by that point; bodies went pinwheeling into the rafters as she leapt into the fray. I watched her go, shaking my head in amusement, only to feel a pair of impossibly beefy arms wrap around me, crushing the air from my lungs as they drew me back towards a chiseled body.

"Looks like she left you all alone, little mouse," Modi whispered maliciously into my ear, the heat of his cheek against my neck raising goosebumps along my spine. "Let's have some fun while you tell me who sent you, shall we?"

"Your father..." I wheezed, struggling to draw breath, "is...alive."

"What did you say?" Modi spun me around.

Which was exactly what I'd hoped he'd do; I headbutted the bastard, slamming my skull into his nose with as much force as I could muster. I reeled from the experience, seeing galaxies as opposed to stars, but at least the assault had the desired effect: Modi released me, clutching his shattered nose instead of my arms. What I hadn't prepared for, unfortunately, was the backhand that followed.

The blow sent me flying across the room to crash headlong into a gaggle of rumbling drunks who broke my fall with all the comfort of a concrete slab. I groaned, they groaned, we all groaned as the collision took its toll. Eventually, I rolled away, flopping onto my back to stare up at a gap in the rafters from where Magni had hit, just in time to watch the last light of day dwindle and cease. The stars came out, accompanied by the pounding of Modi's footsteps and the wheeze of his threats. Of course, I wasn't listening; I had far more important things to worry about.

Like how I'd gotten here in the first place.

*T*he ugly face of a demigod obstructed my partial view of the night sky, its bulbous-nosed, broad jawed mashup caked in blood that seeped from each nostril like a leaky faucet. Hairy, calloused hands reached for me as though to draw me to my feet. I cringed at the thought of being touched by such dirty fingernails and slapped them away with disdain, glaring at the figure hovering over me, irked by his presumption.

"Can I help ye?" I asked, forced to speak up to be heard over the din; wherever I was, it seemed a fight of some sort had broken out. Even now I could hear guttural shouts, the occasional crow of victory, and the splintering of wood.

"You can die!" the demigod snapped, abandoning all pretense of civility as he lunged for me.

"Oh?" I flicked my wrist, and a ribbon-like tendril of shadow answered; the dark shape flew towards the demigod's throat and encircled his flesh like a lasso, yanking him backwards like a dog hitting the end of his leash. The oafish creature groped at his neck, fingers passing right through his shadow collar, his unfortunate face purpling so quickly it felt like I was staring up at a grape about to burst.

I sat up and flung the demigod sideways so he wouldn't obscure my view. Scowling, I took stock of my surroundings, noting the beer-soaked floor and my blood-stained shirt with equal disgust. I pawed at myself, aware that even my mouth tasted of that coppery substance. Had some pious soul offered me their blood as a sacrifice, or had I torn out some mortal's beating heart and eaten it? Neither notion appealed to me, but I knew there had to be some explanation. Unfortunately, judging by the melee raging inside what appeared to be a massive wooden hall, anything was possible. As I watched, a swarthy, bearded man began pounding on a red-haired giant with a series of hammerfists, beating on him in fits and spurts to form some sort of primal language that defied translation.

Norse Code.

That voice again, tinged with amusement. Still, I supposed it made sense: the brawlers looked like vikings with their animal skins and vibrant fabrics. They also fought like what you'd expect from a race of plunderers—albeit more ferociously than I would have thought possible. No mortal, after all, should have been able to take a dozen blows to the head from an attacker and keep drinking, or get body slammed into a table only to leap to their feet a moment later. And yet, these improbable things happened again and again.

"Where am I?" I wondered aloud.

Valhalla.

The answer slid across my mind like a caress, and with it came the faintest memory. I suddenly remembered where I was and how I'd gotten here, though the latter was a bit murky. Another goddess had sent me to...spy for her? That couldn't be right. Why would I have agreed to something like that?

I'd only just risen to my feet, prepared to find answers, when the blonde demigod I'd dismissed moments before came hurtling between two tables and barreled into me, wrapping his arms about my legs and lifting me off the ground like a child. I ended up half over his shoulder, staring down at his rippling back as he slammed me against, and then through, the nearest wall. The demigod slipped as his feet hit a plot of slick grass, and within seconds the obscene weight of his body fell on top of me, his shoulder goring into my stomach with the full force of his momentum.

The experience as a whole was...unpleasant.

I grunted, raised a hand, and punched the demigod in the ear before he could think to try anything so foolish a second time. The angle was awkward, but the blow landed well enough; the blonde reeled, rolling to his side and cradling his injured organ, whimpering like a whipped dog.

"Not goin' to do that again, are ye?"

I huffed as I found my feet, forced to brush off more dirt and grime from my ruined clothes. At this rate, I'd have to steal an outfit from those vikings—preferably something befitting a goddess of my stature. I eyed the writhing demigod. Too big. Maybe there would be someone my size inside?

Before I could find out, however, a body came careening through the mead hall wall, thrown so hard it blasted shards of wood everywhere and ended up bouncing across the lawn like a skipped stone. A figure stepped through the gaping hole she'd created, her body bathed in moonlight and roiling with power. I took an inadvertent step back, wary of the newcomer; her power lashed at the very air, tasting of ice and bone-chilling cold. And yet she kept it contained, somehow, refusing to let it loose on this place, perhaps aware that—if she did—she'd be dooming us all to a blizzard the likes of which I could only imagine.

"Who are ye?" I called.

"I see you are still figuring things out, child," the blonde goddess replied, grinning wolfishly. "Come find me when you have finished with those two."

I followed her gaze, realizing the demigod who'd tackled me had wandered off to help the hapless soul she'd sent hurtling through the wall. Together, leaning on each other for support, seething with anger and wounded pride, the two figures rose. I turned to ask a follow-up question, but the blonde goddess had retreated back into the mead hall.

"Now you've done it." The demigod I'd punched stepped forward, threatening me as though he hadn't been whining like a child only a few minutes ago. "Separate, my brother and I are stronger than any mortal."

"But together," his companion continued, his rusty beard comically askew, "even gods bow down before us."

"Not this one," I drawled.

"Magni," the blonde demigod said, throwing out one arm so dramatically that I'd have thought they were trying out for a play.

"Modi," replied the other, mimicking him.

Power began to build as the two locked hands, their energy shifting from one to the other and back again with a rocking sensation—like the tide rushing in and out. With every oscillation, the power grew. The two demigods began to glow with it; the blonde's hair seemed to catch fire, his eyes burning golden beneath the night sky, while the ginger's skin became a canvas of swirling blue light. I watched with interest as they began hyping each other up, shouting their names like berserkers.

"Magni!"

"Modi!"

"MAGNI!"

"MODI!"

Just as their voices reached an impossibly loud crescendo, their combined luminescence enough to make me squint, I caught sight of a dark figure lurking behind them. A serving girl, judging by her attire. I thought to warn her to step away from the crazy bastards before they erupted, but she didn't give me a chance. Instead, the girl spread both arms wide, holding them outstretched like wings...and slapped the shit out of both demigods from behind.

Their combined light went out like a snuffed candle as the two brutes toppled to the ground, limp and unmoving. I blinked away spots in my vision and cocked an eyebrow as the serving girl approached, moving more sinuously than I'd have expected given her slim body.

"Who are ye?"

"You know, I knew there was something special about you the moment we met," the serving girl replied, her eyes gleaming yellow in the moonlight. "Asking about these two, badmouthing Thor. And in Valhalla, no less. So risky."

"We've met?"

"Of course we have. I see I must not have made enough of an impression." The serving girl pouted, though the expression failed to account for the amusement twinkling in her otherworldly eyes. "That's alright. I'm sure you won't forget me after tonight."

She raised a hand to her face as if to pull away a mask, pale yellow smoke trailing from her fingertips. I caught the barest glimpse of another face lurking behind her own, the briefest sense of a power that rivaled—if not surpassed—my own. But then, like a faucet being turned in the opposite direction, the sensation fled, and the serving girl's pout returned.

"Looks like Freya sent her pet pigeons to ruin the fun," she said, her arm falling limp to one side as she studied the night sky. True to her prediction, a flock of winged creatures soared towards us, their silhouettes visible across the face of the moon. "Such a shame. Things were just getting interesting, too. Oh well, I guess it's time to go."

"I don't t'ink so" I said, throwing out a hand, binding the serving girl's limbs with chains formed from shadow. "Tell me who ye are."

But the girl's body simply dissolved, turning into yellow smoke that coiled into the air, leaving only a floating head to speak three solitary words before it, too, faded like a mirage.

"See you around."

15

I found myself surrounded by armored women with their weapons drawn, their metal wings tucked out of sight beneath the folds of hooded cloaks the color of arterial blood. I studied each in turn, struck by a nagging sense of familiarity that left lingering impressions of hands braiding my hair and smiling faces leering over my shoulder as I studied myself in the mirror. Only it wasn't my reflection I saw staring back at me, and there was no way I could have spent time with these mortals without knowing it; I couldn't even recall their names.

Valkyries.

Before I could locate the source of that voice, a Valkyrie with a crude lighthouse etched across her breastplate stepped closer than the rest, dragging the two unconscious demigods across the lawn by their wrists. She dumped them at my feet like discarded trash and threw her hands up into the air, clearly irate.

"What were you thinking?" the Valkyrie demanded. "You were supposed to spy on these idiots, dammit, not incite a riot!"

"I was spyin' on these two?" I arched an eyebrow, bent down, and snatched up both demigods by their tunics. I lifted them up high overhead, studying their slack faces and wondering what could possibly make them worth my attention. Finding nothing of note, I began looking for traces of whatever magic the serving girl had used to short circuit the meatheads. I didn't find any; whatever she'd done, it had been too quick, too subtle, for me to follow. I grunted, annoyed—between her and the blonde goddess with literal ice in her veins, I was beginning to feel a little outclassed.

"How the hell are you doing that?"

I craned my neck, looking past the demigods to find the Valkyrie who'd accused me of starting the brawl in a fighting stance, the razor sharp prongs of her trident pointed directly at me as though I'd threatened her with some form of violence. I gave her the look that deserved and swiveled to face her directly.

"Doin' what, exactly?"

"That." She tilted her chin towards the demigods, jabbing her glorified pitchfork in their general direction. "Lifting them over your head. When did you get that strong?"

"When?" I echoed, frowning. I shrugged, confused by the question, and dropped the bodies. They landed with a thud, sprawled across each other like exhausted lovers. "I've always been like this."

"Not always," the Valkyrie countered. "When we fought, you weren't capable of that."

"Don't be ridiculous. We've never fought."

"Did you hit your head, or something? Of course we did. I sliced your wrist. Look!"

I glanced down at the wrist she indicated, saw the grubby bandage binding it, and began immediately tearing the wretched thing off; blood and beer were one thing, but any material stained that particular color could only have revolting origins. Fortunately, once removed, I found the flesh underneath as pale and unblemished as ever.

"Lady Freya's magic must have healed you," the Valkyrie muttered, dubiously. "I'm telling you, we fought, and you were barely able to pin me."

"That's impossible."

"Why impossible?"

"Because," I replied, exasperated by her insistence, "if we'd fought, you'd be dead."

The Valkyrie's mouth fell open, then clamped shut, her jaw clenched so tight I could practically hear her teeth grind. She narrowed eyes of two different colors, shaking her head.

"I don't think so."

"No? Well, you're welcome to prove me wrong. Otherwise, I suggest ye drop it."

"Don't be ridiculous. We came to retrieve you, not beat you senseless."

The first rule of Valhalla.

"I challenge any one of you to try."

The Valkyrie's two-toned eyes widened at the challenge, her trident dipping several inches as though she'd expected me to back down. Realizing that wasn't the case, she tensed, her grip tightening perceptively around the shaft of her chosen weapon. I flashed her an inviting smile, daring her to make the first move.

But then a hand landed on her arm.

"Allow me, sister."

"Róta?" The trident-wielder flinched, startled to find another Valkyrie at her side. "No, this is my challenge to answer. Lady Freya asked me to look after her...even though kicking her ass probably wasn't what she had in mind."

"The spy issued the challenge to all of us. As your elder, I insist you allow me the honor." The Valkyrie—Róta, I assumed—patted her younger companion's shoulder. "Stand down, Kára."

I could tell Kára, the younger Valkyrie, didn't like it, but still she stepped aside with a slight bow of her head. Róta stepped forward wielding a spear that appeared carved from lava rock; veins of fire spread along the shaft, consolidating at the tip to form a blade of pure white heat. She let that blade graze the grass, and, within seconds, the blades began to curl and brown.

"I will try my best not to do any permanent damage," Róta said, addressing me for the first time. "Lady Freya warned us of your frailty. Submit quickly, and we will take you back with us to give your statement regarding what happened here. But, if you insist on being difficult, you should know that I—"

A loud crash from inside the mead hall caught everyone's attention, cutting the Valkyrie off mid-sentence—which was just as well, seeing as how I had no interest in listening to her ridiculous threats. Clearly, the Valkyries had me confused for someone else; there was nothing frail about me. A series of shouts and groans erupted after a brief silence, chased by a booming laugh I thought I recognized.

So, the goddess was still inside wreaking havoc.

"Kára, take the others and go see what's happening inside," Róta insisted. "I'll handle this alone. Oh, and avoid the einherjar, if you can."

"And if I can't?"

"Then at least try not to break anyone," Róta replied, a smile tugging at the corner of her lips. "We wouldn't want relationships to deteriorate any further than they have already. In fact, take the Allfather's grandsons and drop them somewhere inside when no one's looking. We wouldn't want anyone to think we had anything to do with what happened to them."

"Understood."

The Valkyries marched off without another word, though I noticed Kára casting a dubious glance my way before ducking through the hole the goddess had created, the fallen demigods in tow. I had a moment to replay Róta's instructions in my head and to wonder what sort of political quagmire I'd stumbled upon, but I didn't bother dwelling on it. Now that the fight was imminent, I couldn't afford to get distracted.

With her fellow Valkyries gone, Róta seemed considerably more at ease; she began whipping her chosen weapon about, arcs of flame trailing wherever the speartip passed. The effect was actually rather pretty, despite the circumstances, and I told her so.

"Thank you," she replied, bowing her head. The metal plume atop her helmet caught the moonlight, and I was suddenly able to discern the design: a bird in flight, the wings thrown back to flare like horns on either side of her head, the neck and beak descending to rest against the bridge of her nose.

"Fantastic workmanship, too," I noted, pointing.

"If you keep complimenting me, I may start to think you don't want this fight," Róta said, resuming her fluid spear twirling routine.

"Well, we can't have that. Tell me, why didn't ye want your underlin' fightin' me? Afraid I'd hurt her?" I asked, tracking her graceful, flowing movements out of the corner of my eye.

"Hurt her? No, Kára is more than capable of taking care of herself. I should know, I trained her when she first came to us."

"Still, ye stepped in on her behalf. Why was that?"

"Kára has been distracted lately, and I could tell she didn't want to fight you. I also noticed that you shared none of her reservations in that regard." Róta stilled and studied me, her eyes peering out from beneath the sloped curve of gleaming steel. "Do you agree to the terms of our bout?"

"We fight until one of us submits, is that it?"

"Succinctly put, but yes."

"Fine by me."

I swept out an arm, swatting the Valkyrie with a wave of shadow thick enough to send her flying in a way she wasn't used to. Except that wasn't what happened. Instead, the shadow crashed against her breastplate and shattered like a window pane, sending her stumbling—but certainly not soaring—backwards. Róta muttered a curse, staring wide-eyed at my exposed arm. A glance revealed the shimmering emerald veins beneath my skin, visible where the leather of my coat had been torn and the bandage removed.

"How is that possible?"

"I should be askin' ye the same question," I replied, eyeing her intricate armor appreciatively. "That's magic shieldin' ye, I take it? But not your own, I t'ink, or I'd have sensed it."

"Our armor is tied to our bond with Lady Freya and the Allfather. It protects us." Róta assumed a much less relaxed stance, her spear leveled over her forearm in a pose I thought I recognized. "But it is our life force which powers that bond. Our will to win."

"Ye know, you're very forthcomin' for a mortal," I noted. "I appreciate that. Tell ye what, let's make this interestin'."

I held out my hand and waited for a sliver of night to form, felt it coil and lengthen beneath my palm until it was roughly the same length as Róta's spear. The instant I clasped it, green flames burned along the shaft as if mirroring my foe's weapon. I fell into a stance that felt eerily familiar, the tip of the spear pointed towards the ground, the shaft across my back.

Róta's eyes widened further.

"You've fought with a spear before, I see."

"Only one way to find out."

The Valkyrie grunted, grinned, and lunged. Her strike came startlingly fast; the white hot blade of her spear licked my cheek as I pivoted and brought my own to bear, flicking it up to crack against her pole and send it skyward, leaving her wide open for a counterattack. I took the opportunity to spin, using my body rather than my weapon to get in close, and felt the tip of my spear score a hit across the Valkyrie's belly that would have sliced her open were it not for her armor. Still, by getting past her guard, we both knew I had her at a significant disadvantage; she couldn't defend against my blows with her spear overextended.

Except it seemed defense wasn't her main concern.

Róta dropped her spear entirely, letting it tumble to the ground in exchange for a free hand—one she balled into a fist the instant I swiveled to strike at her a second time. She struck me across the face with it, her gauntleted hand taking me just below the eye with enough force to send me sprawling. I rolled with the blow, coming up with my spear in a half-guard, but Róta was busy retrieving her own weapon, her fingers probing at the wicked scratch I'd left across her midsection.

"That was expertly done," she said, sounding impressed.

"Would've been better if you'd ended up cradlin' your guts," I admitted, marveling at the taste of blood in my mouth from her blow. "That was some punch."

"The trick is putting your back into it. So, do you submit, yet?"

"To a juiced-up mortal?" I laughed, amused by her cheekiness. "Not a chance."

"You keep saying that like you aren't one. And then there's your arm. Reminds me of when the Temple boy came to Asgard." Róta rolled her shoulders. "Well, Lady Freya did warn us not to underestimate you. Suppose I can't be too surprised."

"I have no idea what you're talkin' about," I admitted, though her words did stir a vague...something. Whispers bubbled up inside my head, promising answers if only I would listen. But I shook them off, focusing instead on the task at hand: tearing my opponent apart. "Once this is over and I've peeled ye out of that suit, you'll have to explain what all this nonsense was about."

"You sure do talk a lot."

I ran my tongue across one of my eye teeth, amused by the Valkyrie and her endless gall. If I wanted, there were at least a dozen ways I could silence her for good. I could smother her with a blanket of night, for instance, or bind her with the chains I'd used on the serving girl. I could even reach out and call to the fire that burned inside her breast, draining her will to win even as I drank the life force she was so proud of. But none of those methods would satisfy me as much as beating her at her own game.

A goddess has to have a little pride.

"Your move," she insisted, beckoning.

I jerked my chin in acknowledgment, accepting her challenge in complete silence.

This time, I'd let my actions do the talking.

16

The second round of my fight with Róta lasted perhaps another couple seconds before we were rudely interrupted by a half-dozen Valkyries crashing onto the lawn through a series of brand new holes —just long enough for us to square off before turning to stare at a mead hall that was beginning to look more and more like a block of Swiss cheese. The Valkyries who'd been thrown lurched to their feet, groaning, their armor dented and charred in places, their cloaks shredded or gone entirely. The one with the dual-colored eyes, Kára, was not among them.

"What happened in there, and where's—" Róta began.

The remaining Valkyries came pouring through the breach to join their companions, forming a vanguard of deadly warriors that looked capable of standing firm against any threat. Any threat, that is, but the overwhelming power of a goddess; the blonde I'd spoken to earlier emerged holding a battered but still lively Kára by one arm, their silhouettes looming large against the torchlight at their backs.

"Who does this one belong to?" the goddess called, ignoring the Valkyrie's incessant squirming.

"Wait, Skadi? Is that really you?" Róta asked, her mouth agape.

"Róta, get over here and help me stop this thing!" Kára shouted before the goddess could answer, firing off a savage kick that glanced harmlessly off the blonde's thigh. "She's the one who started the brawl inside!"

"I did no such thing." The goddess chucked Kára across the lawn to land just a few feet away from where I stood, then pretended to brush her hands clean as though she'd just finished taking out the trash. "That was all her," she continued, pointing in my direction.

Everyone's eyes turned to me.

"Well, I'm sure I had a good reason."

"Reasons make no difference," the goddess replied, grinning. "It is Valhalla. Everyone fights. Anyway...Róta! It is good to see you. Sorry about your sisters. I did not recognize any of them, or I would have held back a little."

"Valkyries!" Róta called, her voice quavering with what might very well have been fear. "Stand down. Now!"

"Róta, come on, together we can take—" Kára began but was immediately cut off by a sharp look from her superior. The younger Valkyrie rose to her feet, glaring at the blonde goddess as though looks alone could kill. Still, I had to at least admire her spirit, if not her common sense; not many mortals had what it took to threaten not one but two goddesses in the same night.

"What brings the jötunnar here, Skadi?" Róta asked. Her question was immediately met with whispers and sidelong glances from the other Valkyries. Even Kára seemed taken aback by the news; she stopped glaring to rub at the wrist the goddess had held only moments before, her eyes wide and disbelieving.

"She brings me here," Skadi replied, pointing at me a second time. "This one freed me from a Tiny God's prison."

"You freed one of the jötunnar?" Kára hissed, her voice so hushed I doubted anyone else could have heard her. "Are you freaking insane?"

"I didn't. Or at least, I don't remember..." I struggled to find the words, suppressing a sudden headache as a superimposed vision of Skadi's face appeared before me, the pupils of her eyes so large I could see myself reflected in them, the spread of her impossibly huge rosebud lips like watching a cave mouth undulate. I looked around in my mind's eye and saw her manacled wrists, saw the chains that bound her. But then the vision shifted, and the chains were no longer there; all that remained was a trunk of twisted metal, its jagged edges reaching for the sky. Suddenly, I felt ridiculously overwhelmed by that nagging voice within, my equilibrium so disrupted I could no longer stand.

Kára caught me before I hit the ground.

The Valkyrie hoisted me upright with a firmer grip than was strictly necessary; I could feel her fingers burrowing into my shoulders blades. I shook my head, trying to clear it, and pushed her away, resolved to stand on my own two feet. I was a goddess, dammit, not some fragile mortal with a weak constitution.

Something had to be wrong.

I closed my eyes and stretched my senses only to find the night fading fast. But how? The night had been young only a couple hours before. There was no way I'd lost track of that much time, was there?

"It's no good. Dawn is comin'," I said, drawing strange looks from all but Skadi. "I have to go."

"Go where?" Skadi asked.

I looked up to find the goddess approaching, her arms spread wide as if to appear less threatening. But I wasn't fooled; her frigid power remained, leaking from her like a cool breeze. Indeed, frost licked at her boot heels, turning blades of grass into shards of ice wherever she stepped. Still, I didn't run. Something about her question made me hesitate, made me turn it over and over in my mind like a puzzle box. Where would I go? What was I doing here? I wasn't sure. Why wasn't I sure?

"What's happenin' to me?" I whispered, drawing a cluster of shadows together to form a cloak and wrapping myself in it. Kára gasped and danced backwards at the display of power, mirroring her companions. Only Skadi and Róta seemed unperturbed, though—if you asked me—the pity written across their faces was far worse.

"Nothing we cannot fix, Quinn." Skadi stepped close to place her hands on my shoulders, her voice surprisingly gentle. "You freed me from an eternal prison in exchange for a flower."

"I don't remember that."

"That's alright. You did not know what you were then, either."

"I know what I am," I countered, angrily. "I'm just not sure what I came here for, or what I want to do, next…"

"Give it a minute, and it will come to you."

17

*I*n the end, it didn't even take that long; the sun broke over the horizon mere seconds later, painting the cloud-strewn sky in shades of pink and purple that might have brought tears to eyes far less cynical than mine. I blinked rapidly, and found Skadi studying me in the dim light of dawn, her glacial blue eyes probing for signs that I was still in there, somewhere. For a brief moment, I considered pulling a prank on the earnest giantess, like feigning amnesia or faking a schizophrenic episode. But truthfully, I was too tired to bother.

"So, who won the bar fight?" I asked, wearily.

"Ah, there we are! Glad to have you back!" Skadi bellowed, slapping my shoulder with enough gusto that it sent me stumbling sideways, my arm throbbing as though she'd punched the shit out of it.

"Back?" a familiar voice asked. "Back from where?"

I turned to find a very ragged looking Kára leaning on her trident, looking skeptical at best. Not that I could blame her; I hadn't warned Freya or her Valkyries about my...condition before going into this. Of course, that was at least partially because I'd sincerely hoped that—between Fólkvangr's eternal sunshine of the endless time and the afterlife's general disregard for physics—it wouldn't come up.

"Say, why is it mornin', already?" I asked once I realized Skadi intended to ignore Kára's question. "Shouldn't it still be nighttime?"

"Time works differently here," Róta explained, her gaze lingering on my face as though I'd said something more interesting than I'd intended. "The day progresses faster in Valhalla so that Fólkvangr may remain largely unchanged."

"Two sides of a flipped coin, is that it?"

"They are connected, yes. Even in the afterlife, there must be balance. Right and wrong. Joy and sorrow. Day and night," Róta added, giving me a meaningful look. "So, now that you've regained your...senses, would you care to tell us what happened here?"

"Ah, well..." I hesitated, surprised to find my memories weren't the jumbled mess I was used to, but rather a montage of notable moments—a highlight reel I could access at will. Of course, that didn't mean I wanted to; recalling how I'd mistreated the Valkyries, how I'd threatened them after they'd only tried to help, made me cringe. I found myself wondering how much they knew or suspected. And then there was Skadi, who—according to her cryptic comments over the course of the evening—seemed to have a better idea what I was than I did.

Or, at the very least, what made me tick.

"Listen, I should have told ye lot before," I admitted, sheepishly, "I'm a—"

"She is a witch," Skadi interjected, cutting me off before I could expose myself in front of everyone.

Well, my divinity, that is.

"A witch?" Róta asked, dubiously.

"Yes."

The Valkyrie and the jötunn exchanged meaningful looks that didn't go unnoticed by the rest of us. Still, when Róta accepted Skadi's explanation despite its obvious inconsistencies, no one argued or complained. Perhaps because the lie was more convenient than the truth, or perhaps because plausible deniability was a valued commodity even in the afterlife. Either way, it seemed—for the time being, at least—I was a falsely-labeled witch. A logical occupation in the afterlife for a six-foot-tall redhead, I figured.

Now all I needed was a broom and a pointy hat.

"Well then, witch, why did you start the bar fight?" Kára asked, cutting through the momentary silence with her snark.

"I didn't *start* it," I replied, glaring at Skadi for ratting me out. "Magni and Modi were stirrin' up trouble, tryin' to get the warriors inside—"

"The einherjar," Kara supplied.

"Sure, whatever. They were tryin' to get the *einherjar* to mob us."

"And how did they know to do that in the first place? Wasn't the whole point of this operation to disguise yourself and keep out of sight?"

"Ye try spyin' on someone with *her* tellin' everythin' with ears who ye are," I replied, jabbing my thumb at the giantess. "She's not exactly built for stealth."

Skadi beamed as though I'd given her a compliment but contributed nothing else to the conversation, clearly content to let Kára grill me as she saw fit.

"And Odin's grandsons? Were you the one who brought them down? How did you do it?"

"No," I replied, thinking back on the beginning of the evening. "That was someone else. A servin' girl. She took 'em both out with one blow."

"A serving girl?"

"It's fuzzy," I admitted. "I remember she was in the mead hall. We spoke before I eavesdropped on the brothers. She even pointed 'em out to me when I asked. But she wasn't what she seemed. There was somethin' about her eyes. And I remember seein' yellow smoke...and...someone else's face hidin' beneath hers?"

"That's enough questions, for now," Róta said, her gaze shifting to the mead hall, a scowl plastered across her face as several bleary-eyed drunks poked their heads out to stare at us. "We should go before our presence draws more notice than it already has. She can tell the rest to Lady Freya in person."

"Freya?" Skadi barked, her expression darkening as she reached out to grip my arm. "You are working for the Vanir?"

"More like freelancin', if I had to put a label on it. She's got somethin' I need."

"And you, Róta? Since when do the Valkyries answer to Freya?"

"She took command of us after the Allfather disappeared," Róta explained. "Without him to reign in their baser impulses, we could no longer walk freely among the einherjar. Times have...changed, Skadi. The world is not what it once was."

"I can see that." The giantess scowled, and the air began to grow chilly, sending goosebumps rippling along my arms and shivers up my spine. Interestingly, I wasn't the only one who noticed; the Valkyries shifted uncomfortably, eyeing Skadi as one might a volcano about to blow.

"We have our orders," Róta insisted. "I would ask that you allow us to bring her back. We don't mean her any harm."

"Very well, then," Skadi replied, her eyes bright with barely restrained amusement. "Let us all go see Freya."

"I'm sorry. You wish to, um, come with us?"

"Of course. I have my own affairs to settle with Quinn. Besides, I have not seen any of the Vanir since my wedding to Njord. I look forward to experiencing my daughter-in-law's hospitality firsthand."

"Hold on, your what?" Kára asked, her expression mirroring the surprise on everyone else's face, excluding her superior, who seemed more mortified than surprised. "Róta, what did she just say?"

"Njord is Lady Freya's father," the Valkyrie replied, exchanging a meaningful look with her subordinate. "Which means we would be more than happy to escort them both to Fólkvangr."

"Much as I appreciate this whole talkin' about me like I'm not here t'ing ye lot keep doin'," I said, waving my hand like a child looking for attention, "what exactly d'ye mean when ye say 'escort'? Can't Freya just make us a Gateway?"

"Unfortunately, no. There wasn't time once we realized your cover had been blown to set anything like that up. In fact, *Lady* Freya sent so many of us because she was concerned Magni and Modi would be loathe to hand you over unless they had no other choice. The plan was to fly back once we retrieved you."

"To fly back," I echoed, recalling the awkwardness of dangling from Kára's grasp the day before, not to mention the discomfort that had followed. "Aye, well...I t'ink I'll pass, if it's all the same to ye."

"There are other ways," Kára supplied, barely able to suppress her smile at my obvious unease. "But they aren't as fast. And you did say you were on a deadline."

"I'll show ye a deadline," I muttered under my breath.

"If it is speed you need, I will carry you."

Everyone turned to stare at Skadi, who stood with her fists on her hips like some Nordic rendition of Wonder Woman. Everyone, that is, except Róta, who'd removed her helmet to cradle her head in her hands, mumbling what sounded an awful lot like obscenities.

Or maybe prayers.

"Come," Skadi insisted, grinning so wide I found myself instantly on edge. "It will be fun."

18

*F*un was decidedly *not* the word I would have chosen to describe what Skadi had meant.

And yet, here we were.

A brisk wind whipped my hair into a frenzy, my helmet lost somewhere back in the mead hall, as the world sped past in a blur far below my feet—not that I planned on looking down anytime soon. In fact, I was actively doing everything in my power to ignore what was happening, going so far as to cover my eyes like a child playing hide and seek. I'd already tried counting backwards from a hundred, reciting lines from my favorite movies, and singing—anything to pretend that the breeze itself was a byproduct of an exceedingly windy day and not the aftermath of being carted around on the shoulder of a giantess.

Unfortunately, the counting only made me *more* aware of how many hundreds of feet up I was, the sole line I could remember was "I see dead people" from *Sixth Sense*, and the only tune that came warbling out from my lips was the final refrain from "Ring Around the Rosie."

Ashes, ashes...

We all fall down.

"Doing alright down there?"

I pried open one eye, scowling, and found Kára soaring alongside us with a malicious smile marring what would have been an attractive face. I flipped her the bird, which only made her laugh.

"Punk ass Tweety-bird bitch," I muttered.

"What was that?"

"Nothin'!" I replied, sweetly, wishing I could convince Skadi to swipe the Valkyrie from the sky like an errant insect. Maybe then she'd stop harassing me. Of course, that wasn't going to happen; now that Skadi had returned to her gargantuan height, she'd become a force of nature, answering to no one.

The transformation had taken place mere seconds after Skadi extended her proposition to me. So suddenly, in fact, that it had sent all of us flying backwards with the release of so much pent up power. When the dust finally cleared and we were able to find our feet, we discovered the space the giantess had occupied replaced by a boot roughly the same size as the mead hall. Even now, I couldn't shake the memory of looking up, my eyes tracing the impossible line of her leg until I reached her kneecap, after which point the giantess became less and less visible, her top half swallowed by clouds and mist.

And now here I was, riding on one of her mountainous shoulders, shivering uncontrollably as we passed through said clouds, fighting off the bouts of nausea that accompanied the idea of riding what amounted to a moving skyscraper. Oh, and let's not forget the presence of my Valkyrie escort, a diabolical woman who seemed to find my discomfort hilarious.

"We're almost there!" Kára called in a rare display of mercy that I immediately distrusted. "Then she can put you back down!"

And...there it was.

I groaned, my stomach lurching at the thought of departing Skadi's shoulder; despite the giantess' careful handling of my fragile body, the arrival flight had been a little like riding an elevator attached to a rocket, if the elevator had no walls and the rocket was one spasm away from squeezing you into oblivion. So not really like that at all, I supposed. Either way, saying I wasn't eager to repeat the experience was an understatement of jötunn proportions.

"It'll be fine," Kára said, though her barely suppressed chuckles suggested otherwise. "Need a distraction?"

Another understatement.

"Depends," I replied, skeptically. "D'ye have to be involved?"

"Not necessarily." Kára dove and banked, her wings braced against the wind even as her scarlet cloak fluttered behind her like a cape. "Why don't you tell me about being a witch? I think that sounds *fascinating*."

"Sure t'ing," I shot back, patting the fur next to me. "How about ye come down here so I can turn ye into somethin' pretty? That way it doesn't hurt me eyes to look at ye."

Kára barked a laugh.

"I guess I deserved that. Fine, something else, then. You pick the topic."

I considered telling the Valkyrie what all I'd already tried but suspected she'd find it more amusing than anything. Instead, an idea formed from something Róta had said—a mention of Kára being off her game for some unspecified reason.

"Why don't ye tell me why you've been distracted, lately?" I called. "Ye don't seem the type."

"Who says I have?"

"Róta, durin' our fight."

"You and Róta actually fought? I figured you'd have started posturing as soon as we left. And you're still standing...that's impressive."

"Nice try." I swallowed down another wave of nausea as I swiveled, studying the Valkyrie's body language. "Quit tryin' to change the subject."

"Why would I do that?"

"Because you're afraid to answer me question."

"Don't be ridiculous. I'm not distracted, no matter what Róta told you. I'm fine."

"Fine, huh?" I narrowed my eyes, a suspicion forming. "Guy troubles?"

"No!"

"So...girl troubles?"

"Odin's beard, you don't let up, do you?" Kára made a disgusted noise in the back of her throat and ducked beneath a cloud before continuing. "It's not 'guy troubles' so much as it is that I'm worried about someone. Someone...special, to me. He's gone missing."

"Sure he isn't just avoidin' your ugly mug?"

"I'm sure," she replied, nonplussed.

"Well, shouldn't ye lot be able to locate him? Or find someone who can?" A thought occurred to me. "Is that how ye know the Horseman?"

"No! No. The Horseman and I know each other from...somewhere else." Kára began drifting on the currents, oscillating back and forth, her single braid whipping behind her like a flag. "But even the Horseman has no idea where he is. No one does. Not even Lady Freya, and the Allfather has been searching harder than anyone."

"So, he's a big deal then? Your 'special' guy?"

"Something like that. More than I ever thought he'd be, I have to admit."

"What d'ye mean?"

"It's just I've known him for a long time, and never thought he'd have ended up mixed up in all this. But then, I didn't think I would, either. Funny what dying does to your dreams."

"I hear that," I drawled, showcasing my surroundings with a smirk. "So, what's his name?"

"Master Nate Temple," Kára replied, wistfully, her fingers trailing across the lighthouse carved into the meat of her breastplate. "I remember the first time he told me. He was so puffed up and self-important back then. Always acted like the smartest guy in the room. But sometimes he'd surprise me with some incredibly topical quote, or by standing up for someone without asking, or by listening when other men would've talked."

My mind spun with the abrupt revelation—doing nothing for my vertigo, I might add—as I began processing what Kára told me; it seemed not only did she *know* Nate, she had a romantic interest in him that predated the others I knew about. Of course, that raised all sorts of curious timeline concerns—especially what with Callie Penrose, a friend from Kansas City who'd done me a solid on more than one occasion, crushing hard on the wizard from St. Louis.

Naturally, however, none of that concerned me as much as the fact that Nate had gone missing, and what it meant that I'd seen him as little as a few days ago. Well, a facsimile of him, at any rate. Either way, assuming Circe hadn't tricked me when she showed Nate chained up on Mount Olympus, it was entirely possible I was the last person to see him alive.

"So, Kára," I began, startling her from her wistful reverie, "I'm not sure how to tell ye this, but I t'ink I know where your boyfriend is...though I have a feeling ye aren't goin' to like it."

19

*P*erhaps an hour later, three of us stood before Freya on the top floor of the tower I'd failed to break into, the two Valkyries at my back like bodyguards. Or corrections officers, depending on your point-of-view...not that I knew *anything* about what that was like. Kára was a nervous ball of energy, shifting from side-to-side like a child doing the pee-pee dance, barely able to contain herself after discovering Nate's where-abouts. Róta, on the other hand, stood rigid in the presence of her benefac-tor, waiting for Freya to address the bombshell I'd dropped at her feet.

"I'm having trouble deciding which questions to ask first," Freya admit-ted, massaging her temples.

"Maybe we should start with what ye sent me to do," I suggested, hoping to get that out of the way before yet another member of Team Aryan grilled me regarding all things Nate Temple; I'd already laid it all out for Kára and then again for Róta on our way here.

"Oh?" Freya cocked an eyebrow but waved for me to continue. "Alright, go ahead."

"It turns out Magni and Modi were plottin' the Allfather's downfall, just like ye thought."

"Those fools," Freya muttered.

"I heard 'em say they'd found a weapon they thought could do the trick."

"A weapon?"

"Aye. Mjolnir. That would be Thor's hammer, right?"

"You're sure that's what they said?" Freya dipped her chin, giving me the full weight of her gaze from the dais upon which she sat. I felt the tension in the room climb even higher as Róta stiffened and Kára stilled; apparently I was bearing all sorts of bad tidings, today.

"I'm sure. I didn't get any of the details, but they did mention someone else before Skadi blew my cover. And it sounded a lot like that person could be involved, somehow."

Freya's expression darkened at the mention of her mother-in-law, but she didn't ask me to elaborate on that subject. Instead, she asked whose name I'd overheard in connection to the hammer.

"Loki."

"Of course," Freya mumbled, then sighed. "Well, at least we have our answer on that front. The rebellion continues." The goddess turned to Róta, dismissing her with a broad, sweeping motion. "Return to Valhalla and collect the mutineers before they cause any more trouble. Perhaps they can tell us what Loki has been up to, or—if we're lucky—where he's hidden Fenrir."

"As you command, my lady."

"Oh, and Róta!" Freya barked as the Valkyrie turned to leave, her sudden shout catching all of us by surprise. "I had almost forgotten. Is it true you fought this mortal?"

The Valkyrie grunted.

"The person I fought was as mortal as you are, my lady. I would stake my wings on it."

"I see. Well, was she any good?"

"Ye know I can hear ye both, right?" I asked, raising my hand.

But Freya ignored me completely; the goddess locked gazes with her Valkyrie, giving the question more weight than the circumstances would have suggested.

"Was she?"

"Had she not resolved to fight on my terms, my lady, I doubt I would have walked away intact," Róta replied, earning a startled gasp from her subordinate. "In terms of skill, well, let's just say I haven't had to work that hard since I fought Brynhildr on Himinbjorg."

"Truly?" Freya cracked a genuine smile that emphasized that vibrant beauty she was known for, the look in her eyes vaguely wistful. "Ah, Bryn-hildr. My husband's champion. You never did get over that loss."

"I failed you, my lady, and shamed myself. Plus, she kicked me off the side of the mountain."

"And right into Heimdall's arms, as I recall. Do you two still keep in touch?"

"All due respect, my lady," Róta said, grinning wryly, "that is none of your business."

"You see, Kára," Freya went on, shifting her attention to the other Valkyrie in the room, "you aren't the first to fall."

A glance over my shoulder revealed a flushed Kára, her eyes averted as though embarrassed, or perhaps simply reflecting on what Freya had said. I considered asking what the goddess was talking about but decided against it; Kára's feelings were none of my business. In any case, the moment passed the second Róta bowed and left the room.

"Speaking of, I think it's high time we move on to the matter of Nate Temple's whereabouts," Freya insisted. "I must say, the timing of all this is a tad...circumspect. If it weren't for the Horseman's testimony, I'd have mistaken you for a spy passing along false information."

"I guess that's fair," I admitted, seeing how that could be the case. After all, what were the odds of some strange mortal showing up to demand a blessing only to reveal a plot to overthrow the Allfather, the whereabouts of not one but two missing allies, *and* a prior relationship with one of the jötunnar? Hell, even *I* was beginning to wonder whether circumstance alone had brought me here, or if fate had intervened, yet again.

"She was meant to come," Skadi grumbled as if reading my thoughts. As one, the four of us shifted our attention to the tower window to find a single eye staring back, its pupil so large I could see myself reflected in it. It wasn't a flattering view; I looked like I'd been chewed up and spit back out, my hair falling loose from its braid, my clothes tattered and stained.

"Tell me what you told Kára," Freya said, ignoring Skadi's comment as though she hadn't heard her—which was, for anyone with functioning ears, impossible.

I did as Freya asked, relaying everything I knew about Nate's situation, which—unfortunately—wasn't much; despite our time together in Morpheus' dreamscape, Nate and I hadn't bothered discussing current events and had instead spent the bulk of our time together rehashing the past. Which, in hindsight, seemed like a mistake; maybe if we'd focused on discussing the future, I'd have more to offer than his location and the conditions of his captivity.

"I wish I could tell ye more," I admitted.

"Why you?" Freya asked, cocking her head.

"What?"

"Why did his astral form appear to you? Why not my husband, for instance, or one of his close friends? Grimm, Gunnar, Alucard, Talon...these names I know, but not yours. I guess what I want to know is the nature of your relationship with Master Temple. What makes you so special?"

I sensed Kára's abrupt attention like a gun barrel pressed to the nape of my exposed neck but did my best to ignore it; I had more important things to worry about. Like quantifying my turbulent relationship with Nate Temple. I licked suddenly dry lips, giving the question the consideration it deserved under the circumstances.

I mean, sure, we'd become friends in another world, rescuing each other from imagined threats and saving each other from reliving horrifying mistakes. But did that make us close? I'd struck a deal to hunt him down, once. He'd broken into my apartment. Hijacked my Uber. Ryan wanted him dead more than anything in the world, and yet the Templefriends had saved my ass more than once. His parents had reportedly committed their fair share of sins, but that included conspiring with mine.

The scales were tipped, but which way did they fall?

"I'm not sure what we are to each other," I admitted, glancing back at Kára. "We're not romantically involved. Not at all. But it seems we are...bound to each other, somehow. It has somethin' to do with our parents. A deal they made before we were born."

"Like an arranged marriage?" Kára asked, alarmed.

"Jesus! No! I told ye, no romance. Zero. Zilch. He's...a friend. An idget half the time, but a friend all the same. Beyond that, I'm not sure. But, for whatever reason, he *did* come to me. And I know for sure he's being held by Zeus. I saw it in Circe's pools."

"And you swear he was alive?" Kára asked, her voice a whisper, her eyes pleading.

"I do."

"I knew it."

"Well," Freya interrupted, "that's good enough for me. Kára, you've met Temple's friends before, haven't you?"

"A few," she said, dabbing at her eyes before putting on a brave face. "Want me to round them up?"

"Yes, go to them, first. Then send word to everyone you think may want to take part in the rescue effort. But be sure they know to keep the knowledge from falling into enemy hands, and that this *has* to be a coordinated response, not some half-baked scheme. Zeus will not give him up easily. We may only get one chance."

"Yes, my lady!"

Kára reached out and grasped my arm, squeezing it, with a smile so broad that it made me feel a bit guilty for ever daydreaming about the various ways I would torture her once we reached solid ground. I found myself grinning back and watched the Valkyrie bolt for the stairs with no small degree of amusement.

"Well, now that we're alone," Freya said, drawing my attention, "it seems we have our own business to discuss."

"Not alone," Skadi insisted, her voice echoing like thunder throughout the chamber. "Have you forgotten I am still here, Freya?"

"Tell me what you want with her, and I'll invite you in!" Freya snapped, repeating the same demand she'd made when we first arrived.

"That is our concern, not yours, little Vanir."

"Small wonder my father left you," Freya muttered under her breath. "Wasn't the thunder he got tired of on that damned mountain."

"What was that? You have to speak up when you talk to one of the jötunn, or else we cannot hear your whining, high-pitched voices."

"Gah!" Freya sighed and threw up her hands, exasperated. "Give us a few moments to ourselves, then I will send her out to you!"

"Very well, but do not take too long or I will bury this land in snow."

Skadi rose from her crouch and departed, sending faint vibrations rippling through the stone with every rumbling step. I had a brief moment to wonder whether she would follow through on her threat before Freya rose, as well, and descended her dais to stand before me, her honeyed perfume filling the air, her vines twitching along my skin.

"So," she began, a wolfish look in her eyes, "is the imposter ready to receive her blessing?"

20

a thrill of alarm rippled up my spine, forcing me to straighten under Freya's probing gaze. Imposter. The word settled like a noose around my neck as the reality of my current situation dawned on me; Freya and I were alone in the tower, which meant there were no witnesses should she take exception to anything I said or did. Like, for example, hedging the truth.

"Relax," Freya said, smirking. "Róta sent word ahead. I know what happened in Valhalla." She let that set in before continuing. "You should not have hidden what you were."

"And what is that?"

Freya gave me a flat look.

"I mean it," I insisted, earnestly. "As far as I know, this hasn't happened to anyone else. At night, I can do t'ings that shouldn't be possible. I can bend shadows to me will, I don't get tired, I barely register pain, and I am hardly meself. But durin' the day, I seem to be as mortal as I have ever been. Or at least I thought I was. Now even that is up for grabs."

"How so?"

I gestured vaguely at Freya as if for emphasis. "I could sense your power the moment I met ye. Hell, I managed to chase it back, somehow."

"Yes, you did..." Freya drifted off and began pacing the room with measured steps, her arms folded behind her back. "I should have suspected what you were, then. Unfortunately, it has become harder to gauge the gap between mortals and gods, of late. It's clouded my judgment."

"Wait, does that mean ye know what I am? Truly?"

"I...have an idea."

"Well, d'ye care to share?"

"It is not for me to say." Freya held up a hand, cutting off my response. "Some answers must be earned to be appreciated. This is one of those instances."

"And until then I'm supposed to, what, fumble around like an idget? I could've hurt Róta, ye know. And it wouldn't have been *me*. D'ye know what that's like?"

"We all behave as our nature dictates," Freya replied, cryptically. "If you feel you lack control, maybe that's because you are meant to. Not all gods represent order."

I opened my mouth to respond, but something in Freya's expression warned me not to; she looked expectant, as though she'd given me something to chew on, not spit back out. I clamped my jaw shut, thinking furiously about what she'd said. Unfortunately, I'd never had a gift for puzzles or riddles; I scowled, dwelling on the latter portion of what she'd said, playing it again and again in my mind.

Not all gods represent order.

Fair enough, I thought. Circe had made similar claims, as I recalled, though she'd referred to a god's "aspect" as opposed to his or her "nature." Mine, according to the goddess within me, was bound to night. But there were many deities who represented more than one thing. Was I one of them? I considered Freya's enigmatic response but kept coming back to the notion of order, triggered by the way she'd emphasized it. What was the opposite of order? Chaos? Was she calling me an agent of chaos?

That didn't feel right. If anything, it seemed like I was the victim of chaos, not the perpetrator. Indeed, the more I thought about it, the more I felt something was missing—some measure of control, a sense of unity and purpose, a conduit for all this raw power.

"And what if I feel...incomplete?"

Freya beamed at me as though I were a prized pupil who'd just given her the correct answer to a particularly complicated question. I, on the other hand, felt even less sure of myself than I had before. Until now, I'd managed to put off thinking about it, but what if I ended up facing Ryan as I was, now? What if I couldn't talk him down? Despite my brief display of competence when challenging Freya, I couldn't be sure that would be enough to dissuade the monster he'd become. And worse, what if we did square off with the goddess in control? Would I be able to sway her as I had before? What if I couldn't?

What if even *she* wasn't enough to stop him?

"I need to be able to control this power," I admitted aloud, sighing. "If I'm goin' to do what I came here to do, that is."

"I am afraid I cannot help you with that." Freya crossed the room and placed a hand upon my shoulder. "But I can give you my blessing. And, perhaps, offer you the means to enter Helheim, provided you agree to do something for me."

"Somethin' else, ye mean?" I shook my head, fighting the sudden urge to pull out my own hair. "Ye do realize I'm not some hired hand, right? Or do ye not care what happens to Helheim?"

"Come with me," Freya replied, stepping away and angling for the stairs as though I hadn't just asked her several pointed questions.

"Why should I?"

"Because," she said without turning around, "you look like a fate worse than death. We can talk more after you've changed."

Before I could reply, Freya took to the stairs and disappeared from sight, the sound of her footsteps receding faster than should have been possible. I cursed, glanced down at my shabby appearance, and followed after her, muttering under my breath.

"'Ye look like a fate worse than death,'" I mocked, mimicking Freya's voice, "I said because I t'ink I'm *so* funny, but really I'm a classless, ungrateful cow..."

The windowless stairs were as dimly lit as I remembered from our ascent, the braziers spread so few and far between it was as if the Vanir were concerned about the gas bill. Unfortunately, I didn't have a chance to tease Freya about it; the goddess was nowhere in sight by the time I reached the first landing, though I thought I could make out the sound of her progress on the flight below. A nagging sensation, however, kept me from descending further. I lingered, though I wasn't certain why until I heard it.

Whispers.

The language was unfamiliar, but the tone was insistent, luring me towards the nearby wall. The whispers grew louder, and I could have sworn

I heard my name being called. I pressed my hands to the stone, feeling its seams until my fingers brushed against something the gloom had hidden: more runes. I hissed as they stung me once again, but didn't jerk back. Instead, I bit back my cry and traced them, marveling as they blazed in a kaleidoscope of colors, shifting from one shade to the next like a shimmering rainbow. Moreover, they were beautifully rendered—carved so seamlessly that there were no jagged edges to speak of, as if molded into the stone itself.

The wall gave way beneath my hands so abruptly I nearly slipped and fell, revealing a door so heavy that it barely shifted an inch even after I regained my feet and set my full weight against it. Resolved to find out what lay behind the door, I dug my heels in, driving with everything I had, but it only budged another few inches. Daylight poured through the gap, casting golden shapes on the far wall as I continued to apply pressure, which meant there had to be a window beyond. I redoubled my efforts, groaning from the strain.

Of course, that's when Freya found me.

"What are you doing?" she barked, alarmed to find me pressing my face against the gap, trying to see what was on the other side. "How did you get that open?"

I froze.

"If I say I used me magic fingers, would that make ye more or less likely to get mad?"

"Get away from there, it isn't—"

The door gave way before she could finish, swinging so easily on its hinges that I yelped as I fell into the antechamber within, my knees banging so hard against the floor that I didn't immediately look up to see what I'd found; I swore up a storm, instead, oblivious to the whirling dust motes and the scent of rusted metal until at last I managed to clamber to my feet.

"So, what's the big deal about this room..." I drifted off, my eyes widening as Freya stepped into the room behind me, her own gaze decidedly less surprised to find the treasure I'd uncovered.

And it *was* a treasure.

"This can't be," Freya whispered, her voice laced with so much disbelief that it bordered on horror. "Odin said her armor would lay unclaimed until..."

The goddess drifted off, seemingly captivated by the sight of the armored mannequin. I was focused on the armor itself, which—despite the rust stains, dents, and other signs of wear and tear—looked impossibly regal, if a bit vicious. The set as a whole reminded me of a bird of prey with its wickedly-spiked pauldrons, tapered gorget, and black steel vambraces. Even the artfully crafted chainmail coat mimicked a crest of feathers, obscuring a breastplate dominated by a single, indecipherable rune. And that was to say nothing about the unique shape of the helmet, the visor of which protruded like a beak, leaving the lower half of the mannequin's face exposed.

"Sorry," I said, only half paying attention at this point. "Until when?"

"No, don't be." Freya shook her head. "It doesn't matter. Come with me, this armor was not meant for you. There is another set below, much newer, that I—"

The stone door slammed shut behind us with a deafening clang before Freya could finish. The goddess waved a glowing hand, forming shapes with her fingers, but to no avail; the door refused to open no matter what she tried. I watched her with mounting apprehension, worried what she might do to get us out of here, but it didn't take long before the goddess ran out of steam. She pressed her arm against the door and bowed her head over it, her shoulders tight with unspoken tension.

"Very well," she said, though I had the distinct impression she wasn't speaking to me. "But she will have to agree to my terms. Otherwise, mark my words, we shall stay here until the Norns speak their final peace and the Great Winter comes."

"Um," I interjected, clearing my throat, "who are ye talkin' to?"

The light in the room burgeoned for a moment, so blinding I had to look away. Freya, as if awaiting the sign, sighed and turned her attention to the armor once more. She approached it and pressed her fingers against the helm, caressing the feathered cheek guards like a lover, her expression soft.

"Brynhildr. My husband's champion, until she was led astray. This was her armor."

"Led astray by what?"

"By that which even gods cannot overcome. Love," she explained, catching my incredulous expression. "Brynhildr fell for a mortal, a hero, who woke her, tricked her, and betrayed her. She was the first—though not the last—to bear the name Sleeping Beauty."

"Why was she sleepin'?" I asked, unable to disguise my innate curiosity. "If she was Odin's champion, I mean, shouldn't she have been by his side?"

"First you have to understand that my husband has always been prone to wandering in his pursuit of knowledge. He craves it more than anyone I have ever met, and even traded an eye for its sake. Except that meant he would often disappear without warning, leaving the rest of us behind to do as we wished. For someone like Brynhildr, who loved to fight and would do so often in his absence, that meant all manner of trouble for Odin to sort out when he returned."

"Sounds like me kind of Valkyrie," I noted, appreciatively.

"Under the circumstances, that isn't surprising," Freya replied. "Anyway, the Allfather tried to get Brynhildr to marry, hoping that would distract her, but she refused to do so unless he could find her a man without fear. Except no such men lived, then, and so the Allfather cast a spell on her to sleep whenever he journeyed elsewhere. It was during one such stretch that Sigurd found her." Freya sighed and shook her head. "It is a long story."

"Well, apparently we aren't going anywhere anytime soon," I replied, refusing to keep the snark out of my voice. "So, let's hear it."

"Very well. In the beginning, there existed the abyss, fiery Muselpheim, and frozen Niflheim. From their joining came Ymir, first of the jötunnar, who lay with himself and bore—"

"That's not funny."

"You asked me to tell you the whole story."

"Of Brynhildr and...who was it again?"

"Sigurd."

"That one."

"If you insist," Freya acquiesced, though I could tell she'd been messing with me from the get go. "Sigurd found Brynhildr guarded by a wall of flame my husband created to keep her safe from harm as she slept. He was a bold mortal. Strong enough to slay a dragon and passionate enough to weep for having done it. Sigurd took one look at Brynhildr and strode through the blaze, insisting his love for Brynhildr was hotter than any flame."

"Ye don't have to oversell it, ye know," I interjected, eyebrow raised.

"Hush and listen. As I was saying, Sigurd survived the wall of fire, freed Brynhildr from her armor, and woke her with a kiss."

"Hope she knocked his ass out."

"They were engaged days later," Freya went on, ignoring my commentary, "but Sigurd was also a restless man. One day, he left to seek greater adventures. After that, Brynhildr changed. She renounced her role as champion, fretting over Sigurd's increasingly long absence. Unbeknownst to her, however, Sigurd had been given a tonic during his travels that wiped his memory."

"Startin' to t'ink I shouldn't have asked for this story" I grumbled, eyeing the battered suit of armor and the sad ending it promised.

"I never said it was a happy tale. Anyway, Sigurd ended up married to the mortal woman who'd drugged him. Worse, the mortal woman's brother sought to trick Brynhildr by pretending to be Sigurd. When she discovered the deception, Brynhildr was devastated. Distraught, she demanded Sigurd be held accountable for his betrayal. And he was. She found his body the next day on the funeral pyre. Then, in a fit of remorse, she joined him."

"Jesus," I muttered. "Couldn't ye have just said 'it didn't end well' and have been done with it?"

"Perhaps. But her armor called to you. I believe it's right that you know her story. Besides, some good did come of Brynhildr and Sigurd's affair. They had a child. A daughter who, after her mother's death, was raised by Valkyries until—it seems—she left for Midgard on the orders of someone posing as Odin."

"Ye mean Hilde," I said, shocked to make the connection. "Hilde was Brynhildr's daughter?"

"Yes."

"Wait, shouldn't Hilde have her mother's armor, then?" I gestured to the mannequin. "Why is it here?"

"Hilde earned her own set, one she had forged by the dwarves of Svartalfheim. The legacy of this armor is not an easy one to carry. After it was removed from Brynhildr, she used it as a shield to escape the wall of flame before returning it to the Allfather in this sad condition. I was there when he received it."

Freya looked away, then, clearly troubled.

"What is it? Is this armor cursed, or somethin'?"

"No, not exactly. It's curse is on the world, not the wearer. You see, when Odin last laid his eye upon it, he told me it would be worn again by another champion...in the days leading up to Ragnarök."

I pointed at my chest, my eyebrows climbing so far up my forehead I thought they might disappear beneath my bangs at any moment. Was Freya seriously talking about *me*? She thought I was the "champion" meant to wear Brynhildr's armor? And what was with this Ragnarök business? I shook my head as I repeated the questions buzzing around in my head out loud.

"You have been chosen," Freya replied with a shrug, as though that should have addressed all of my concerns at once.

Spoiler alert: it didn't.

"So what? Listen, I'm not goin' to lie to ye and say I haven't dreamed about gettin' me own fancy suit of armor—especially after I saw Hilde in hers back in Boston. But that doesn't mean I want her mom's hand-me-downs, or to kick off Doomsday in the process. I mean—"

"Stop being so disrespectful," Freya snapped, her power swatting at me so fast across the face that it was a full second later before I clutched at my stinging cheek. "Brynhildr's warrior spirit chose you. It called to *you*."

"And what if I refuse?"

"Then you refuse. But you should know what you are walking away from." Freya gestured to the armor, her eyes flashing with barely restrained anger. "This is the armor of the first of the Valkyries, forged by Sindri and Brokkr, themselves. Whoever wears it, provided the armor is whole, can pass through the mists of Niflheim unmolested. Indeed, she could even walk through the gates of Helheim without drawing unwanted attention."

I gaped at the goddess, then turned to stare at the suit of armor. So, this was the key Freya had mentioned—the aid she'd promised. Except...she hadn't known I would find this room, so what *had* she intended?

"What's the catch?" I asked suspiciously, still studying the armor, my eyes drawn inexorably to its flaws.

"Before I let you take it, before I give you my blessing, I want you to swear fealty to me as Brynhildr once swore to Odin. To serve me as a Valkyrie."

I'd have been lying if I said I was shocked by her condition. Frankly, I'd expected something like this from the moment Freya experienced my power firsthand. In her eyes, I was an asset—a valuable tool to be employed. Indeed, in that context, our earlier conversation made a lot more sense; she hadn't been trying to help me sort through my existential crisis, she'd been trying to recruit me.

"I don't t'ink so," I replied after pretending to give it some serious thought. "I'll take the blessin' ye promised and be on me way, if it's all the same to ye."

"Please, don't be so hasty. Think about it. You told me yourself you felt incomplete. That you lacked control." Freya laid her hand on my arm. "You would be welcome with us. I could help you discover your true potential."

"And what d'ye get out of it?"

Freya jerked her hand back as if I were a stovetop. Indeed, it appeared I was; her hand smoked, the flesh pink from contact as white heat roiled off of me in waves. The goddess shook her head, looking forlorn.

"Something is coming," she said. "I only want to protect what is mine."

"And d'ye really believe strong armin' me was goin' to get ye what ye want?" I shook my head, trying hard to see past the white flames licking at the edges of my vision. "Doesn't anybody *ask* for help, anymore? Or are goddesses too good for that?"

"Are you saying you'd have agreed to help out of the goodness of your heart?" Freya retorted, her own temper flaring. "Do not think me a fool."

"Then stop actin' like one and t'ink, really t'ink, about what I've done for ye so far. I told ye about Nate, told ye about what Magni and Modi said, told ye about Hilde, and all I asked in return was your help to save someone *I* want to protect. And instead ye offer me slavery? Fuck that."

"Not slavery!" Freya flung out one arm. "Do my Valkyries act like slaves? Do I control their every action? Do I tell them who they can and can't love? Of course not. So you can stop pretending like you understand the bond we have. Do you have any idea what it meant to me to find out Hilde was alive? What it meant to see Kára's face when you spoke of Nate Temple? They are like daughters to me."

I started to say something, then thought better of it; our fight was about two more tirades from devolving into a literal altercation, and I wasn't eager to find out how much power I did or did not have in her realm. Instead, I took a deep breath, letting that white fire peter and die out. After several more just like it, an idea occurred to me—a possible solution that might satisfy both of us.

"Give me the armor, and I'll find Hilde for ye."

"That's—wait, what did you say?"

"Ye wanted to make a deal, so this is me negotiatin'. I won't swear fealty to ye. Not to anyone. Ever. But I don't expect ye to give it to me for nothin'. So, in exchange, I promise to find Hilde and pass on the message that ye want to talk to her."

I watched the gears in Freya's head churn, her expression shifting so slowly from anger to acceptance that I wasn't certain until the last moment whether she'd even consider my terms.

"Two weeks," she replied, finally.

"Excuse me?"

"I'll give you two weeks after you leave here to find her and get her to return. If you fail, then you will swear to serve me in her place." Freya held up a hand. "I swear not to interfere, in any way. If Hilde comes home, the armor is yours to do with as you see fit."

"Home?"

"Asgard."

After a brief review of Hemingway's hierarchy of realms, I realized Freya was talking about the first of the Nine Worlds—home to the Aesir, by all accounts. I felt immediately daunted by the request; I had way too many loose ends to tie up back in Boston without tacking on a time-sensitive reconnaissance mission. What if I couldn't get to the Valkyrie in time? Or worse, what if Hilde refused?

"Two weeks isn't long enough," I argued, hoping to renegotiate. "Me body isn't even *in* the mortal realm right now, and I'm not sure how long it'll take me to return."

"Where did you leave your body?"

I hesitated, uncertain whether to tell Freya the truth.

"I promise I intend you no harm," the goddess added, perhaps sensing my discomfort.

"It's bein' guarded by a witch on an island in the Titan Realm. A realm that has no exits, from what I've been told."

"Nonsense. Every realm connects. You simply have to find out where the veil is thinnest. But I take your point…I'll give you a month. *After* you return to the mortal realm. But no longer."

I closed my eyes, weighing Freya's offer. On the one hand, agreeing would give me the means to infiltrate Helheim and find Ryan—essentially the reason I'd agreed to die in the first place. On the other hand, failure to find Hilde for any reason could land me back here in a month's time, provided I survived this and ever made it back to Boston. Only this time I'd be Freya's freshest cadet, forced to polish steel boots until they gleamed and to ruin my excellent posture with all that ridiculous bowing.

Of course, there was really only one answer to give, no matter how I rationalized it.

"Alright," I said, praying I wouldn't regret this. "Ye have a deal."

22

The armor was made up of perhaps a dozen intricate parts, each of which had to be applied in a specific order, and most of which required the tightening of some strap or the snap of some clasp until I began to seriously worry whether I'd ever be able to take it all off when the time came—because I certainly wasn't going to get it all back on without help. Perhaps sensing that would be the case, Freya began naming and describing each piece as she went, bidding me to recite after her like a priest extracting wedding vows.

"You'll have to come up with a name," Freya said as she adjusted the last few bits, tugging the chainmail down and brushing some debris from the plackart.

"A name for what?"

"For your armor," the goddess replied, as though that were obvious. She rapped her knuckles against her breastplate, seemingly pleased by the resounding clang, before holding the last remaining piece out to me. "Every Valkyrie must name her armor. Often these names live on as an extension of their wearer."

"Didn't Brynhildr give it a name?"

"She did, but the armor no longer belongs to her. It is not so strange a practice. A sword used to kill and a sword used to protect may appear the same, but their legends will never coincide."

"Aye, that makes sense. What about Róta's armor? What name did she give hers?"

"Róta dubbed hers 'fire-slayer' in our tongue. Even then, she dreamed of taking on the sons of Surt when the fire giants come to destroy the world." Freya shook her head, her tone far too wistful for the context of what she was saying.

"Right." I turned the helm over in my hands, captivated by its savage appearance; the beak was cruelly pointed, the sides swirling, the comb and back spiked with steel tail feathers. Indeed, the armor as a whole had a vicious cast to it that seemed at odds with the sets I'd seen until now.

"Something wrong?"

"Ye said this armor was crafted by someone important—"

"Sindri and Brokkr," she supplied. "The finest craftdwarves this side of Asgard. Loki once lost a bet to them and ended up with his mouth sewn shut for thirty years. Good times."

"What was the bet?"

"That they couldn't create something as pleasing as he had. In the end, they created several exceptional pieces, including Mjolnir."

"And did they forge every Valkyrie's armor?"

"Ah, so you noticed." Freya was quiet for a moment, then shook her head. "No, they did not. Brynhildr was Odin's champion, and to honor her was to honor him. So they fashioned armor that could change at the whim of the wearer with the slightest understanding of *seiðr* magic. They even gave Odin the design, which spawned the creation of the sets you've seen until now. But this...this was the first."

"The prototype, huh?" I ran a finger along the beak of the helmet. "Does that mean it's better than the others, or worse?"

"Hard to say," Freya admitted. "Many of us thought it a clever creation, but the Allfather always suspected the dwarves had outdone themselves in crafting such a thing. Nothing as devastating as Mjolnir, of course, but the fact that it was the last they ever forged together always concerned him."

"What about this?" I asked, tapping the rune that had been engraved in the center of the breastplate, obscured once more by the blackened chainmail.

"*Dagaz*," Freya intoned, her eyes tracing what appeared to be an hour-glass turned on its side. "The dwarves never explained why they chose that symbol. You see, the rune has many meanings. But it is best known for its most noble translation: Hope."

Hope.

The word was accompanied by a thrill of recognition, a nagging sense of familiarity. I turned the helm over and slid it on, the beak obscuring the top half of my face. And yet, somehow, the instant I secured the strap beneath my chin, I could see as though nothing obscured my vision. Indeed, once complete, the armor—which had felt almost oppressively heavy to this point—lightened to the point I felt like I was wearing the world's comfiest pajamas.

"D'ye have a mirror?"

"Of course, come," Freya said, her voice catching with emotion at the sight of me in Brynhildr's armor. She escorted me through the secret door —no longer locked—and down two flights of stairs before angling into another room. A chamber full of gleaming steel piled high along the walls, separated categorically.

Valkyrie armor.

A whole freaking room full of Valkyrie armor.

"I was going to bring you here and have you choose your own pieces," Freya admitted. "That is traditionally how we have done it. What they pick often says a lot about the wearer and the path they will take."

"And what does me choice say about me?" I asked, trailing the goddess, marveling at how freely I could move despite the wealth of metal layered upon my person.

"Nothing. But then you didn't do the choosing."

Freya reached a small recess covered by a scarlet curtain and peeled it away, revealing a gilded floor-length mirror. She then held up a hand, however, as if to stall me.

"First, the blessing."

"Ah, right," I replied, having almost forgotten. "Is there somethin' special I need to do?"

"Yes. Stand still and stay silent."

"Easier said than done," I joked.

Freya shot me a dark look, and I clamped my mouth shut and mimed locking my lips with an invisible key. The goddess nodded, satisfied, and reached into a pouch on her hip. From it she drew out what looked like multicolored, irradiated sand; it shone brightly against the skin of her palm.

As I watched, she licked two of her fingers, dipped them into the magic dust, and drew a rune across the visor of my helm, then the palms of my gloves, and finally over the space where my heart lay. The symbol—an angular "B"—began to pulse and throb with light, brightening so quickly that I had to shut my eyes to keep from being blinded.

When at last I could open them, I found Freya beckoning me towards the mirror, then stepping away as though allowing me to look for myself. I didn't hesitate; I wanted to see the whole package.

I wasn't disappointed.

"I look..."

"Scary," Freya finished for me, admiring her handiwork; whatever she'd done had made the armor appear good as new. "Like a mortal child's nightmare come to life."

"I was goin' to say 'badass', but I guess I can't argue with ye."

I ran my gauntleted hands over the freshly fixed armor, awed by the brazen nature of its accentuated curves and fearsome trimmings. True to Freya's assessment, I looked like something out of a demented dreamscape —both terrifying and captivating all at once. And yet, the rune across my chest read "hope," as though the contradiction were worth acknowledging. Like a parent standing in front of the dream car with the keys dangling in hand saying "I know it's pretty, but don't you dare drive too fast and wreck this thing."

"And it filled me with fantastic terrors never felt before," I murmured, struck by a half-remembered line of poetry from an old favorite of mine. I patted the breastplate. "I t'ink I know what I want to call her."

23

*F*reya and I stood at the base of the tower after I'd spent perhaps the past half hour relearning the signs Hilde had shown me back in Boston while Freya fed me relevant information about Niflheim. We'd even exchanged the occasional pleasantry, including a few anecdotes about Hilde; Freya had been quite relieved to discover that her Valkyrie hadn't given me a set of contraband armor but the uniforms the Valkyries passed out to the *hugr* to keep them appropriately outfitted. I, of course, had been less than pleased to learn I'd been given some poor phantom's hand-me-downs from Pluto's Closet.

Hah.

As I prepared to depart, however, Freya got serious again, repeating the terms of our deal as though I might have forgotten in all the excitement. I hadn't. Indeed, I was more aware than ever that I had responsibilities waiting for me in the mortal realm once this was all over—starting with Max, who still hadn't arrived to honor Hades' side of the agreement. At this rate, I was beginning to think I'd have to track the brujo down, myself. Of course, if I did, that at least meant I could avoid meeting up with the Temples and passing along the god of the underworld's enigmatic message.

Sulfur linings.

"And you're sure about the name?" Freya asked, drawing me back to the moment at hand, her head cocked as though my choice had baffled her. But then, that didn't surprise me; I wasn't sure how much Edgar Allen Poe the Norse gods had access to.

"Nevermore," I said, relishing the sound of it even as I flicked the edge of my pauldron with a closed fist, transforming the armor into a pair of boots, jeans, and a white crop top under a leather jacket. I wasn't going for fancy; according to Freya's description of where I was headed and what waited for me there, flashy wasn't my best bet.

"Does it mean something special to you?"

"It's from a very well-known poem written by a rather troubled mortal. This armor reminded me of a few stanzas, that's all."

"Ah, so like the title of a bard's song," Freya replied, appreciatively. "That's sensible. Many tools of war are honored in such a way."

"I suppose so," I replied, shrugging. "Nevermore isn't the title, though. The poem is called 'The Raven.'"

Freya's face went shockingly pale.

"What, is that like some Nordic taboo?" I asked hurriedly, startled by her reaction. "I didn't just guarantee me own death by callin' me armor that, did I?"

"No! No, it's nothing like that. It was just a surprising choice, that's all."

"Why?" I showcased my body as though she could see the intricate armor lying beneath the illusion. "I mean, its design practically screams bird. It's black. Lots of sharp, pointy bits. Why shouldn't I have thought 'raven'?"

"Quite right," Freya replied, though I could tell she was holding something back. "I am sure it was an innocent coincidence."

"What was?"

"Sorry, it's nothing. Forget it."

"Doesn't sounds like nothin'," I countered, growing exasperated by her caginess. "Why not simply tell me?"

"Because honestly, I'm not sure if it means anything or not, yet. Only time will tell. In fact, let's table this until you come with Hilde to Asgard. If you still want to know, then, I should have an answer, one way or another."

Sensing this was the best offer I was going to get, I agreed—despite the fact that I had no intention of traveling to Asgard alongside Hilde. Not because I wasn't curious to see the mythical realm the majority of the Norse gods called home, but because I wasn't interested in becoming embroiled in another pantheon's politics. Between the deals I'd made in Fae, the debts I owed the Titans, and my unresolved issues with the Otherworlders, I had plenty to keep me occupied without sticking my sweet new beak into Nordic business.

Speaking of which…

"Assumin' I make good time through Niflheim and can sneak past the mutt guardin' Helheim, what should I expect from the goddess in charge?"

"From Hel?" Freya shrugged. "She's Loki's daughter and one of the jötunnar, but more trustworthy than most. My husband appointed her the realm's guardian long ago, and by all accounts she has carried out her role as dutifully as anyone. But I have never met her, so I cannot say for sure."

"D'ye t'ink she'll help me?"

"I do not know. From what you've said, it seems the being you're after is capable of far more than most in the afterlife. His power may even rival Hel's own."

"Even in her own realm?"

"It is possible. Our power grows weakest when it is unused, when we gods become negligent," Freya replied, sounding as though she was speaking from personal experience. "Hel has ruled unopposed for millennia. The dead do not covet power so much as mourn the loss of it. You will see that for yourself, soon enough."

"Cheery thought."

"Where you are going, joy does not exist," she warned. "Once you leave Fólkvangr, despair will be your greatest enemy. You must not let it win."

"Don't ye worry, I've got all me happy thoughts right here." I tapped my temple for emphasis, amused by how seriously the goddess was taking herself. "Any other advice before I go meet with Skadi?"

"Yes. Be wary of her," Freya urged.

"Of Skadi? Why?"

"Her father once warred with the Aesir and was slain as a result, which is actually how she came to marry my father. It is another long story. One I don't wish to tell. But you should know that she was not imprisoned by accident. She was betrayed by Loki, who she has always feuded with. If she has discovered that for herself, I cannot say what plans she may lay to see him caught."

"I thought Loki was your enemy, also? Why not combine forces?"

But Freya was already shaking her head.

"Loki has always been an outsider looking in, helping or hurting as his whims decide. We cannot know what he is planning, or who will suffer for it, and so we prepare as we are able. But a vendetta between us and him? That would serve no one, and cause even more damage than my son-in-law did when he tried to supplant his father."

Yikes, I thought, talk about family drama; Freya's description of life among the Nordic gods struck me as some sort of incestuous rendition of a backstabby soap opera. The Jötunn and the Headless...or The Slays of Our Knives. Either way, I suddenly found myself grateful to have had the upbringing I did—parents or no.

"I'll be careful," I said, at last. "I promise."

"See that you do. I'd hate to have to track down the armor if you succumb to its mists and get lost in Niflheim for eternity."

"Gee, t'anks."

"You are welcome," Freya replied without so much as a trace of sarcasm before reaching out to squeeze my shoulder in some semblance of solidarity, looking as though she wanted to say more but either wouldn't, or couldn't.

Realizing our time together was at an end, I offered the goddess the slightest bow of my head and ducked out the doorway hidden behind the trees, emerging in the pass Hemingway had taken me to what seemed like weeks ago, though it must only have been a day or two by conventional standards. Of course, when he'd dropped me off, there hadn't been a gargantuan leg swinging to and fro from the edge of the nearest cliff. I found Skadi's right knee raised like an impossibly sheer mountain in the distance, her left lying flat, the rest of her sprawled across the land as though she'd decided to lay down and take a nap. Hell, for all I knew, she had.

I considered flying up to meet her but realized with a jolt that I hadn't learned the sign to create wings; that I hadn't thought to ask was a testament to how many knives I'd been juggling since I arrived. Dismayed, I whirled, planning to march back in and demand Freya show me how it was done. But the door was already shut, its Nordic security system armed and ready to zap me the instant I tried to break back in. I cursed, distantly aware that Freya had probably kept that tidbit to herself on purpose—anything to keep me under her thumb. That, or I was simply being paranoid after her shady recruiting pitch.

Either way, it seemed I'd have to get Skadi's attention the old fashioned way.

"Oy! Big fuckin' giantess!" I yelled at the top of my lungs. "Shrink your fat ass down and say what ye came to say!"

I felt Skadi sit up before I saw it; the world beneath my feet shook as her torso soared towards the heavens, her face so far away and so high up I could barely make it out. Still, I waved, making it as obvious as possible that I was ready to talk if she was.

"Do you still intend to go to Niflheim?" Skadi rumbled, her voice like thunder overhead.

"I do!"

"Then let us walk and talk."

That bright light shone—far more brilliantly than the late afternoon sunlight that permeated Fólkvangr—and suddenly Skadi stood at the edge of the cliff, her fists on her hips. She beckoned me to join her as though all it would take was a single bound. But then again...why not? I began pacing the base of the cliff, getting a feel for how the armor moved beneath the illusion I'd placed upon it; while my base speed seemed largely unaffected, a brief test of my reflexes and overall strength revealed noteworthy improvements. Maybe not enough to leap a couple hundred feet in the air...but enough to climb a cliff without a harness.

"I'll be right up!"

Of course, that turned out to be a bit of an exaggeration, though I did manage to reach the top some ten minutes later feeling pleasantly spry. Skadi, on the other hand, seemed less than impressed; she took off in the general direction of Niflheim without so much as a word, forcing me to race after her to keep up.

"Hold on!" I shouted to no avail.

"I do not wish to be within earshot of Freya or her Valkyries when we speak. The faster we walk, the farther away we get. Now, we move."

And move we did; I ended up jogging after the taller, leggier giantess to keep from falling too far behind. After several minutes of that pace, however, she finally slowed and took stock of me for the first time since we left Valhalla. I watched her eyes wander up and down my body like some creep at the bar and immediately covered my vulnerable bits out of sheer habit.

"What?" I asked, alarmed.

"Your armor. It is...familiar."

"Ye can see it?"

"Of course I can see it. We jötunnar were the first to create this magic you are using to hide your true self, though we did so far less frivolously."

Well, that was news to me; I'd assumed the jötunnar's magic was of the raw, untamed variety. The fact that the Aesir had somehow bastardized it was another thing Freya had failed to mention. That, or we were dealing with the Norse equivalent of "he said, she said."

Regardless—now that Niflheim was finally in my sights—I wasn't eager to debate revisionist history with a jötunn. So, thinking it would save time, I quickly summarized what all had happened in the tower after Skadi left, including the deal I'd made with Freya and the origin of the armor I'd been given in exchange. To her credit, the giantess stayed quiet throughout my explanation, waiting until the very end to pass judgment.

"You are a fool."

The words hit me like a bitter slap, accompanied by the faintest downtick in temperature; my skin pebbled beneath Skadi's withering glare. I may even have taken an inadvertent step backwards—prompted of course by my trusted survival mechanism.

"What d'ye mean? Why?"

"Because if you had come to me, first, I would have given you my blessing and escorted you to Helheim, myself. Without demanding anything from you."

"Why didn't ye say somethin' sooner?!"

"You did not ask."

"Well, when I made the deal in exchange for the blessin', I had no idea ye were comin' down from your mountain." I ducked my head a bit as Skadi's scowl grew even fiercer. "Look, I'm sorry. But how was I supposed to know you'd do somethin' like that for me? So far it seems every deity this side of the River Styx believes in a barter system."

"That is because they owe you nothing, child. Whereas I owe you a debt. But that is not why I would have done this thing on your behalf."

"Really? Why then?"

"It is my belief that only you can defeat the creature who has invaded our realm."

"Ye mean Ryan?"

"I can feel him," Skadi insisted, her glacial blue eyes staring into the middle distance as if imagining someone—or perhaps something—that wasn't there. "His power is too close to my own for comfort, and his will is as destructive as any I have ever felt. He must be stopped."

"Are ye still offerin' to help me, then? I could seriously use an escort to—"

"No, I cannot," Skadi said, making a cutting motion in mid-air. "It is too late. You wear the armor of a Valkyrie. Any who saw us together would be too suspicious of one or both of us to leave us be. Even the jötunnar who have made peace with the Aesir avoid their pets, as a rule."

I cursed, wishing I'd have spoken to Skadi earlier. Maybe then I could have avoided Freya's bargain—albeit at the cost of what was, admittedly, a sick set of armor. I sighed and shook it off, realizing there was no use crying over spilled blood.

"Alright, well if ye can't come with me, then what d'ye want to talk to me about?"

"I have something for you. A gift that will help you accomplish what you came here to do. The thunder in Thrymheim told me what you would need to succeed, and so I have come to give it to you."

"The thunder?" I echoed, reminded of the bizarre phrasing Skadi has used back in the mead hall. "Are ye sayin' the sky spoke to ye?"

"Does it not to you?"

"Not generally, no."

"Well, perhaps you are simply too short to hear it speak."

"Must be it," I drawled, though I was barely able to repress my skepticism.

"Stop here," Skadi instructed me a few seconds later, flinging her arm out like a mom at a crosswalk. I halted in my tracks, startled by the abrupt command, but even more surprised to find the giantess turning towards me cradling a wonderfully ornate box in her other hand—a jewelry chest that hadn't been there a moment before. "This is for you, child."

"Uh, t'anks," I replied, eyeing the would-be present as I replayed Freya's warning in my head. Was this some sort of trick? Some elaborate plot cooked up by the jötunn? I decided I couldn't be sure, but knew I was reticent to take it from her. "Can I ask what it is?"

"Of course you can."

We stood in silence for a moment before I realized Skadi was genuinely waiting for me to ask the question.

"Oh, right. What is it?"

"It is my father's heart." Skadi flashed me a roguish smile as she opened the chest to reveal a glittering black jewel that seemed to swallow up the nearby light the instant it was uncovered, its facets throbbing to the beat of my own pulse. "I hope you will cherish it."

24

I must have made an appropriately disgusted face in response to Skadi's grisly offering, because Skadi snapped the lid shut and pulled the chest close with a hurt expression. Of course, I wasn't sure how she'd expected me to react after opening a box containing her father's "heart"; where I came from, organs didn't look like the sort of jewels a maharajah might wear to his serial date night. Still, I'd been raised to say thank you no matter how awkward the gift, and so I held out my hands and put on my most grateful smile.

"Sorry, Skadi. I thought ye were givin' me your father's *actual* heart. That is a lovely gift."

"But it *is* my father's heart. The heart of Thiaza, greatest of the jötunnar."

I frowned, struggling with the glaring anatomical discrepancy, and pointed at the gilded chest in her hands. "Your father's heart is a precious stone?"

"Yes, as are all hearts belonging to those of us who walked the world before mankind was conceived," Skadi replied matter-of-factly, as though such knowledge was commonplace. Then again, maybe it was; Skadi had spent millennia imprisoned in a pocket realm, which meant it was entirely possible there was a sizable gap between what was known then and what was known now.

"And ye want me to have it?"

"Yes."

"Not to sound ungrateful...but why?"

"Because you will need his power where you are going."

"In Niflheim? Or d'ye mean Helheim?"

"I cannot say. All the thunder told me was that you would require the power of a jötunn if you hoped to survive." Skadi continued as though that tidbit of information were far more trivial than she made it sound. "This is perhaps the last unclaimed heart of my people, but if it means my debt to you is repaid, and it rids the Nine Worlds of this abomination, then it will be worth it."

"Well, then...uh, t'anks. I will do me very best to honor ye and cherish your father's...heart. And when ye say I'll need it to survive..."

"I do not know the details," she admitted. "I wish I could tell you more."

"Right. Well, t'anks anyway."

"Another word of caution before you go," Skadi said as she passed the box over. "Keep this hidden, even if it means using the pathetic magic Freya taught you. If any realize you carry it, they will try to either steal it from you or take it by force. The heart of a jötunn is a precious and incredibly powerful thing."

"I appreciate the warnin'. I'll be sure to do that." I slid the chest under one arm, surprised by its density; the box had to weigh twenty pounds, at least. I extended my other hand awkwardly, unsure whether to shake hands or squeeze Skadi's beefy shoulder as Freya had mine. But it turned out neither was necessary; Skadi yanked me to her and wrapped me in a bear hug that would have shattered every bone in my body if it weren't for Nevermore. As it was, I heard the fabled metal creak under the strain.

"You must return as soon as you are able," Skadi muttered, her voice ragged with emotion.

"Skadi, are ye cryin'?"

The giantess drew back, her cheeks stained with frozen tear tracks, and clapped both my shoulders hard enough to make me whimper. She smiled, her eyes shimmering with unspoken sentiment.

"I will miss you, child."

I grinned despite myself, realizing I would miss her, as well; no matter what Freya said, my gut said to trust Skadi's intentions, if not her actions.

Some people—even giants capable of leveling whole cities Godzilla-style—were just inherently well-meaning and therefore, in my not so humble opinion, worthwhile. And I had a sneaking suspicion Skadi was one of them.

"Don't worry, Skadi. We'll always have Valhalla."

25

I headed north after saying farewell to Skadi, skirting the boundary between Fólkvangr and Valhalla so that Freya's eternal sun grazed my left side as I walked towards Niflheim. Unsure what to do with the jewel in my possession, I used the trick Freya had shown me to stow my helmet away, tapping my hip and then the box with my pinky and pointer finger. The box vanished, though I felt its weight on that side of my body, forcing me to adjust my gait to avoid walking with a noticeable limp.

Despite the inconvenience, I found myself touched by Skadi's gift; I doubted any of my friends would be so altruistic as to hand over their patriarch's still-beating heart, no matter the reason. Or maybe I was simply being uncharitable to my friends. Either way, I appreciated the gesture—even if I had no idea what I was supposed to do with the thing, powerful though it undoubtedly was.

Resolving to solve that mystery when the time came, I turned my full attention to the journey at hand, scouring the horizon for signs of Niflheim's border. Of course, I need not have bothered; after walking perhaps another mile, I came upon a dip in the flatlands that led to a valley smothered in dark mists which rose into the sky like a dome, swirling so violently that I could see nothing beyond.

"The entrance to Niflheim," I said aloud as I strode towards the eye of that lethal cloud, recalling what Freya had said of the border between her lands and the true realm of the dead.

"Keep your eyes shut and do not breathe when you enter," she'd cautioned. "The mists will burn your eyes and sear your lungs. Your armor will protect your flesh and my blessing will keep you safe from most of the creatures you might run into within, but you should still avoid the mists at all cost. Stay away from the bogs and out of the caves. Head straight for Helheim and you should be safe."

At the time, I'd been duly concerned by the goddess' caveats and stipulations—especially when they included words like "most" and "should." Now that I saw the wretched looking realm for myself, however, I couldn't help but wish I'd extracted a few more promises from the Vanir. Like, say, a medical evacuation clause should I sneeze in the middle of a mist pocket.

Fortunately, according to Freya, there was a path that led directly from the edge of Fólkvangr to the gates of Helheim, reserved for Valkyries and their freshly collected souls. Apparently—assuming they weren't chosen by Odin or Freya—the leftover spirits were escorted to either Niflheim or Helheim, respectively. Neither seemed like a punishment in the strictest sense of the word—nothing like the fiery pits of Hell I'd been threatened with as a child. And yet, neither had sounded particularly appealing, either.

"And now ye get to experience both firsthand," I muttered, chastising myself as I stood before that wall of writhing mist. "And ye always did say ye wanted to travel to new and exotic places, didn't ye, Quinn? Ye damned idget."

Before I could talk myself out of it, I took a deep breath, closed my eyes, and marched into the mists the way you might leap into the deep end of a swimming pool.

Geroni-freaking-mo.

26

*P*erhaps only a few minutes—but what felt like at least an hour—later, I caught my foot on an outstretched tree limb, stumbled, and crashed to the ground with my pulse beating in my ears. Shrieks and howls followed me like some demented laugh track, playing over and over again as I scrambled back to my feet, searching desperately for the path Freya had urged me to find and stay on. The path I'd been looking for since I first arrived and been set upon by the horrific monsters which hunted me. If I could only locate it, I thought, maybe I would be safe, or at least able to make a break for the relative safety of Helheim.

Anywhere was better than here.

How had things gone so wrong? The answer was simple: I had no fucking clue.

It had all begun the instant I cleared the wall of mist, after which I'd been immediately tracked and hounded by terrifying beasts of unimaginable size and speed, surviving only thanks to the integrity of my armor and my improved reaction time. Since then, I'd been swatted and gnawed on, slashed and smacked around—forced to flee before I became some buga-boo's permanent snack. At first, I'd assumed I must have stepped into some Niflheim nest full of revolting critters, but the longer I ran the more of them I saw. Indeed, between them and the haphazard pockets of mist, it had quickly become all I could do to stay one step ahead of my assailants. Now, it felt a lot less like I'd upset Niflheim's ecosystem and more like I was being herded.

Like I was being led somewhere.

Somewhere that rhymed with water.

I panted heavily, sprinting between two sickly looking trees weighed down by thick, mossy vines just as an enormous snake-like monstrosity curled its massive body around the nearest trunk. It saw me and reared back to reveal a muck-covered, white-scaled belly complete with chitinous legs. I dove instinctively, rolling to my right as the beast struck the tree, barreling into the rotten trunk with enough force to snap it in two. I leapt to my feet, immediately aware of a sense of movement beneath the creature's flesh as though its insides were trying to emerge. A second glance revealed dark, man-like shapes writhing beneath its skin, their mouths open in silent screams.

Disgusted, horrified, and verging on exhausted, I took off once more, this time moving towards the chill that lingered in the air; Freya had mentioned something about the heart of Niflheim being more of an icy wasteland than a terrifying jungle, with Helheim at its center. If I couldn't find the path, I decided, perhaps this was the next best thing.

Unfortunately, as the air grew colder, the landscape grew more bleak, leaving less cover for me to duck behind and catch my breath. I began to see shadows flit across the ground as beasts from above wheeled in mid-air, flinching every time I heard one of their ear-splitting shrieks.

Why hadn't Freya's blessing worked? I asked myself that question over and over again as I bolted from tree to boulder to bush, skirting patches of mist that hovered like a poisonous fog. But the answer eluded me. It was possible Freya had betrayed me, of course, but unlikely. She'd gone through too much trouble to outfit me and extract a promise. Skadi, too, might have done something to negate the Vanir's power, but why? If she wanted me dead, all she had to do was step on me and claim it was an accident. That left the possibility of either a defective blessing or a rule change even Freya hadn't known about.

Could Ryan have done something to upset the balance? The thought made me sick to my stomach; if Ryan had enough influence to do this, I wasn't sure I stood a chance against him no matter which version of me was steering the ship. Worse, if this was the fallout from his mere presence, I doubted there was anything left of my friend to save.

Before I could dwell on any of that, however, a pair of glowing eyes emerged from a nearby bog, attached to the seething silhouette of what looked like a gigantic wolf. I recognized the bastard immediately as one of the first monsters to find me, recalling how its canines had crunched against my armor as it flung me about like a rag doll. Realizing it would be futile to hide, I made a break for it, charging in the opposite direction even as the dread wolf loped towards me, its ragged panting growing louder and louder, until I thought I could feel its fetid breath on my neck. Seeing a cave entrance looming in the distance, I changed direction. But there was no way I was going to make it.

This was it.

The second it caught me, the others would catch up and pull me apart by my limbs, armor or no armor. Which meant I would never save Ryan. I would never find and save Max. I would never see my friends or loved ones again. Indeed, at that moment, it wasn't my life that flashed before my eyes, but the life I would have had.

The dread wolf pounced.

And suddenly a bigger creature appeared, spiking the dread wolf's head like a volleyball before snatching its torso up in jaws that could easily have clamped around an apartment building. Perhaps three times as large and twice as wide as its opponent, the hairy monstrosity snarled and snapped, tearing the dread wolf to pieces before my very eyes. I had perhaps a second to admire the ferocious creature, to realize I was looking at a jötunn wolf that made its prey look like a cheap, dime store knock-off by comparison, and to wonder at the collar around its thick neck before a hand clamped over my mouth and someone snatched me up by the waist and drew me back into the recesses of the cave.

27

*T*he hand pressed against my lips fell away before I could so much as utter a muffled scream or—even more likely—lick the offending palm; few things weird people out as thoroughly as sliding a sloppy wet tongue across their skin without their permission. The arm around my waist followed suit as the person it belonged to backpedaled deeper into the cave, his hands held out to either side, fingers splayed as though assuring me he meant no harm. Which was good, because as abductors go, something told me he wasn't the sort I'd have wanted to square off against.

Several inches taller than I was, with lean, ripcord muscles on display beneath his shabby, tattered clothes, the man who'd snatched me up—if only for a moment—reminded me of a wild animal, though I wasn't entirely sure why. Perhaps it was his crazy mane of dark, curly hair or the fluid way he moved as he leaned to look past my shoulder at the fight raging outside, or perhaps it was the feral grin that tugged at his pouty lips. Either way, I found myself on edge as the madman, with a movement so slow and sinuous that it became mesmerizing, brought one of those spindly fingers to his lips, his pale grey eyes flicking meaningfully to the sounds of the dread wolf being ripped to shreds and devoured.

He beckoned me to step further into the cave, then retreated as though I'd have no choice but to follow. Of course, he was right; at least in here I could catch my breath and hide out from the beasts who'd been after me up to this point, maybe even get some answers. Still, I knew better than to trust some madman in a cave in a realm that was supposed to cater exclusively to dead people. I grabbed a flat rock big enough to clock my abductor upside the head with and crept forward, prepared for whatever shenanigans he might have in store.

Fortunately, the madman seemed to have gotten it out of his system when he abducted me; nothing untoward happened until I was another twenty feet further in, and—when it finally did—all that came of it was a fire being lit in the recesses of the cave. I hid my face from the sudden blaze, but lowered my arm once I saw that it illuminated what remained of the cave's interior with its flickering light. The madman squatted beside it, poking the flames with his bare finger.

"Who are ye?" I whispered once I reached the fire. "And what is this place?"

"You can speak freely," he replied without so much as a glance in my direction, waving his hand idly at the cave ceiling. "We won't be overhead, here."

I looked up and gasped, marveling to see so many runes carved into the stone. No, not carved, I realized. Branded, their designs burned into the stone itself. The stone bore scorch marks elsewhere—evidence of past fires. Oh, and bones. Lots and lots of bones.

"For when my son grows hungry," the madman went on, gesturing to the pile of discarded remains.

"Your son?"

"Yes, he's the one making all that noise outside."

"He..." I drifted off, realizing the madman was talking about the ginormous wolf that'd inadvertently saved me. "Ye can't mean..."

"I hadn't planned to stay here very long, you see," he continued as though I hadn't spoken. "But Fenrir is so fond of hunting down those creatures outside, how could I deny him?"

Fenrir. The name instantly struck a chord; I took a halting step backwards, my skin crawling with the knowledge that I'd been saved by the wolf prophesied to kill Odin and kick off Ragnarök...after he devoured a good portion of the earth and sky, of course. Worse, if the madman was telling the truth, that meant I was talking to Fenrir's father.

Loki, the Norse god of mischief.

"Relax," Loki insisted, turning to stare at me, the firelight bathing half his body, the other lost to shadow. Except it wasn't Loki lookin at me; a single yellow eye danced with amusement in the socket of a serving girl's familiar face. "I did say I would see you around."

"It was ye! You're the girl from the mead hall!"

"Allegedly. You know, I do love that word. Also the phrase 'innocent until proven guilty.' And rumors! All those tools of misdirection making equally useful tools out of people...and gods, of course. Let's not forget those preening fools."

"Why were ye there?" I asked, unable to let go of the deception even after his face shifted back to normal. "And why d'ye hit on me?"

"Curiosity, mostly. I've never lain with a woman pretending to be a man while I pretended to be a woman. It was all so...meta. Another great word." Loki leaned back, his lean muscles bunching as he looked to the ceiling. "And I was there for the same reason as you, obviously. Though I confess I make a much better spy. It's all in the body language. And, well, the body."

"Ye were spyin' on someone? But who? Wait..." I drifted off, sensing the answer before he could respond. "Magni and Modi. They were talkin' about Mjolnir, and they said somethin' about ye..."

"I know." Loki's tone was displeased to the extreme, and the fire seemed to react to his displeasure; it flared up for a moment, forming a brilliant column of flame. "Those imbeciles. They had one job, and they couldn't even do that right."

"To kill Odin?" I asked, tentatively.

"Those morons? Kill Odin? Of course not. They weren't ever going to lay a hand on the Allfather. They were simply meant to keep him busy. Preoccupied. *Distracted.*"

"Why?"

"That's my business. And I'm much more interested in hearing about yours." Loki swiveled, produced a rocking chair out of mid-air, and plopped down with a sigh. "What brings you to Niflheim, my little imposter?"

"What d'ye call me?" The nickname sent a shiver up my spine, reminding me of the private conversation between Freya and me. Or what I'd assumed had been a private conversation, at any rate. Had Loki been listening in, somehow? But then, why hadn't either of us noticed him? For that matter, why couldn't I sense him, now? I scented the air, trying to determine the flavor of Loki's power, but found it masked by the odor of burning wood and the vague sensation of warmth.

Loki's grin simply widened in response.

"I came here to find someone," I replied eventually, breaking the awkward silence, my voice barely carrying over the crackle of the fire. "Well, not here, exactly…"

"Helheim," Loki supplied.

"How d'ye know that?"

"Educated guess. Tell me, do you know what that thing out there chasing you was? Ah, I can see that you don't. Allow me to share." Loki rocked back and forth in his chair, his fingers steepled at chest level. "Those, my little imposter, are souls. Spirits sewn together by foul magic that is not of this realm."

I scowled, baffled as to why Loki would freely share this much information with me, but also caught up in the content of what he was saying. Those were souls I'd seen swirling beneath that creature's flesh? It was the word "sewn" that I kept coming back to, however; I only knew of one asshole who used magic to create monsters.

Frankenstein.

"Now *that* you know something about," Loki said, leaning forward eagerly.

"That's me business," I retorted, spitefully.

"Ordinarily, I might agree. Not that it would stop me from flaying you alive to find out what you knew, but I respect the commitment to one's secrets. In this case, however, I think it is also *my* business."

"Why is that?" I asked, my mouth dry after having processed Loki's not-so-idle threat.

"Because Niflheim is considered the outskirts of my daughter's realm, and I know my own flesh and blood perhaps better than they know themselves. Hel is a gloomy, depressing creature, but she was never cruel. What animates those beasts out there are hundreds of tortured souls, and I am a god."

Struggling to put the pieces together, I found myself recalling not what Freya had said about Loki back at the tower, but *how* she'd said it. She hadn't spoken of him in glowing terms or anything like that, but she had seemed to respect whatever Loki brought to the proverbial table. Which meant the question wasn't whether the god of mischief was lying to me, but whether he thought telling me would serve his agenda.

"What's bein' a god got to do with it?"

"When souls are in pain, they pray to anyone who will listen. Which means I can hear their *screams*."

A shiver ran up my spine.

"Why are ye tellin' me this?"

Loki reached out to touch the fire with his bare hand, letting the flames lick his immortal skin as he adjusted a log about to tumble and collapse into the ash. The fire grew hotter, chasing away even the faint chill from outside, and I realized the sounds of Fenrir's chomping had died away, leaving a stillness in the air that made me want to squirm.

"What if I were to tell you that my daughter is no longer running Helheim?"

*D*espite knowing the trouble Ryan's arrival could mean for this realm and its inhabitants, the news that its ruler had been supplanted came as quite the shock. So much so, in fact, that I had to spend at least a minute processing Loki's pronouncement. Of course, the next logical question was the obvious one.

"Then who is in charge?"

"The individual responsible for those malformed monsters that hunt you, I expect. I haven't been able to sneak past my daughter's guard dog to find out for myself." Loki pinched his shirt between his fingers. "Illusions are one thing, but getting the smell of dog out of your clothes? Good luck."

"That's why you're tellin' me all this," I said, clapping a hand to my head for being so dense. "Ye want to know who it is."

"Oh, but that's where you're wrong."

I lowered my arm, slowly.

"You see," Loki continued, "I don't much care who it is. I just want them stopped. Murdered, actually, assuming they're alive. Oh, but also tortured, if you can manage it."

"Would ye like me to make ye a cup of coffee while I'm at it?"

"No thanks. I'm stimulated enough as is."

I rolled my eyes. "And what makes ye t'ink I stand a chance against him if he managed to overthrow your daughter? Isn't she one of the jötunnar?"

"So it's a him, then?" Loki pursed his lips, amused to see me squirm with the knowledge that I'd given him a clue. "Hel is very powerful, it's true, but also easily fooled. She gets that from her mother, obviously."

"Obviously," I drawled.

"It's quite possible she was taken in by this usurper. Tricked, somehow. Helheim has been her home for a long, long time. Few gods ever visit who aren't already dead, and Valkyries make for poor company." Loki eyed me up and down with disdain. "Anyway, she makes an easy mark."

"So ye want me to, what, rescue her? After I torture and murder the person responsible, of course."

"I'll leave that bit up to you. Keep in mind, however, that Helheim without Hel would be a lawless wilderness full of abandoned souls with no one to shelter or guide them. If you can live with that on your conscience, then far be it from me to try to convince you otherwise."

So, that was his plan: use me to do the dirty work and help his offspring, aware that the only way to right the wrongs that had been done here was to see order restored. Of course, that meant he was relying on my altruism—my sense of justice.

"So, what's in it for me?"

"Pardon?"

"Well, it seems to me ye get to see your daughter returned to her throne, these beasts returned to their less horrifyin' states, and all ye have to do is sit on your ass in some cave, keepin' your son as far away as ye can from an old, one-eyed man and his stick."

This time it was my turn to smile as Loki flinched, betraying the reason he'd holed up in this cave with all its runes. He, along with Fenrir, was hiding—avoiding the fulfillment of the prophecy that would doom the Norse to the end of times. That's why he wanted Odin distracted; with his own grandsons on the warpath the Allfather couldn't hunt Fenrir down, which meant a rebellion from within was just what the Trickster ordered.

"So, and correct me if I'm wrong, it sounds like I'm doin' ye quite the favor. Only that's not how t'ings work down here, is it?" I folded my arms across my chest. "What will ye give me for it?"

"It?"

"The death of the bastard responsible for those creatures and the return of your daughter to the throne."

133

"Ah, a negotiation," Loki said, rubbing at his cheek, his half-mad smile spreading wide as his thoughts churned. "What do you want?"

"I want Odin's eyepatch."

Loki's smile disappeared and his jaw dropped. Indeed, for a moment, he reminded me of a guppy; his mouth opened and closed with such regularity I thought I might have broken him. Eventually, however, he shook his head.

"Why in the Nine Worlds would you want the Allfather's eyepatch?"

"Can ye get it, or not?"

"I...maybe."

"Ah, so ye have a way to get close to him that he doesn't know about."

Loki's expression flipped from perplexed to furious, the flames at his side roaring with such ferocity that they caught his rocking chair on fire. Not that he seemed to care; the god of mischief sat amidst the flames like some infernal demon, pinning me with his eyes.

"You...tricked me."

"And here I thought you'd be impressed."

"I ought to kill you."

"But ye won't," I replied, sounding more confident than I felt. "Ye need me to do somethin' ye can't, and I already know how far you'll go to keep your children safe." I jerked a thumb over my shoulder, clearly referencing Fenrir. "Which means right now I'm more valuable to ye alive than dead."

"Assuming you aren't the walking dead already," Loki replied, his eyes dancing. "Whatever you've done to get yourself down here is wearing off, you know. I could see it in Valhalla. The dead aren't supposed to wield such power. Of course, if you're still here when it does, you won't ever leave. But I'm sure you knew that already."

Guess I should've read the fine print.

I stored that bit of trivia for later, knowing I'd have plenty of time to worry about the efficacy of Circe's potion once this conversation was over. Until then, I couldn't afford to show weakness. Loki's power, from what I could tell, hinged upon how he could make others feel, or what he could provoke them to do. Having to lift a finger to kill me wasn't in his nature. If he wanted me dead, he might arrange it, but he'd never pull the trigger.

Which meant—at this moment—I had all the leverage.

"I'll need an escort to Helheim," I said, at last. "To keep the beasts from attackin' me. Send Fenrir with me, and I'll consider us even."

"You want *Fenrir* to keep you safe?" Loki asked, his voice laced with incredulity.

"He'd have to shadow me. I can't risk his scent gettin' on me, or I'll run into the same issue ye did and we'll both be up the River Styx without a paddle."

"Do you have any idea what you're asking? Fenrir is not the sort to take orders. Getting him to keep a low profile requires every ounce of cunning and patience that I have. And I'm his father."

"That may very well be. But technically I'm not askin' Fenrir to help me, at all. I'm askin' a big brother to help save his baby sister. Granted, I may not know a whole lot about how ye Norse bastards do t'ings, but I do know that when a family member is in trouble, sacrifices can, and will, be made. The question is whether Fenrir is prepared to do his part."

"You were right," Loki said after a long period of hesitation, during which he rose and paced the room like a convict doing laps in his jail cell.

"Which time?" I asked, flippantly.

"Funny." Loki cocked his head. "I have to admit, I am impressed."

"That's sweet, but don't get any ideas." I held up a finger. "I also want ye to promise not to get all backstabby once I leave. I have enough on me plate without addin' your carcass to it."

Loki's eyes narrowed to slits, but he didn't argue.

"Very well, you have a deal."

I left at a trot, headed in the direction Loki had indicated as we emerged from the cave, confident of the arrangement we'd come to. The god of mischief had already gone and spoken to Fenrir. I, naturally, had opted to stay inside and hang out with the remains rather than join them. I spotted the jötunn wolf some fifty yards to my left as I took off, his bestial frame rising above the nearest trees, his breath steaming into the air as if from the mouth of a chimney, his muzzle slathered with gobs of drool. To me, he looked both pissed off and...hungry. But he hadn't met me at the cave mouth and gobbled me up like a post-dinner breath mint, so I could only assume Loki had told me the truth when he claimed his son was on board.

Thank Dog.

The instant I hit my stride, the cacophony I'd become accustomed to while in Niflheim resumed as a veritable horde of dread beasts came out to play. I saw the grotesque snake with its chittering legs weaving across the ground, the misshapen birds circling high overhead, a bear with porcupine quills protruding from its back, and a dozen other shadows lurking in the distance. Of course, if I could see them, that meant so could Fenrir.

Soon, the sounds of torn flesh and splintered bone were all that followed me; even the birds fled lest Fenrir leap into the sky and drag them down by their tail feathers. I had to admit there was something reassuring about having a guardian hellhound at my back, even if he was a crazed monster destined to kick off the end of days. Of course, it was also possible I was feeling nostalgic; for a good while there, I'd had Cathal at my side for moments like these. Of course, he'd have been bitching about how much we humans sucked or how shitty the dread beasts tasted.

I found myself grinning as I finally reached the path that led to Helheim, charmed by the conjurings of my imagination. But my smile only grew wider once I spotted the fuzzy outline of Helheim's walls and realized this leg of the journey, at least, was nearly over.

Not that I was getting cocky, of course.

I still had no idea how I was going to defeat Frankenstein, especially if Ryan was standing between us. My strategy—though far less comprehensive than I'd have liked—had always been to separate the two at first opportunity. To divide and conquer. The way I figured it, once I got him outside the mad doctor's influence, my odds of knocking some sense into my old friend went way up. Maybe then I could make him see that what he was doing—what he'd done—wasn't really *him*. Then we could take on Frankenstein as a team, find Max, briefly confront the Temples, and get the hell out of Hell before Circe's potion wore off—assuming Loki hadn't lied about that.

Unfortunately, that was beginning to feel like an overly simplistic, highly idealized approach. What if Frankenstein's hold was too strong and Ryan didn't want to leave the dark side? Worse, what happened if I never got a chance to talk some sense into him, at all? Having seen Ryan's power firsthand in the Titan Realm, I doubted my armor would be enough to save me. Unless my inner goddess took the reins, Ryan could turn me into a popsicle and keep me around as a decorative ice sculpture for all eternity if he felt so inclined. Indeed, for some reason, all I could picture was Darth Vader beheading Luke before he could spout his do-gooder rhetoric.

Bye bye, Skywalker dynasty.

Unfortunately, I couldn't worry about any of that, yet. First, I had to sneak into Helheim. Which—I found out very quickly as I closed in on Hel's realm—came with its own less-than-ideal challenges.

Like getting past Fenrir's meathead stunt double.

I froze on the path, staring past the black river surrounding Helheim's towering stone walls—the sound of its gurgle eerily like the murmurings of a deranged maniac. Past the narrow bridge that rose over said river to end at the foot of Helheim's gates. Past the gates themselves, to look with awe upon the beast which lay between them, a hound unlike any I'd seen before. With russet fur so short he appeared nearly hairless and more muscles than should have been anatomically possible, Garmr would have looked like a pitbull on steroids *without* being as big as a house. As it was, I suddenly understood Loki's unwillingness to risk sneaking past, even for his daughter's sake.

Too bad that's exactly what I'd come here to do.

I slid my helm from my hip and dismissed the illusion covering my armor in one smooth motion, donning the beaked headpiece with a murmured prayer to whoever might be listening—even if that *was* Loki. For simplicity's sake, I kept my message both ambiguous and direct.

To whomever god it may concern.

Please let this work.

Despite knowing it made no difference, I stepped onto the bridge thinking Valkyrie thoughts as hard as I could. I told myself I was there on business, even concocted some ridiculous backstory in case I ended up stopped and questioned—just an innocent Valkyrie stopping in for the bimillennial inspection, nothing to see here, folks. Of course, the instant I realized Garmr's fur was actually khaki-colored, and that what I'd mistaken for a russet coat was in fact dried blood, all rational thought went out the window.

"Please, please let this work," I muttered.

Garmr's ears flicked and his eyes opened. They were tinted a shade of lavender—and would have been gorgeous, really, if they'd belonged to a domesticated pooch as opposed to a monstrous guard dog. He yawned, his pinkish tongue lolling like a rogue wave between canines I couldn't have comfortably wrapped my arms around. I, meanwhile, kept right on walking, my feet moving inexorably forward despite every instinct in my body screaming for me to turn and run away.

I was halfway along the bridge when Garmr clambered to all fours and poked his head out, thrusting his muzzle between the gates, scenting the wind. His eyes found me a moment later, and that's when his expression changed; wrinkles curled along the hound's snout as his hackles rose. He snarled, the sound alone enough to make the stones tremble beneath my feet.

Or maybe that was just my legs giving out.

"Good doggie," I said, holding up both hands as though I could talk him down.

Garmr lunged forward, snapping his jaws and barking his head off as he thrust the gates open wide with his massive, blocky head. Mercifully, his shoulders met the walls on either side, refusing to budge, otherwise the hound would have rushed out onto the bridge and rent me to pieces— assuming he didn't swallow me whole.

I cursed, pissed to learn that neither Freya's blessing nor my Valkyrie armor had really paid off down the stretch; I might just as well have rubbed grease all over my naked body and gone running through Niflheim like a slice of bacon with legs for all the good they'd done me. But complaining wouldn't help now. What I needed was to find another way in, or to distract the bastard long enough to sneak by without him noticing. I scoured the landscape, studied Helheims's walls for handholds or holes big enough for me to slip through, but saw nothing I could use.

Fortunately, I wouldn't have to.

Fenrir, my deadly shadow and willing accomplice, appeared along the furthest bend of Helheim's walls, his hulking body suddenly at least as large as Garmr's as he emerged like a shaggy mountain from a distant tree line— maybe even bigger if you took into consideration all that fur. As I watched, Loki's son plopped his monstrous ass down, raised his muzzle to the sky, and howled, hurling his challenge to the heavens.

And it worked.

Garmr's eyes popped open so wide I could see his lavender irises swimming in a sea of white. I, meanwhile, pressed my hands to either side of my helmet, trying to block out the primal howl before it made my ears bleed. Then, before you could so much as spell "t-r-e-a-t," the hound backpedaled and shot off towards the sound of Fenrir's cry, barking his godsdamned head off.

Realizing it was now or never, I waved in gratitude to the jötunn wolf and sprinted for the gates, which had already begun to swing closed on their hinges without Garmr's thick neck to stop them. Every breath came fast and hard as I raced forward, the sound of my boots on the cobblestones like shotgun blasts in my oversensitized ears. Realizing I wasn't going to make it, I leapt, diving for that slim divide...and crashed into Helheim, forced to pull my legs in before the gates could slam shut and cut me in two. I thrust a fist in the air, panting, and sent out a thank you prayer.

So, I had officially broken into Helheim.

Now the question was, would I ever make it out?

3 0

*H*elheim was not at all how I'd pictured it. In my mind, I'd anticipated an icy wasteland full of wandering souls dragging their feet in the snow, their faces locked in expressions of numb horror as they waited for eternity to end. The reality was somehow both better, and worse. Instead of a frozen tundra full of restless spirits, I found a city seething with life, its denizens milling about the streets in their thousands as though they all had places to be and people to see.

Except no one spoke.

Indeed, the only sound came from the tolling of bells that hung like streetlights from a series of stone arches that led towards the city's epicenter. And it was there—in the space dominated by a single dark tower looming over the city in the shape of a twisted tree, its limbs protruding like jutting parapets upon which knelt dozens of pious souls—that I knew I must go. It wasn't merely the faint miasma of evil I sensed lurking about the place, but the way the spirits below averted their eyes, refusing to look up at the Helspire for fear that they, too, would be called forth to worship whoever or whatever lay inside.

A chill wind blew past, fluttering hair and fur alike as I waded among the silent phantoms, their flesh not unlike mine—if a bit paler, which was remarkable in and of itself. It was their movements, however, which gave them away; they shuffled about like automatons, miming actions that made no sense. I watched a mother rock a nonexistent child as she crossed the street, a man with no axe strike an invisible tree, and dozens of other behaviors I couldn't account for. It was like these souls had been displaced, removed from the everyday toil of their afterlives.

I grabbed at the arm of the nearest woman, an elderly lady wrapped in a thick, woolen shawl, hoping to ask if she knew what was going on here. But the second I touched her, I felt my hand go numb, then my wrist, then my forearm. I jerked back with a hiss, flinging my arm about to get the blood back into it. The old woman stopped, tilted her head, and stared up at me with rheumy eyes.

"Sten, is that you?"

Her voice was a gravelly whisper.

"No, me name is Quinn, I—"

"Do not dally with that girl, Sten. Her brother will kill you in your sleep, and you will never reach Valhalla." She reached for me, her fingers splayed like claws. "Do not make the mistake your grandfather did, or you will end up old and alone. Sail east with your cousins. See the world, Sten, or—"

I turned to avoid her touch and bumped into another spirit, a man with a limp this time. Despite my armor, my shoulder went instantly numb, and I was forced to dance away from both specters.

"I should have joined the shield wall!" The man spoke with more passion than his ruddy face would have suggested as he turned to me. "Why did I run? I should have fought, and maybe the arrow would never have taken me in the knee and Erik wouldn't have slept with my wife..."

More voices began chiming in as I whirled, angling to avoid the meandering spirits before any could brush up against me. The lost souls, seeming to sense my presence, called out to me like dementia patients at a nursery home, declaring their regrets, citing their failures, and lamenting their cowardice. Was it because I was likely the first warm body they'd encountered in centuries, or maybe some side effect of being a Valkyrie? Or was this Frankenstein's handiwork? I couldn't be sure, but the effect was alarming. Soon, everywhere I went I was followed by reaching hands and pitiable faces, by tales of woe and loss that made *Schindler's List* seem like *The Sound of Music*.

Mercifully, once I cleared the third archway and its tolling bell, the spirits began to thin out, almost as though they were avoiding the base of the Helspire, leaving me to walk the last hundred feet or so in relative silence. Surprisingly, there didn't appear to be any guards stationed outside, nor any other forms of security as far as I could see. Perhaps Garmr was considered deterrent enough, I thought. Or perhaps there was simply nothing to fear from spirits like these. Either way, I was glad; the less they suspected an intruder, the easier it would be for me to slip in undetected.

And yet, as I closed in on the tower, I found myself dragging my feet, blissfully unaware of the chill that had nipped at me only moments earlier. I sighed as warmth flooded my chest, then yawned with exhaustion I hadn't realized I'd been staving off. My thoughts became sluggish, then plodding. What was I doing here? Why was I walking when I could be lying down?

Why bother doing anything?

I felt a burning sensation in the center of my breast and looked down to find a sigil shining beneath my chainmail, its white-hot light bringing tears to my eyes. The discomfort brought me back to my senses, and I frowned to realize I'd hesitated a mere foot away from the base of the Helspire, my hand inches from the open doorway. The rune on my chest faded to a dull glow but didn't dim entirely. I pressed a gauntleted hand to it and made a closed fist, extremely grateful for the assist.

Dagaz.

Hope.

I supposed I could do a lot worse than to have a little of that on my side.

For as dark as the Helspire was on the outside, it was equally light on the inside. Diamond and quartz spanned the walls of winding corridors, while the floors seemed made of glass and cast long reflections in either direction depending on the location of the nearest brazier. As far as I could tell, there were no stairs, and every hallway led to the top; my calves ached from the steady incline. The hallways were also completely deserted, which gave the eeriest impression of walking alone through some sort of living dreamscape—like those surreal scenes set in a room full of funhouse mirrors that no one actually finds fun anymore.

I'd estimated I'd gotten about halfway up—though frankly I had no way to gauge distance in a place like this—when I finally heard the first voice that wasn't my own. It was a woman's, and she was crying. Not great, pitiful sobs, but the sort of tears we reserve for ourselves and ourselves alone. I pressed myself against the glittering stone wall and inched forward, peered around the bend, and saw a pitiful figure chained so that her body formed an "X", her hands and feet bound and stretched to their limits, attached to the floor and ceiling respectively. It was a horrifying sight and all the more so because I knew exactly who I was looking at.

Mabel.

The elven lass looked somehow even worse than when I'd last seen her on Polyphemus' island. Back then she'd been covered in blood and sores, woefully malnourished, and begging me to kill her rather than leave her at the mercy of her master—who I'd assumed was Ryan at the time, but now I wasn't so sure. Either way, Mabel currently bore so many bruises and scrapes I hardly recognized her, and her clothes were tattered rags. Worse, whoever had hung her up had either neglected or refused to cover her exposed bits. Strung up like that, she looked every part the victim, and even I felt terribly sorry for her.

But then her tears stopped.

"Is someone there?" she called.

I wavered, uncertain whether to step out and help her, worried I'd fall into some sort of trap set by Frankenstein or Ryan or both. The fact that either could have done this upset me almost as much as the fact that it had happened at all; if Ryan was capable of this, I'd be doing the known universe a favor by slitting his throat, and I knew it. The trouble was, Mabel had tried to kill me before—more than once. Could I afford to risk confronting Frankenstein for her sake? Unfortunately, the answer was no.

But I did it, anyway.

"It's Quinn," I replied, popping my head out to make sure the coast was clear before slipping into the hallway and creeping towards the chained Faeling, my soft-soled shoes making hardly any noise in the process. I'd used Freya's magic to hide my armor, hoping the illusion would offer me a strategic advantage.

"Quinn?"

Mabel's voice was thready and full of pain. I noticed she didn't so much as turn her head when I spoke, and saw why when I got close: they'd used iron shackles. I hissed at the damage to her wrists and ankles, getting angrier by the second. Whoever had done this had wanted her to hurt —a lot.

"Aye, it's me. Don't worry, I'm goin' to get ye down in no time."

"Trap."

I froze, my hands hovering inches above the shackle around her right ankle, prepared to snap it in two with my newfound strength. I scanned either side of the hallway, trying to figure out where the trap was coming from, but no one was in sight.

"What trap, Mabel?"

"Frankenstein," she replied, weakly. "He wanted you here."

Well, that much I'd already suspected, at least. Why else would his dread beasts have hunted me across Niflheim? Still, it wasn't exactly reassuring to know that the mad scientist had what he wanted.

"And Ryan?"

"Gone."

"Gone? Where's he gone?"

"Atlantis."

"That's not possible," I replied, my pulse speeding up at the mention of the City of the Lost. Unfortunately, Mabel wasn't up to a debate; her head lolled forward, her chin pressed against her chest. I cursed and snapped the shackles binding her legs in quick succession. She jerked upright and screamed as the restraints fell away, her wrists now bearing the brunt of her weight. I took care of those next, allowing the shockingly light creature to fall over my shoulder like a bag of kibble.

Mabel whimpered as I lowered her to the floor, her eyes pinched shut so hard I thought they might get stuck and never open again. Part of me wished I'd have asked Freya for a cloak before I left so I could cover the Faeling up, but as it was, the best I could do was adjust what little fabric remained and keep my eyes averted for modesty's sake.

"Mabel," I said, worried her scream would soon bring reinforcements, "I need to hide ye and find Frankenstein. D'ye know where he is?"

Mabel nodded, still refusing to open her eyes, but her sudden grip on my arm reminded me that I wasn't dealing with a frail mortal woman; she held on so tight I'd have been bruised were it not for Nevermore's layer of protection.

"Take me with you," she insisted. "I know where he is. I can show you."

"Mabel, I can't. Ye aren't in any condition to—"

"You can't leave me here. Not again."

I bit my lip, cursing inwardly. She was right; I'd abandoned her once, and they'd strung her up knowing she wouldn't die. What happened if I failed and they found her a second time? Better that she be at my side where at least she'd stand a chance against her captors than forced to hide and await the outcome.

"Ye have to do everythin' I say," I hissed as I helped her to sit up. "That means if I say 'run,' ye run. If I say 'hide,' ye hide. I'm not your babysitter, and I haven't forgotten the time ye tried to stab me."

"I'll do it." Mabel opened her eyes, her expression hardening as she sought my face. "I want the one who hurt me to pay. To suffer for eternity."

Well, *that* we could agree on.

"Alright, then," I said, drawing her to her feet despite her raspy groans. "I'm sure the doctor will see us, now."

*W*e reached the tower's uppermost floors after several excruciating detours that whittled down Mabel's early enthusiasm until she was all but slung across my shoulders, her toes sliding along the ground. It turned out that her knowledge of Frankenstein's whereabouts was more theoretical than actual, which meant we'd had to try multiple hallways before finding the one which led to what my elf companion had dubbed the "throne room." It was there, apparently, that she'd last seen Ryan.

"Frankenstein made a deal with the goddess who ruled this place," she told me as we moved towards the massive double doors at the end of the hall. "Ryan was part of it."

"What was the deal?"

"I don't know. I was tied up on the floor and couldn't overhear much. All I saw was their feet. One second Ryan's were there, then they weren't. Poof." Mabel looked up at me with a dazed, slightly manic gleam in her eye that spoke of more trauma than I could possibly relate to. "He left me, too. Why does everyone do that?"

I felt a twinge of guilt in response to her question but refused to dwell on it; I had enough people to take care of without picking up strays who had a history of biting the hand that fed them. Once I'd confronted Frankenstein, found out where Ryan had gone, and gotten us all out of here, *then* I'd see about securing the psychological help Mabel would need to recover from what all had been done to her.

"So, he's through here, ye t'ink?" I asked, jerking my chin towards the double doors. "Frankenstein?"

"That's where he was when I last saw him."

"Here?" I cocked an eyebrow. "But then who tied ye up?"

"Oh, that was Ryan," Mabel replied, sounding distracted. "He used his new magic, the stuff he learned from the witch on that island."

"But I thought ye said he was gone by then?"

"Shit," Mabel cursed, her voice dripping with such scorn that alarm bells began ringing in my head. "I knew I was going to screw this up."

I turned to ask the elf what the hell that was supposed to mean when I felt the tip of the syringe plunge into the side of my neck, just below my ear and above the protection of my armor. Somehow, Mabel had known exactly where to strike—probably from having hung on me for the past hour, I realized. I wobbled, my legs giving out almost immediately after she pushed the plunger home, and this time it was Mabel's turn to catch me. The elven backstabber lowered me to the floor and took hold of one of my arms, dragging me casually behind her as though I were a doll who'd wandered off during tea time.

I tried to speak but nothing came out. I was paralyzed, unable to so much as twitch. And yet I could feel everything; I knew she hadn't bothered to remove the syringe from my throat, for example, just as I knew she'd tear my arm out of its socket soon if she didn't slow down. I wanted to ask why, to demand she stop and explain herself, to curse her for tricking me after I'd saved her miserable ass...but in the end all I could do was listen as she kicked the door open and flung me across the threshold.

"Here she is, Master. It happened just like you said! I had to use the syringe you gave me, but she didn't suspect a thing until it was too late."

"Excellent work, Mabel. Well done."

The vaguely German voice would have stopped me cold in my tracks if I weren't already lying on my side and completely unable to move. A pair of brown loafers approached, but the monster they belonged to didn't bother squatting down to look me in the eye. But then, nothing about that shocked me; from everything I'd seen of him, Doctor Victor Frankenstein enjoyed looking down on everyone.

"I'm so glad, Master!" Mabel jumped up and down, her bare feet caked in the blood from her chafed ankles, clapping her hands excitedly. "Does this mean I'll get to assist you? You did promise."

"Of course you may, but only after you get cleaned up. You know how I feel about contamination, and we have ourselves a very special operation planned today. Now, hurry along or I'll be forced to dissect this creature without you."

33

The stone was cold against my naked back. Thick leather straps pinned my bare legs and chest to the table, making it impossible to do anything but turn my head away from the blinding overhead light Mabel had procured on Frankenstein's orders. But that only made me feel worse. All I could make out from where I lay were the tools on the neighboring table, the majority of which looked exactly like what they were: torture devices. I'd taken one peek and immediately regretted it. Indeed, the fact that he hadn't yet used any of them on me was all that kept me from screaming for help. That, and the realization that no one who might have cared could hear me anyway.

It was a morbid, unpleasant thought.

But accurate.

After all, if anyone was going to step in on my behalf, I expected they'd have done it before Frankenstein and his demented nurse stripped me out of my illusory clothes with absolutely no difficulty and strapped me naked to the table. The fact that I could still feel their hands on my pliant, unresisting body—the press of Mabel's chest against my shoulders as she carried me to the table and dumped me like trash onto its unforgiving surface, the pinch of the mad doctor's fingers as he took my measurements—made my stomach churn.

"Any questions before we begin?" Frankenstein asked as he donned a pair of thin, brown leather gloves, his peppered mustache twitching above his pale lips. "I suggest getting them out of the way, now. You may not be in your right mind to do so later."

"Where's Ryan?" I managed, struggling to form the words; I'd only recently regained the use of my limbs and voice.

"Ah, Herr Frost. I am afraid he and I parted ways not so long ago. He had other business to attend to on my behalf."

I felt the dim ember of hope that Ryan might somehow find me lying here and free me for old time's sake flicker and die like a blown out candle. There would be no rescue. No white knight to ride in and save the day—not that I'd have anticipated one. Still, that meant it was up to me to figure a way out of this. But what could I do? Even if I weren't recovering from a paralyzing agent, I'd never be able to escape these restraints. No ordinary human could.

"No more questions? Excellent. Mabel, hand me the scalpel. Yes, the smallest knife, there. Remember, we want to make a clean incision."

"Wait," I interjected, weakly.

"Oh, you weren't done." Frankenstein looked disappointed but passed the knife back to his eager assistant, his decorous manner at odds with the egomaniacal lunatic I'd met on the island of the Vegiants. Of course, back then my inner goddess was the one with all the power, foiling all his plans.

"Atlantis..." I struggled to clear my throat.

"The toxin will make it difficult to speak, fräulein. The muscles in the throat are most susceptible, I've found. But I think I can grasp what it is you wish to say. You want to know where the lost city lies, is that it?"

I shook my head.

"Oh? I must admit *that* was what I would have wanted to know in your position. What is it then?"

"Why...Atlantis?"

"Ah, an abstract thinker!" Frankenstein smiled, his teeth sitting strangely perfect, their glossy whiteness at odds with the fleshy ruin of his leathery face. "You'll have to forgive me. Most seem obsessed with its location, more so than its relevance. Of course, having never been there, myself, I am not equipped to answer your question as thoroughly as I would like. Suffice it to say that Atlantis holds a certain...proximal value."

Proximal, as in proximity? Meaning Atlantis was *close* to something worthwhile? But that didn't make any sense. How could something so sought after offer so little? I felt like I was missing something. Unfortunately, I didn't know the right questions to ask, and time wasn't on my side; the longer I stayed quiet, the more likely Frankenstein was to resume his operation.

"Why...send Ryan?" I prompted before he could speak again, hoping to delay the process indefinitely.

"And not go myself, you mean? Yes, I must admit I was terribly intrigued to see the lost city with my own eyes. But the road to get there, losing one's mind...I must confess, I had not realized Atlantis would be so well guarded. It was very cleverly done."

"Ryan...lost...his mind?"

"Oh yes, but don't fret, the effect is not permanent. His mind belongs to me, you see. He won't find getting rid of it so easy as all that. Indeed, once I understood what needed to be done to reach Atlantis, all that was left was discovering the how. Something at which, and I do hope you will not think me too boastful for saying so, I excel. No, in due time, I expect Herr Frost will set about pilfering the city's treasures, looking for a weapon worthy of his devourer. Such an enchanting jewel. So much raw power. A shame they cannot be harvested as readily as one would like."

"A...weapon?"

"Indeed. One he can use to thwart a Master," Frankenstein replied, putting significant emphasis on the title. "Though, truthfully, I have no intention of allowing that. We already have too many nuclear-level threats unaccounted for as things stand."

The doctor waved his arms about as though none of that mattered, before being reminded of our current situation thanks in part to an impatient comment from Mabel; the elf still held the requisitioned knife out where I could see it, waving it back and forth like a treat. He clapped his gloved hands together and slid them against each other briskly.

"Quite right, Mabel. In any case, simply put, Herr Frost is doing me a favor, though he is, as of yet, unaware of that. Of course, it will not matter to him one way or the other, in the end."

"Why...not?"

"Doctor..." Mabel growled.

"Yes, Mabel, I know. But as our patient, she is as entitled to her questions as we are to take her apart. Such is the contract we make." Frankenstein flashed a doting smile on his deranged assistant, then returned his attention to me. "As for your question, fräulein, you should know by now that Herr Frost *belongs* to me."

"How?"

"Ah, well, I would like to think he would have served me of his own free will, eventually. But unfortunately, I found myself pressed for time. So I used the devourer he procured for me some time ago to...ease his troubled, inconsistent soul. The poor creature had lost his purpose, you see, and purpose for beings like him is everything, as knowledge is for men like me." Frankenstein smirked at my withering scorn, anticipating my reaction. "You may not care for my methods, but it was for his own good, was it not, Mabel?"

"Of course, Master!" Mabel replied, leaning forward so eagerly that she pressed her bony chest against my arm. "Ryan never would have left that stupid bitch if you hadn't convinced him to."

"Ah, yes. Calypso. Fascinating creature. Did you know nymphs have stomachs, but no need to eat or drink? Nor do they produce waste of any sort. I would not have believed it if I had not cut her open, myself."

I licked my suddenly dry lips, my pulse speeding up at the doctor's casual reference to the dissection of a witch who'd kept Odysseus in her clutches for years before releasing him to return home at the gods' behest. Worse, of course, was the knowledge that he'd used the devourer Ryan had stolen from me to gain control of my old friend.

"Then why..is Ryan...in Atlantis?" I asked, retreading old ground in a desperate grab for more time. I'd already begun calling to the goddess within, begging her to lend me the power I'd used to back Freya down. But nothing came.

"I see we are going in circles now. Let us say that access to the city is of particular interest to those I work with and leave it at that," Frankenstein replied, patting my naked shoulder and ignoring my subsequent flinch. "You should know I intended to send you along with Herr Frost, before I saw what you could do. He was quite adamant that you join him. Remarkable, really, considering how little of his personality was left by the time I was through. It is too bad we will have to disappoint our mutual friend, but I really must see how you work. As I said before, knowledge is everything."

Frankenstein reached over me as though our conversation were at an end whether I liked it or not, taking the knife from Mabel's trembling fingers. I began to shake, chills running up my spine as I caught sight of the raw fascination lurking behind the doctor's wire-rimmed glasses. This, I realized, was what a brilliant man without scruples could become given immortality and an unhealthy dose of curiosity.

"Now, I usually prefer my subjects be dead when I perform this procedure," Frankenstein said, leaning over me so that his face was obscured by shadow, the light overhead forming a halo around his head. "But, as I have no desire to kill you for some time, that will not be possible in your case. So, I would ask that you not thrash about, or this may become a messy affair. Feel free to scream, of course, if you think it will help you keep still."

"No, I—"

Mabel clamped a hand over my mouth.

"Scream into my hand," she said, sweetly.

The full horror of what Frankenstein was about to do registered a moment before he pressed the tip of his knife to the base of my sternum. Then, with a suddenness that stole my breath away, he began. A line of fire lanced along the length of my body as I convulsed, gasping for air, my flesh pressed so tight against my restraints that I slammed the back of my head on the table when I came back down. A jagged line of pure, searing pain ran from my crotch to my chest—so much of it, in fact, that I could hardly breathe, let alone cry out. The rest of me tingled, my limbs rigid and spasming.

"Well, that could have gone better," Frankenstein said, sounding put out as he studied the wound he'd created. "I did warn you to stay still. Now I'll have to sew you up, myself. Provided you do not heal on your own, of course."

"But Master," Mabel whined, "you promised I would get to do the next one."

"Once you have had more practice, Mabel." The doctor reached out to pat his assistant's head, staining her blonde hair with the blood coating his gloves.

My blood.

Dear God, it really was *my* blood.

"Go...fuck...yourselves," I ground out, every syllable sending new waves of pain which flowed down my body until I began hyperventilating, my mind abruptly overwhelmed with panic and fear. This wasn't a game, or some ploy to get me to talk; they were actually going to dissect and then kill me. And then I'd be dead, for real, and stuck in this city of lost souls, assuming Frankenstein didn't turn me into some sort of monster.

No, I wouldn't let that happen.

I couldn't let that happen.

"Ah, she is going into shock," Frankenstein said as he stepped back from the table, his blade gleaming red. "I had hoped she would be able to heal some of the damage. I believe we can safely assume she has lost the power she once had. Very well, let us start with her heart while we still have her. Pass me the—"

The rest of what Frankenstein said was lost, drowned out by a series of ferocious barks, each yawp splitting the air like a thunderclap. Distantly, I realized I'd heard them before. Garmr—it had to be. Was it Fenrir out there, antagonizing him some more, or was there someone else at the gates trying to gain entrance? I realized it didn't matter; I was already losing consciousness and could feel the blood seeping from my wound, bathing my torso and the table beneath.

"That mongrel," Frankenstein muttered between barks as he stripped off his gloves. "I have always hated pets that refuse to behave. Mabel! Apply pressure to the wound and keep our patient awake while I deal with whatever is going on out there."

"Gladly."

"And remember, we cannot allow her to die!" the doctor called over one shoulder. "Once she becomes a wandering soul in truth, she will lose all sense of self and our opportunity to uncover her secrets will be lost. Do not forget, an education is a terrible thing to waste!"

"Yes, Doctor."

I watched Frankenstein's silhouette disappear mere seconds before Mabel pressed her hands against either side of my open wound and proceeded to push the edges together—her version of applying pressure, I gathered. I screamed for real, then. Screamed until my throat was raw and my vision began to tunnel.

"Oh no you don't," Mabel whispered in my ear, her voice so sickly sweet it made me want to vomit. "Not before I see you suffer the way I have. In fact, I think it's time I pay you back, for real." The elf stood to her full height, pinched my nose, and made a honking sound. "Don't go anywhere, I'll be right back. And I'll be bringing company, so be on your best behavior."

34

I lay there, the pain stretching time until it felt like I'd spent my whole life on this table. Existence became a miserable thing—a waking nightmare I could not escape simply by opening my eyes. The light overhead was a searing sun, baking me alive. The stone at my back was a solid patch of ice, eating away at my skin. Part of me, the part that shut all the doors and hid from the pain, thought it ironic that it'd taken me this long to experience true hell, given my itinerary. The rest of me, of course, could only scream.

"Still awake?" Mabel called, her footsteps drawing nearer from somewhere to my right. Except it wasn't only hers; a heavier tread slapped against the floor, and a moment later I saw both the elf and the hulking silhouette of a man looming over me. "Oh, darn. I was hoping I might have to wake you. That can be *very* pleasant."

I tried to speak, to say something hurtful if only to strike back at the bitch the only way I still could, but all that came out was a pathetic whimper. I closed my eyes, felt tears of pain roll down my cheeks, and pretended I had managed to land a witty zinger, that even now Mabel's expression was one of bitterness and rage. I fixed that image in my mind, willing it to be true. Except when at last I opened them again, what I saw was not the face of a psychotic elf, but that of the man; Mabel held his face inches from mine, her hand wound in the thickness of his remarkably dark hair, forcing him to look down at me with eyes that seemed to stare at nothing.

Still, they were eyes I recognized.

"Max..."

I whispered his name like a prayer, my eyes tracing the lines of his familiar face. He looked not so much as he had on the hospital bed in Circe's pool but as he had when we first met; with an iron jawline and knee-weakening bone structure, Maximiliano Velez was the sort of man whose masculinity bordered on cruel, saved only by his easy manners and confident swagger. In repose, his was the sort of face which belonged on the statue of an avenging angel or a conquering king. In the flesh, however, the brujo was more scamp than statesman.

Except there was no personality playing across that face, no smile tugging at his full lips, no dimples breaking the smoothness of his cheeks— nothing of him at all, in fact. He looked drugged, anesthetized. Perhaps even lobotomized. I squirmed, trying to see past the brujo, to lock gazes with Mabel and demand that she reveal what they'd done to him, but she stayed hidden behind the much larger man.

"Before you ask," she said, her voice materializing as if from thin air, "we found him like this. And no, the doctor has no interest in carving him up."

Mabel drew Max back by his hair, adjusting the line of their bodies with a violent flick of her wrist until they stood front to front. Now that Max's face wasn't dominating my vision, I saw the brujo wore a pair of ill-fitting trousers slung low across his narrow hips, his upper body completely nude. Unfortunately, seeing his body made me acutely aware of my own in a way I hadn't been before; I felt defenseless and vulnerable, the unrelenting pain momentarily overshadowed by the shame of exposure.

Mabel must have mistaken my response for jealousy because she watched me eagerly as she ran her hands over the swell of Max's chest, tracing a nail along the scar that remained from his time with the witches of Ipswich. When I didn't immediately react, she bent down and leaned in, pressing her cheek against the brujo's taut stomach so that she was looking me directly in the eye while she slid her hands down the line of his body.

"The doctor is incredible, isn't he? Especially for a Manling. It took me a while to realize how important it is to do as he asks, but now he treats me better than Ryan ever did. He even gave me this one to play with, can you believe that? You two were an item once, weren't you?"

So, that was her game.

Apparently, Mabel meant to make me pay through Max, somehow. To punish me for what I'd done to Ryan, for how her life had ended up. I wished I could have convinced her none of this was my fault, but crazy is as crazy does; no matter how pointy her ears were, logic would fall deaf on them. Unfortunately, she was right about Max and me: we'd had a connection, once. A powerful connection—perhaps too powerful; I'd avoided the brujo for fear of its potency.

"Apparently, he and the doctor go way back," Mabel purred as she played with the hem of Max's trousers, running her finger along the edge. "But then you knew that already, I bet."

Memories of my time with Max and his sister surfaced, including the tale of their escape from Frankenstein's clutches. I felt a stab of pity for them both—a degree of kinship now that I'd experienced firsthand what the mad scientist was capable of when he held someone in his sway. Of course, if I recalled correctly, they had spent *years* working for him. The idea alone was enough to make my skin crawl.

"It's a shame he's like this," Mabel continued, pouting, lifting one of Max's arms only to watch it fall and land with a thunk on my table. "Feels like playing with a doll. But at least he won't complain about the things I intend to do to him, the way I'll use his body..."

As if to demonstrate, the elf rose, grazing her lips along the brujo's skin as she went. Once upright, she planted her mouth over his nipple, glanced my way to make sure I was watching, and bit down with all the savageness of a dog with a bone. Blood quickly trickled down her chin and began streaming down Max's body in crimson rivulets. I winced, disturbed both by the sight itself and the fact that Max's expression never changed once during the abuse, though his body did twitch of its own accord. I felt but could not see his fingers as they accidentally brushed against mine...and they burned.

Something in the air changed.

Mabel's eyes widened perceptively as a large, calloused hand grabbed a fistful of her hair and pried her away from his chest. She looked up, her bloodstained mouth gaping wide to find a pair of smoldering brown orbs glaring down at her. But the heat was not restricted to Max's gaze; his skin shone with flickering light as if an inferno blazed just below the surface, and the hand currently gripping mine was feverishly hot.

Of course, from the moment we'd touched, so was I.

My flesh ached with power, surging from me into Max and back again until we glowed with it. The tunneling of my vision was abruptly replaced by a rim of white hot flames—the same, strange manifestation I'd seen when I'd snapped at Persephone and shrugged off Freya's will. On a whim, I reached out with my senses only to find Max's power waiting for me; his unique signature rode the air, smelling bitterly of roasting ozone but feeling absurdly plush—like the fur of a mohair teddy bear. Neither sensation was as overwhelming as the gods' had been, but there was nothing minor about his power, either.

And it seemed Mabel knew it.

"What's happening?" she asked, breathlessly, as she caught sight of our linked hands. She traced the line of my wound with her eyes, her expression frantic. "What are you two doing? How are you healing so fast? And why are your eyes like that?"

I craned my neck and realized I *was* healing; the pain was receding swiftly beneath our combined heat. My eyes I couldn't explain. Without a mirror, I had no idea what the elf was talking about. What I did know, on the other hand, was that I had been wrong to dismiss the possibility of a white knight, even if he had shown up half-naked without a white horse. I squeezed Max's hand, basking in the glow of his effervescent skin, only to release it immediately as an alien thought slammed into my mind.

Dónde estoy?

I glanced up at Max's face, saw his sudden confusion, and watched him release Mabel as though he'd found himself holding a snake. The elf, taking full advantage of her sudden liberation, scrambled backwards and fled the room screaming Frankenstein's name. Max twitched at the mere mention of the doctor, his posture suddenly defensive, eyes scanning the room. When they settled upon me, however, they widened with surprise.

"Quinn? *Dios Mío*, is that you? What happened to you?" Max asked, his accented voice less resonant aloud than it had been in my head. The glow of his skin began to flicker and dim. Though unsure what instinct prompted the action, I snatched up the brujo's hand once more, twining our fingers before he could pull away.

"Can ye hear me?" I asked, speaking in my own head.

Si. I can hear you.

The glow intensified, fed by our touch, and I sensed Max's immediate acceptance of our circumstances—his tentative grasp of the situation, coupled with my sorry state, left him eager to do whatever I asked of him. Admittedly, the brujo's abrupt pliancy made me exceptionally uncomfortable. But I couldn't afford to question it.

No, *we* couldn't afford to question it, I amended.

"Hurry and get these straps off me," I urged.

Max moved to my legs, took the leather in his hands, and tore it in two as though it were no thicker than a paper sack. The chest strap quickly followed. Finally free, I reached down, pressed my fingers to my midsection, and found it sticky with my blood. But there was no wound to be felt —not even a scar. I sat up, marveling at my unprecedented recovery rate. Of course, my relief didn't last long; despite the distance between us, I felt Max's attention like a physical weight, acutely aware of his desire to stare at my naked body, though he at least made an effort to avert his eyes. It seemed our link—whatever it was—remained.

I slid off the table and began searching for my armor. "Frankenstein will be back soon," I insisted. "Watch the hallway."

Max nodded without turning.

I found my clothes nearby in a discarded pile. It seemed I'd been wrong about Mabel's reconnaissance—she must simply have gotten lucky with her strike, before. Fortunately, the illusion I'd applied had held up even after the armor was removed, which explained why Frankenstein hadn't been more interested in it. Additionally, it meant I'd have to be careful not to misplace my hard earned threads in the future; I wasn't sure they were machine washable and I had a bad habit of losing socks.

Even better, I discovered, was the fact that I could put Nevermore on in its altered state without doing up all the straps and such—another detail which seemed to have slipped Freya's mind.

The goddess and I were going to have a long chat one of these days, I decided.

One she wouldn't enjoy.

Mercifully, I'd already thrown on my jeans and hooked my bra when I heard Frankenstein's loafers padding towards us, which gave me the few seconds I needed to finish dressing. Mabel was sobbing, insisting she hadn't done anything wrong, that her pet Manling had come to life all on his own. I heard a wet smack and something heavy hitting the floor.

Mabel's crying ceased.

Max's power flared, smothering me with its plush softness, the air sharp with the odor of chlorine. Hate swelled in my breast, but I knew it wasn't my emotion I was experiencing; Max held his arms wide in challenge and this time the flame raged above his skin, not below. I pressed myself to the wall, hunkered down out of sight, and peered down the hallway past the human bonfire.

"Maximiliano, is that you?" Frankenstein called. "It seems you have woken up! How fascinating." The doctor began rolling up the sleeves of his shirt as he stepped over Mabel's limp body, revealing thin, pasty forearms. "I suppose I have more work to do today than I thought. A shame I will lack the attentive audience I have become accustomed to. But you know what they say...needs must when the devil drives."

Max growled something under his breath, but his response to the doctor's taunts was a booming voice resounding in my head.

Can I kill him?

"It's may I kill him," I corrected in a hushed whisper as I crouched even further down, wary of the doctor's attention; the sight of the bastard alone made my guts churn, unreasonable panic clutching at my throat. I flexed trembling hands, still aware of that unusual power connecting Max and me, sensing I had more to offer than my augmented strength if things turned ugly. They'd caught me by surprise before, I reminded myself.

I was no one's victim.

I took a deep, calming breath. "Ye better, because if ye don't, I will."

Deal.

35

*I*n my experience, very few fights escalate to levels most people would consider life-threatening. They often start small—a shove or a little yank—and build slowly. Curses are routinely exchanged, then more shoving, maybe a fist thrown, or even a kick to the groin. But generally that's as far as most fights go before someone intervenes—usually a friend, but occasionally someone with a black t-shirt or a badge. That's typically all it takes to save face, to show you mean business and aren't to be messed with. But then there are the other kinds of fights, the sort that thugs and professionals get into—the sort which begin with a single twitch, or even the not-so-casual glance. Fights that don't end with someone nursing their bruises and tossing back drinks with friends, but with crowded hospital waiting rooms and cramped prison cells.

This was one of those fights.

The instant Frankenstein stepped within reach, Max took hold of the doctor's shirt collar, pivoted, and threw him across the throne room with all the speed and velocity of a major league relief pitcher. Frankenstein hit the table next to mine, clipped his shoulder, and pinwheeled into the air, his tools exploding in a spray of sharp metal objects. Less than a second later, the doctor crashed into the ceiling with a sickening crunch, then collapsed to the floor in a crumpled pile of twisted limbs. I rose from my crouch, gaping at the man who'd chucked him, marveling at Max's savage efficiency;

as opening salvos went, the attack should have been more than enough to kill anyone—especially a twiggy, elderly bastard.

A quick calculation of the damage was all it took for me to be certain; a shattered clavicle, snapped neck, broken spine, cracked skull, dozens of broken ribs, punctured lungs...any one of those could have done the trick, and my best guess put the prognosis somewhere between "say your good-byes" and "we gather here today." And yet, Max looked anything but relieved; his skin swirled with that flickering light, his blazing brown eyes locked on the broken remains of his former employer as though Frankenstein's corpse were some sort of abstract painting moments from revealing its secrets—a Picasso with hidden depths.

"He can't be—" I began.

Max threw out an arm before I could finish my question, cutting me short. As if on cue, the twisted wreck that was the doctor twitched, his limbs spasming and realigning before my very eyes with various pops and snaps that made me wince and shudder. Not because I hadn't seen or heard worse, but because Frankenstein had begun speaking throughout the experience, his voice cutting in and out until his head at last sat comfortably upon his neck.

"That was...*rude*. There are very few things...I despise...but I must admit rude behavior...is chief among them. What an ungrateful creature you have become, Maximilliano. And after all I did for you and your sister. My lovely Camila." Frankenstein's voice grew wistful as he rolled his narrow shoulders. "I trust she at least would have had the decency to accept her fate with grace."

"You are *el Diablo*, himself," Max spat. "I would never let you lay a hand on Camila. Nor will I allow you to touch any woman, ever again."

"You speak of the Devil, here?" Frankenstein fetched his eyeglasses from the floor, dangled them between his fingers, and waved his hand about as if showcasing the throne room's quartz tables and diamond walls, its glass floor and obsidian ceiling. "There are no true devils, boy. There are only those who know they are in a dream, and those who do not. One group makes the rules, while the other abides by them. That is what it means to be a Master."

"You are not my master. Not anymore."

"Is that so?" Frankenstein asked, his perfect teeth appearing below his hairy upper lip in a sneer. The doctor snapped his fingers. Then, when nothing happened, he snapped them again...but to no avail. The doctor replaced his eyeglasses and squinted through their shattered lenses, his right eyebrow twitching. "Maximilliano, what have you done?"

"I traded in your cold authority for something better. Something warmer." Max pressed a hand to his finely sculpted chest and the fire within seemed to blaze hotter, strobing so brightly that I had to monetarily shield my eyes. "I have a new master, now."

I blinked away the spots in my vision to find the brujo looking at me, his expression gentle and far too close to adoration for my liking. Wait, was he talking about *me*? There was no way, I decided. I wasn't his master. I was no one's master. And yet, the instant I read the deep undercurrents of his thoughts, I knew both that he'd meant what he'd said and that, bizarrely, the notion of serving me—of *belonging* to me—gave him significant comfort.

Which must have meant he'd been down here *way* too long.

"You can deny it all you want," Max told me, his expression chiding and a little pouty, "but you can feel it, too."

"Her?" Frankenstein tilted his head, his beady eyes widening at the sight of me clothed and ambulatory. Or at least that's what I assumed had surprised him; there was frankly no way to tell what he meant by his use of the singular gender pronoun.

"Her," Max declared, as though that was a logical response.

Maybe it was a guy thing, I thought. Some sort of caveman dialect that boys are taught as infants while their moms' backs were turned. Either way, I wasn't having any of it; if I was going to be the subject of the conversation, I had every right to participate.

"Me," I said, mimicking Max's tone as I folded my arms across my chest. So there.

"Look at you both!" Frankenstein shouted, throwing his hands up in the air. "You have no idea what you have done, do you? Either of you."

"What I know," Max began, "is that Quinn called my soul back from beyond the veil when your pet torturer tried to kill me. Moreover, she has gifted me with power. True power, the sort that does not come with one-sided contracts and scrupulous fine print."

"You cannot be so foolish as to believe such power comes at no cost, my old friend."

"We were never friends. And I don't care. I will do whatever she asks of me. I will become her servant during the day and her lover in the night. I will become *her* monster."

"Whoa!" I chimed in, alarmed by the brujo's sudden declaration of fealty. "Easy there, Fuego del Toro!"

"Oh, she would be so much more than that, Maximilliano," Frankenstein replied, ignoring me, his tone thick with mirth. "So much more. But it does not matter. I see I have allowed my thirst for knowledge to outweigh my common sense. I am sorry that I will not be able to operate on either of you, but such abominations cannot be allowed to exist in nature."

"That's rich," I muttered, more than a little miffed at being dubbed an abomination by the madman who'd chopped up Chancery members to create a Faeling monster that still haunted my nightmares, not to mention the miserable shit who'd helped turn Ryan into a genocidal sociopath. "Shouldn't ye be the one beggin' nature for forgiveness, ye sick bastard?"

Unfortunately, it seemed Frankenstein was through chatting; the doctor snapped his fingers yet again, except this time a heaving, grinding sound—like what you hear in Indiana Jones movies when one of those ancient doors creep open—accompanied the action. I spun to face the hallway, trying to determine the source of the noise, but there was no one in sight except Mabel, who lay passed out in a shallow pool of her own blood.

Then the floor began to quake.

"What's goin' on?" I demanded, wheeling on the doctor. "What have ye done?"

"He's called them," Max replied, his head cocked to one side as though focused solely on listening, his mouth set in a grim line. "Their spirits. He's told them to come for us, to tear us apart. Can you not hear them scream?"

I felt myself take an inadvertent step backwards before I realized what I was doing, thrown by the severity of Max's reaction. Had he said spirits? I froze, abruptly reminded of all those lost souls prostrating themselves on the Helspire's battlements. That sound before...was it possible Frankenstein had let them in with the mere snap of his fingers? Could he have turned them into his slaves the way he had the undead sailors in the Titan Realm? One glance in the mad doctor's direction revealed the bespectacled man watching us with renewed interest, inexplicably eager to see how we'd react to this newest stimuli.

Of course, Max and I weren't mice in a cage to be studied—to be poked and prodded and sacrificed—without consequence. Indeed, one look at the searing heat radiating off the two of us should have told Frankenstein everything he needed to know but had clearly ignored: Max and I weren't the offering, we were the godsdamned fire.

And we weren't to be played with.

"They'll have to come down that hallway," I insisted, glad to find Max smirking after my little reverie. I performed the necessary sign, tapped Nevermore, and watched with amusement as the brujo's expression switched from appreciation to awe the instant my Valkyrie armor manifested itself, flowing from head to toe like a river until I stood with my helmet in hand. I donned the wicked-looking thing feeling as dangerous as I knew I looked. "I'll slow 'em down."

"And what would you have me do, *mi diosa?*"

My goddess, his head translated for me.

Oh boy.

"Look, we'll have to talk about all that 'servant and lover' bullshit, later," I told the brujo, holding up a stern finger for emphasis. "But for now, go kill that son of a bitch like ye said ye would."

"I am not so sure he *can* die," Max admitted, keeping his voice low so as not to be overheard. "Camila always insisted he was not strictly human, but I wasn't certain until now what she meant. He is a homunculus."

"A what?"

"It is like a...powerful *espíritu* housed in artificial flesh."

"Well then, we're in luck..." I clapped the brujo's naked arm with enthusiasm, the light beneath surging where my gauntleted hand touched. "Because I know someone who can burn that fucker's house down."

36

The spirits of Helheim arrived in a slack-faced, silent mob. Fortunately, the corridor leading to the throne room was narrower than the ones below, which meant only a handful would be able to reach me at any given time. I, meanwhile, waited for those industrious few in the middle of the hallway, curious to see whether they'd trample Mabel into a pulp or avoid her like the trash that she was. I put the odds at fifty-fifty but frankly could have cared less; she'd had her shot at redemption and had used it to drug, strip, and torture me.

If the bitch died, she died.

The horde surged into the bottleneck, each spirit leaping over the elf's unconscious body as though she were a rock to be circumvented. I had to admit, I was a little relieved; part of me was *really* hoping she stuck around long enough to find out how it felt to have all her teeth knocked out...before I slit her throat and loaded the wound with molars like forcing candy into a PEZ dispenser.

Fingers crossed.

The first spirit to reach me was a husky fellow with a gimpy leg, his mouth opened in a soundless scream as he lunged for my shins. I danced back and slammed my knee into his face so hard he literally flew backwards, hitting the ceiling with all the force of a battering ram before crashing down upon a dozen of his fellow spirits. I blinked owlishly as

Frankenstein's de facto slaves scrambled to recover, surprised by the sheer strength behind my blow. Was this the added juice Nevermore afforded me, or a residual effect of the connection between me and Max, or both?

I couldn't be sure...but I sure as Hel wasn't complaining.

A woman came at me next, her hands clawing for the unprotected half of my face. Thinking quickly, I stepped inside her reach, took hold of her fur-lined cloak, and caved her face in with a vicious headbutt. Then, before any more spirits could launch themselves at me, I raised her body off the ground and used it as a shield to keep them at bay while I lashed out at outstretched limbs and delivered body blows with my free hand.

And yet, despite the ease with which I was able to dispatch each of my assailants, I found myself being inexorably pushed back by their sheer weight and obstinacy; they literally clambered over each other in their haste to tear me to pieces. Worse still, if they backed me into the throne room, I knew there was no way I'd be able to keep them all in front of me; eventually, their blows would land—that, or they'd dogpile on top of me until their psychotic master could finish me off.

Worried by the possibility, I took a moment to glance over my shoulder to see how Max was faring with his opponent, hoping he'd have Frankenstein subdued, or at least reeling...but found the opposite to be true. Instead, it was Max who was struggling to stay upright, his wrists bound by diamond-encrusted chains that seemed to have emerged from the walls themselves. Frankenstein, on the other hand, appeared more interested in Max's futile efforts to stand than his own well-being; the mad scientist had leaned in to stare up at the much taller, broader man from mere inches away, probing the brujo's chest with one spindly finger.

"Max!" I yelled, unable to keep my emotions in check.

One of the spirits must have sensed my momentary distraction because she ripped my impromptu shield from my grasp, flung her fellow spirit against a wall, and tackled me to the ground before I could mount a counterattack. I went down hard but was able to shrug off my assailant and rise to a knee before two more took their comrade's place. Within seconds, several more latched onto me, winding their arms around my legs, their hands slipping between the gaps in my armor as if to pry them off and send me to the ground. But I refused to go down—not while Max was in trouble.

"Max!" I screamed again, reaching out for him—not with my arms this time—but with my senses. When at last I found him, it was as if I could see through his eyes, could feel what he felt; I could smell Frankenstein's after-shave. Indeed, the doctor was so tantalizingly close that I could see the pulse in his neck jumping. But Max had no way to hurt him; nothing he'd tried had worked and now his arms were bound by the doctor's peculiar brand of magic, by the dominion he'd established over this place.

"Then don't use your arms, dammit!" I bellowed, thrashing against my would-be captors. I felt their blows raining down on my armored back, threatening to flatten me to the ground.

"Do not bother interfering," Frankenstein called, peering past the brujo to wave me off. "I will be over there to take care of you in due time. Until then, please wait your turn."

"Do it, Max!"

The brujo—having heard and understood the subconscious message I'd sent him—lunged forward like a hound, taking advantage of the slightest give in his restraints to clamp his teeth around Frankenstein's jugular. The doctor jerked at the contact, his expression flitting from startled to baffled and finally to annoyed in a mere matter of seconds. He began to speak, likely to chastise Max for his desperation, but no words came out. Instead, a vermillion light erupted from behind those perfect teeth. Next from his eyes, and then his ears, shining like the rays from the doctor's skull as Max poured every ounce of power he had into the doctor's flesh—enough to raze everything it touched. Indeed, the doctor's skin began to smolder and smoke, to char and blacken. His jaw hung loose, his tongue turned to literal ash in his mouth, and still Max flooded him with that excruciating heat.

The spirits at my back retreated like vampires as the light from the other room swelled, strobing to the beat of Max's thundering heart. Relieved to find them gone, I climbed to my feet, forced to cover my own eyes to avoid going blind. And yet I could feel every pulse of power as though I were being hit by one wave after another, forced to ride them or risk being pulled under. Then, with a suddenness that stole my breath away, the power fled and the light died.

And so, apparently, had Frankenstein.

37

I entered the throne room to find Max stomping the doctor's charred remains to ash and kicking them across the floor for good measure. I supposed I couldn't blame him; one resurrection was enough to make anyone aware of the distinction between "mostly dead" and "all dead." Mercifully, Doctor Victor Frankenstein appeared to have no miracle in the works, which meant Max and I finally had a quiet moment to relax—to sit back, unwind, and congratulate ourselves on a doctor well done.

Or, you know, to make out like teenagers.

In hindsight, I supposed I could blame it on the adrenaline rush, or perhaps that mystical connection which bound us and had saved our collective asses, but—in the end—the why mattered a whole lot less than the how; the second Max turned to face me, I stripped off my helmet, grabbed the back of his thick neck, and drew him into the sort of kiss that got film ratings changed.

Of course, you can't get very far when one person is half naked and the other is armored from the neck down; I pulled away first, my heart hammering away even as I tried to get my bearings. But it was no use, all I could do was think about the kiss, about how good it had felt; his lips had seemed fuller than I remembered, his stubbled jawline more abrasive against my skin, but the underlying passion had never once wavered, not even as I peeled my mouth from his.

"What is it?" Max asked, his voice somehow deeper than when I'd last heard it, more masculine. "Is something wrong, *mi diosa?*"

I shook my head, uncertain of my own voice, not to mention what I might say; there was *a lot* wrong, and yet none of it was expressly his fault. Not really. After all, Max couldn't help the fact that he was categorically my type—and by that I meant, tall, dark, and able to take a punch. Throw in the fact that I found the man so achingly handsome I would have gladly paid to watch him eat cereal and I'd have said we had a huge problem.

Because nothing based so purely on attraction had *ever* led to anything good. Not for me. More often than not, in fact, it led to brutal fights, bitter breakups, and emotional blackmail. All of which I had spent years avoiding, until now.

Perhaps sensing my indecision, Max reached out to brush his fingers along my cheek. And, despite my reservations, I let him. As if to acknowledge my allowance, the brujo bent down to plant a chaste kiss on one corner of my mouth, then the other, his soft lips grazing across mine in a movement that was far more sensual than it had any right to be.

"Tease," I mumbled against his mouth.

This time it was Max's turn to pull me in for a deeper kiss; his hands found either side of my face, cradling it as he raised me onto my tiptoes and explored my mouth with his tongue. Before I could even think to draw back a second time, however, the brujo pressed his body against mine, seemingly oblivious to the discomfort of grinding up against a walking tetanus booster advertisement. Still, I had to admit the sheer size of him, the way his arms enveloped me like a weighted blanket, felt right in a way I couldn't explain. Committed to the kiss at last, I ran my fingers through his thick hair, slid my tongue along the swell of his bottom lip, and made a noise that was more growl than swoon.

Only this time it was Max who pulled away.

The brujo released my face with a startled gasp and stepped back clutching at his chest, his face a rictus of pain. I started to reach for him but then froze, too alarmed to do anything as the man fell to one knee, his breath coming in rasping spurts.

"I...don't...understand," Max said, staring up at me with lost eyes that no longer burned with power. Indeed, the flickering glow which had emanated from him since we first touched seemed to have finally faded, leaving the brujo's skin tanned but otherwise unremarkable

"What is it? What's wrong?" I asked, inadvertently echoing his questions from earlier as I reached his side and endeavored to prop him up.

"Voices. Why...am I hearing...voices?"

The instant I touched the brujo's bare skin, I realized I heard them, too; there were perhaps four people speaking in total, each uncommonly loud and accompanied by a shrill, beeping sound that was both familiar and inexplicably gut-wrenching. One voice cut above the din and asked the others to be quiet, and in seconds all I heard was that sole speaker giving orders which were quickly followed by a single barked command.

"Nurse, clear the room," the voice said.

"I'm not going anywhere!" another replied.

Now *that* voice I recognized.

"Camila?" Max cocked his head as though his sister were standing right beside us. But she wasn't, I knew she wasn't; Camila was at her brother's bedside in the hospital room back in Boston.

"I can see there's been some activity, but we have tests to run, Ms. Velez, before we can proceed. I swear we'll let you come back in once we're—"

"You are talking about my brother," Camila insisted, her authority so absolute it made me *want* her to stay in the room, despite having absolutely zero say in the matter. "I'm not going anywhere. Do your tests. I will stand over here."

"I...fine. But please, don't interfere or I will have to have you removed."

Camila made a sound that was half-laugh, half-snort but said nothing. After that, the voices began to fade into obscurity—little more than a series of mumbles and unintelligible remarks. But it was already clear to me what was happening: Max was waking up.

I couldn't be sure how I knew for sure, or why it was happening now, only that my instincts told me it had something to do with the awakening of our connection and the sudden burgeoning of Max's power. According to Circe, the brujo had ended up in a coma because I'd cut him off from whatever energy had sustained him after he'd nearly died back in Boston. Which must have meant I'd either reestablished the bond between us, or Max had siphoned off enough power to kickstart his own engine.

Either way, I knew I had to be happy for him.

After all, the man had a loving family member waiting for him on the other side.

"I t'ink it's time for ye to go," I suggested, putting on my very best smile. "Ye should tell Camila I said hello. And, if ye see Robin, that I'll be comin' home as soon as I can. Make sure he passes it on. He should know what that means."

"Wait, I don't understand, where am I going?" Max asked, panicked. "And why aren't you coming with me?"

"It's alright, Max. You're goin' home." I squeezed the brujo's densely muscled arm and leaned in to kiss his dimpled cheek. "I have some unfinished business to take care of, but don't worry, I'll be right behind ye."

"No, I can't leave yet! It isn't..."

Max's mouth continued to move, but it was as if someone had hit the mute button; I couldn't make out another word as the flesh beneath my hand dissipated, wavering like a mirage before vanishing altogether, leaving behind nothing but the faintest sensation of a teddy bear pressed against my lips.

38

I seriously considered kicking Mabel until she woke up coughing blood, if only to make myself feel better about Max's abrupt departure, but ultimately decided against it; as things currently stood, she was worth more to me in one piece. So, rather than cave in her lungs with extreme prejudice, I snatched the elf up off the ground, raised her to about eye level, and slapped the living shit out of her.

Twice.

"Ouch!" Mabel cried after the first blow connected, then again following the second. "Ouch, fuck! That hurts, stop it!"

"Sorry to interrupt your beauty sleep," I said, shaking the elf for good measure. "I know how much ye need it, these days. But I have questions I need answers to."

The elf cursed, squirmed, and tried to lash out at me with her feet, only to end up bashing her toes against my armor, instead. Annoyed by the attempts, I chucked her against the wall. She hit with a satisfying crunch, collapsing to the ground in a sprawl that left her looking even more pathetic than before. I nudged her with the toe of my boot.

"Get up. I know you're conscious."

"Why hasn't the doctor killed you yet?" Mabel hissed, glaring up at me from beneath her grimy bangs, two hand-shaped welts forming on either side of her face.

"Who, Dr. McCrispy?" I asked, gesturing to the throne room and the grungy stain spread across its floor—all that remained of the mad scientist's ashes. "What's left of him is over there. So, sorry, but he won't be killin' anyone, anymore. Max saw to that."

"Nice try," the elf spat, craning her neck to look down both ends of the hallway. "Your Manling isn't even here."

"He had places to be."

"Please. More like the doctor took him."

"No, Mabel. Frankenstein's dead. I saw him burn to nothin' with me own two eyes."

"Don't lie to me!" Mabel shrieked, her skin mottled with rage. I didn't know anyone could look so distraught; Mabel glared up at me as though I'd backhanded her a third time for no good reason, tears welling up in her eyes. She began shaking her head over and over again, rocking back and forth, muttering one phrase in an endless loop like a defective children's toy. "The doctor cannot die, the doctor cannot die, the doctor cannot die..."

"Apparently he can."

"No, you idiot, he *cannot* die! I *tried*. I tried to kill him. I poisoned him, I stabbed him, I slit his throat, and every time he came back. And every single time he punished me. Which means he'll be back to punish you, too."

I felt a chill run up my spine but decided to ignore it. After all, Mabel may have done her damndest to murder the bastard using conventional methods, but I sincerely doubted she'd ever managed anything quite as thorough as burning him to ash from the inside. Besides, I had more immediate things to worry about than the ravings of a backstabbing lunatic, like fulfilling my end of the bargain I'd struck with the trickster god and tracking Ryan down. Now that Frankenstein was dead, the glimmer of hope that I could save my old friend had brightened considerably.

"I'll take your word for it," I said, dismissively. "In the meantime, why don't ye tell me where Hel is so we can get this show on the road?"

"Who?"

I seized the elf by her ragged shirt, tearing it until she was nearly as exposed as I had been not so long ago. For some reason, that bothered me a lot more than the thought of smacking her around had. I sighed, looked around, and found a few articles of clothing left behind by the spirits I'd battled. I released the elf and fetched a familiar fur-lined cloak off the ground.

"She's the jötunn, the giantess, who ran this place until you arrived," I snapped, tossing the cloak at Mabel. "The one that throne room belongs to."

"Oh, *her*." Mabel made a disgusted face. "She's probably still in her room, crying."

"In her room? Ye mean Frankenstein didn't lock her up?"

"Like in a cell?" Mabel looked at me like I was the crazy one before barking a laugh. "Not a chance."

"Why not?"

"Because they don't make cells that strong. Besides, the doctor said she wasn't a threat to us. He actually *pitied* her, if you can believe it." Mabel threw the cloak over her shoulders, sneering at the memory. "He called her an endangered species."

"An endangered species…" I echoed, reminded inexplicably of the jötunn heart thumping away in the chest on my hip and Skadi's insistence on its value. I shook my head, resolving to give that more thought when time was less of a factor. "Alright, well I want ye to take me to Hel's room, then. I need to speak to her."

And pray that doing so counted as liberation in Loki's eyes, I added inwardly.

Because, otherwise, we had a problem.

"We'd have to go below ground," Mabel replied, sounding less than eager. "It's a long, long way down."

"Then we'd better get started. I want ye leadin' the way, and keep your hands where I can see 'em. Right now you're more valuable to me alive than dead, but I could go either way. I wouldn't tip the scales if I were ye."

"You need to work on your threats." Mabel snorted indelicately but turned to do as I asked, her hands visible along the cowl of her cloak. "Next to the doctor, you're about as scary as a pixie high on her own dust."

Sensing there was little point arguing with the elf, I refrained from mentioning the numerous pixies I knew personally who'd have skinned Mabel alive for the mere suggestion that they were anything short of terrifying. Besides, I didn't need her to believe my threats, I simply needed her to behave. If the elf couldn't manage that, well, then it was like she'd said: it was a long, long way down.

Especially if someone were to, say, toss her ass out the nearest window.

39

True to Mabel's word, it took a considerable amount of time to reach our intended destination—which, it turned out, was less a room and more of realm unto itself. From my estimation, the cavernous underground chamber reflected the size of Helheim in its entirety, its impossible circumference hemmed with granite walls from which hung black velvet banners and silver braziers blazing with blue flame. The floor itself was even stranger; made of powdered snow, it crunched beneath our feet as we walked. The air of the subterranean space was so cold that I was forced to walk through the fog of my own breath with every step.

"How much farther?" I asked through chattering teeth, already longing for the rejuvenating warmth Max and I had shared back in the throne room.

"You said you wanted to talk to her, right?"

"Aye."

"Well, given where we came in, I'd say her head is a half mile this way," Mabel said, jerking her chin to the left as though that were the obvious direction, not to mention an ordinary distinction.

"Wait, her head?! What about the rest of her?"

"Well I'm guessing those," Mabel said, gesturing to a series of snow-covered hills in the distance, "are her arms. Which makes that her shoulder.

Her head should be somewhere over there. She's moved since we came down here."

I rubbed the bridge of my nose, realizing at last what Mabel had been saying all along: they hadn't thought to jail Hel because, of course, it would have been impossible to do while she held her jötunn form.

Gods, I was struggling lately.

Part of me thought to blame my slow uptake on the afterlife for giving me nothing but moldy, diseased lemons since my arrival, but ultimately I had to admit I'd been off my game for a while. Failing to follow-up with Freya on every little detail, letting first Loki and then Mabel get the jump on me, and now this. Indeed, aside from the rush I'd experienced when connected to Max, I found myself increasingly drained both physically and mentally—making me sluggish and slow-witted. Was it possible I'd overdone it, somehow? Or did it have something to do with what Loki had said about Circe's potion wearing off?

"So, are we going or what?" Mabel asked, impatiently.

"Aye," I replied, realizing I wouldn't find my answers here. "Lead the way."

When we finally reached Hel's head some ten minutes or so later, I was surprised to find her face pressed to the snow as though buried in a pillow. What I could see of it, however, was remarkably lovely; despite being absurdly overblown, Hel had the sort of bone structure that distinguished cover models from their inferior counterparts. In fact, I would have called her downright stunning if it weren't for the silent tears rolling down her face to form a frozen pond.

"Here she is," Mabel said, sounding less than impressed. "Can I go now?"

"Literally no chance in hell."

"Is someone there?" Hel cried out, grinding her cheek further into the snow. "I do not care who you are, just go away! I do not want to see anyone ever again!"

Hel's voice, like Skadi's, boomed overhead. And yet there was far less certainty—if not considerably more whine—to it. Less thunderclap, more tornado siren. Honestly, it reminded me of a teenager's after a bad breakup —all pitchy and overdramatized.

"Hel..." I began, then drifted off, unsure exactly what to say.

"Don't look at me," Mabel interjected. "She was like this when the doctor talked to her, too."

"The doctor!" Hel wailed, pounding her fist into the ground with enough force to send Mabel and me stumbling from the aftershocks. "That vile creature! He stole my palace."

"The doctor is dead!" I shouted.

"Really?" Hel lifted her head from the snow, revealing the rest of her face, her expression hopeful—albeit divided between a beatific smile and a haunting leer.

I flinched, unable to look away from jötunn's horrendously bisected face; on the one side lay the gorgeous mold I'd expected, but on the other there sat a hideous mask of frozen flesh and glistening bone. Bridging the two were nothing but teeth and her father's pale grey eyes, one of which sat full in a gaping socket rimmed in hoarfrost. And yet, both were filled with such hope that I found myself mirroring her expression, dimly reminded of Skadi's guileless nature.

"Really!" I insisted.

"If you say so," Mabel muttered.

"Wait, are you lying to me?" Hel asked, staring wide-eyed at me, her bottom lip quivering as another bout of sobs began to break. "I should have known...not to get...my hopes up!"

"No, I wasn't lyin', I swear!" I grabbed Mabel by the nape of her neck and squeezed until she yelped. "Tell her, Mabel."

"It's true!" Mabel replied, her voice laced with pain. "She was telling the truth. The doctor is dead."

"So, *you*...lied...to me?"

I tossed Mabel to the ground so it looked as if she'd knelt before the giantess, then pressed my boot to her back to keep her there. "Mabel here is sorry, aren't ye, Mabel?"

"I—"

"See? She apologizes. Now, Hel, I wanted to talk to you about what happened here after the doctor came, if you're feelin' up to it?"

The giantess nodded, sniffling.

"Good."

I frowned, trying to decide what to ask. I had plenty of questions—ranging anywhere from what had Frankenstein done to wrest control from her to whether she intended to rule Helheim once more now that the doctor was dead. Unfortunately, any one of those could lead to long, drawn out conversations, and I simply didn't have the time. So, instead, I opted to focus on the most pressing topic: Ryan. I'd already grilled Mabel on every-thing she knew, but it turned out the elf hadn't been remotely privy to their plans; the last she'd seen of Ryan had been when he and Frankenstein left to speak with the jötunn again.

"When the doctor came to visit ye the second time," I began, "d'ye remember whether someone else was with him? A man with blue skin?"

"No," Hel replied. "Not a man. But there was something else. A mean, blue-skinned beast who made it cold in here. He left all this in my room."

Hel picked up a handful of snow on the other side of the room and released it like an avalanche, describing the situation the way a moping child might tell on another for having left out all the toys. But then there *was* something inherently childlike about the jötunn—a naivety bordering on capriciousness which, frankly, rubbed me the wrong way.

Indeed, whereas Skadi had been equally unassuming, she at least had been utterly fearless—the sort of child parents constantly have to check on lest they risk hospitalization, again. Hel, on the other hand, was the trou-bled sort most parents outsourced to a therapist, the kind who came back with so many overlapping diagnoses that it made a Venn diagram look like a mandala.

Of course, part of me knew that I wasn't being fair; I believed we were all products of our environment, to some extent. How long had she been the ruler of Helheim, I wondered? Had any of her kin ever visited? And what about Loki, had he helped raise her? Without her people's encourage-ment and support, could she be blamed for failing to win back what was rightfully hers?

Unfortunately, deep down, I thought the answer was yes.

But then it wasn't my town.

"Aye, that's the one," I said, at last. "D'ye remember if he said anythin' to ye? Or what he and Frankenstein talked about?"

"They wanted to know about the Gjoll."

"The Gjoll? Ye mean the river? The one that circles Helheim?"

In my mind's eye, I pictured the waters of the river flowing beneath the bridge I'd crossed, recalling Hemingway's description of its deadly currents —how to cross it meant death, and how the dead could never do so. Given the city's walls, the security measure seemed a little redundant, but who was I to throw stones at eternal prisons?

"Yes. They wanted to know why none of the spirits will cross it."

"I thought they simply couldn't? Like they were incapable of it."

"Oh, no. Some have tried. A few have even swam across. But none who did will ever talk about it. That is how the Gjoll works."

"I don't understand."

"Neither did they," Hel huffed.

"The Gjoll takes away their memories," Mabel interjected, still kneeling in the snow. "Without their memories, spirits aren't even spirits, anymore."

"See, *she* gets it."

"It's something Frankenstein said after Ryan left," she explained, catching my look. "The doctor told me that he'd gone for a swim and lost his mind. In that order, which is why it stuck with me."

And with that, the pieces began to fall abruptly into place.

Circe had already told me *how* to reach Atlantis but not before making sure I understood the impossible nature of the journey, itself; in order to find Atlantis, you first had to forget everything, including your desire to reach Atlantis. If the effect of the Gjoll was to strip away memories, then it was entirely possible Frankenstein had thrust Ryan into its currents in the hopes that he would stumble onto the City of the Lost.

"Except it is not their memories the Gjoll takes," Hel added, as if suddenly eager to be included in the conversation. "That is what the doctor thought, too. But he was wrong."

"Then what does it take?" I asked.

"Their regrets."

"Wait, it takes what?"

"Their regrets! You see, the dead who end up in Helheim have nothing left *but* regret, and the threat of losing those keeps all but a few from trying to cross into Niflheim."

I frowned, thinking about the spirits I'd come in contact with in the city, how they'd called out to me and chased me down the thoroughfares with angst in their eyes. Perhaps that was what set apart the spirits of Helheim from those in the other realms: a sense of incompletion, of unfulfillment. But then, that raised a whole new concern I hadn't considered until now.

"Did Frankenstein *know* Ryan ended up in Atlantis?" I asked Mabel. "Like, with absolute certainty? Did Ryan send ye lot a postcard, or somethin'?"

"Not a postcard, no. But the doctor seemed sure. I know that after Ryan disappeared Frankenstein was more pleased than usual. He didn't even bother creating another one of his monsters the day it happened. But trust me, if he'd have found out Ryan failed, he'd have taken it out on the rest of us. That's just who he is."

"Was," I corrected, feeling better by the second about what Max had done to the wretched bastard who'd sewn those souls together and tortured his flunkies. Mabel, I noticed, didn't agree with my sentiment—but nor did she argue. It seemed the longer we went without a resurrection, the more inclined she was to believe the doctor was well and truly dead.

"What are you two talking about?" Hel asked, petulantly.

"Sorry! Just one more question," I said, realizing there was little else to be gleaned from the jötunn, "do you know where the Gjoll leads?"

"Leads?"

"Aye. Like where it goes. Where it ends, or becomes somethin' that isn't the Gjoll?"

"Oh!" Hel exclaimed, brightly. "No."

"Great," I muttered, wondering if I dared risk chasing after Ryan with such little information to go on. I mean, what if he hadn't ended up in Atlantis, after all? Or what if, by some stroke of luck, *he* had, but I wouldn't? There were simply too many unknowns to account for. Maybe I could make another deal with Hades? Or double back and demand a little assistance from Freya, considering how worthless her information and blessing had ultimately proven.

"You could always ask Garmr, though," Hel added, perhaps sensing my growing dissatisfaction. "He likes to play in it, sometimes, when he thinks I am not looking."

"Garmr. The gigantic guard dog at the gates, the one with all the blood splattered across his chest, and with teeth as tall as I am? That Garmr?"

"Yes! That is him."

"No offense, but that sounds like a suicide mission. The last time I saw Garmr he was tryin' awful hard to eat me, and that was when I was on the *other* side of the gate."

"Oh, he was probably just grumpy because he has not had his treat in so long!"

"His...treat?"

"Come," Hel said, slapping the ground so eagerly I actually toppled from the subsequent quake, landing next to a seemingly terrified Mabel. "I will show you."

*M*abel and I followed Hel through the streets of her city, watching mute spirits flee at the mere sight of the giantess, much to her initial surprise and eventual dejection. Of course, considering the jötunn had downsized to something far less imposing before leaving her room, I couldn't be sure exactly why that was the case. Perhaps they were put off by the juxtaposition of her improbable height and her ethereal thinness? Despite hovering around a hundred or so pounds, the jötunn stood several feet taller than me, her gangly limbs poking out like those of an emaciated scarecrow. Or maybe they simply failed to appreciate her Two-Face impression for the cosplay award it deserved. Either way, it meant we were able to approach the front gate completely unmolested, which suited me fine—even if that was at the expense of Hel's self-esteem.

"So, this treat ye mentioned," I asked, trying to lighten the mood, "what exactly is it?"

"They," Hel corrected, apparently cheered to have been spoken to. "And you will see. I do not want to ruin the surprise!"

"Ah, the surprise. Right."

As if overtaken by a sudden urge to entertain herself, the jötunn began skipping down the street, humming a dirge under her breath, her heels clipping the ground, sounding like bones rattling together, the whisk of her floor-length skirt like whispers in the dark. Covered from neck to toe in a dark cloak made of what looked eerily like tar and yet moved like silk, the cumulative effect brought to mind an image of the Grim Reaper were he to go frolicking among plague-riddled neighborhoods in broad daylight.

A regular Sickle Me Elmo.

When we finally arrived at the gates a few minutes later, we found them shut but notably unguarded. Fortunately, Hel wasn't as put off by Garmr's absence as I'd expected her to be. Instead, she took a slow look around, planted two fingers between her bisected lips, and whistled—if whistles sounded like the wails of a couple hundred terrified souls being flushed down a toilet bowl.

I clamped my hands to my ears, but it was too late to stop them from ringing, especially once Garmr's raucous barks began; each yawp hit me with the same bone-quivering shockwaves you get from industrial subwoofers at metal concerts. As one, Mabel and I whirled to find the great big hound loping towards us, his tongue flopping along the right side of his muzzle as though he'd forgotten to put it away, the fleshy organ dripping with drool that gathered into steaming puddles wherever it landed.

"You don't think *we* are the treat, do you?" Mabel asked once Garmr's thunderous barks subsided.

"Why d'ye t'ink I brought ye along?" I planted my hands on my hips and tried to mentally prepare myself for whatever Hel had in store once the hound arrived, fighting against the fresh wave of exhaustion threatening to pull me under. "Ye won't be much of a meal, of course, but if push comes to shove I'm bankin' on him gobblin' ye up while I make a break for it."

"I really do hate you, you know," Mabel growled under her breath.

"Welcome to an extremely non-exclusive club," I muttered. "Now, let me do the talkin' unless ye want to end up the Kibble to me Bits."

"Your what?"

"Nothin', nevermind. Just be quiet."

"Fine." Mabel made a face and folded her arms across her stomach. "But if I get eaten I promise you I will haunt you until the day you die, and probably then some now that I know what's in store for you half-breeds. I didn't survive the doctor so I could get swallowed by that thing."

For a fleeting moment, I considered correcting Mabel's assumption, but then "that thing" came barreling at us, his absurdly muscular body flexing with every step, his lips frothing and spread in what looked like a smile. Hel, I noticed, stood with her arms out wide in welcome, beaming—a proud dog lover, for all her faults. At least we had that in common; for the briefest of instants, I pictured Cathal padding towards me, his hindquarters trailed by a cloud of steam, his druidic markings flaring brightly against all that dark, coarse fur.

"Why are you smiling like that?" Mabel hissed. "Don't tell me you've finally lost it."

I shook my head, and the image vanished like a mirage, replaced by the vision of a jötunn hound big enough to wreak havoc in some Japanese city while its citizens shouted "Godzilla!" over and over again until a second monster showed up to cause even *more* damage—something I had to admit I'd never understood. But then, as if realizing at the last possible moment that Hel was not alone, Garmr skidded to a halt and scented the air. He growled at us, sounding a lot like one of those gas-guzzling diesel trucks that tend to piss off environmentalists and somnophiles alike.

"It is alright, Garmr! They were not invited, but they have overthrown the creature who seized the Underworld Tree!" Hel shouted, gesticulating towards the structure I'd dubbed the Helspire. "And, for that if nothing else, we must allow them to come and go as they please."

"Ah, so that's what Fenrir was howling about," Garmr replied, the words rumbling out from between his teeth. "That makes a lot more sense."

"Fenrir!" Hel exclaimed. "You spoke with him? Does that mean my brother is free?!"

"Yes, Mistress. Though the *dunga* has apparently lost his ability to hold a decent conversation. It's all 'eat Odin' this and 'the end of times' that with him, at the moment."

"By the Queens!" Mabel snatched at my arm, shock written all over her face. "Did you know that thing could talk?"

"The thing can also *hear*, Snack." Garmr flicked his tapered ears for emphasis. "So mind what you say unless you want to piss me off."

"He learned for me," Hel hurriedly explained, one side of her face going rosy-cheeked. "I was so lonely when Odin sent me here, but then father brought Garmr and left him with me and now we are the best of friends."

"Only nice thing that trickster has ever done for either of us," Garmr noted, his hackles rising at the very mention of Loki, though his eyes were all for me. "I was certain you were him in disguise when I smelled you on the bridge."

I shuffled awkwardly beneath Garmr's lilac gaze and decided not to reveal who had sent me—or why. If Loki wanted to take credit for his daughter's liberation, he could claim it himself. I had exactly zero interest in getting involved in their familial drama, especially if it was going to land me on Garmr's bad side.

"Fenrir also told me there were souls loose in Niflheim, though I have no idea how they escaped," Garmr continued, swiveling his boxy head to better study his mistress. "We'll have to send for a Valkyrie to bring them back."

"I'd ask 'em to send more than one," I chimed in, panicked at the idea of Kàra or one of her sisters trying to handle all those dread creatures— wounded or not—on their own. "The doctor is responsible for what happened to the spirits who escaped. He turned 'em into monsters, which means they'll need help to get back to normal."

"No wonder none of the citizens will look at me," Hel said, hanging her head in shame. "This is all my fault. I should have protected them, even without her help."

"No, Mistress," Garmr insisted. "The fault is mine. I still don't know how they slipped past me, but if I'd only reached them before they made it to the Tree, none of this would have happened. I'd have torn them to shreds and tossed their corpses in the Gjoll."

I felt Mabel's grip on my arm tighten.

"Listen, all that is over, now," I interjected helpfully, hoping to under-mine the building tension before our hostess broke into hysterics and inad-vertently sent her dog on a rampage. "Hel, I'm sure the spirits will forgive ye as soon as ye get the others back safe and sound. And Garmr—may I call ye Garmr?"

The hound dipped his muzzle, which I took to mean "yes" for lack of any other indicator.

"Great. Anyway, ye should know it wasn't your fault. I know for a fact there's at least one backdoor connectin' all the realms. The doctor stumbled on one, that's all. And, speakin' of other realms...d'ye happen to know where the Gjoll leads?"

"You don't seriously expect me to believe there's a second entrance to Helheim that *I* don't know about, do you?" Garmr asked, ignoring my ques-tion in favor of his own.

"I mean it would explain how the trespassers snuck past ye, wouldn't it? But let's get back to the Gjoll real quick—"

"No. I want to know where this alleged door is. Tell me right now."

"I don't know!" I replied, honestly. Of course, I *did* know someone who'd used it—and recently. I took hold of Mabel's hand and raised it like a prize fighter's. "But she does! And, provided ye tell me everythin' ye know about the Gjoll, I'm sure she'd be happy to show ye where it is."

"Hey!" Mabel yanked her arm free of my grasp. "I never agreed to that!"

"Consider it a lesson in karma," I replied under my breath. "Now, shut up unless ye want to be her bitch, for real. Hel may not have it in her to hold what ye did here against ye, but I'm bettin' the mutt does."

Mabel clamped her mouth closed.

"So," I continued, "what d'ye say, Garmr? Do we have a deal?"

"You want to know what lies beneath the Gjoll, is that it? And, in exchange, this one will lead me to the backdoor?"

"Aye, that's what I'm offerin'," I replied absentmindedly, though I found myself hung up on the peculiar phrasing of his first question—what lay *beneath* the Gjoll, as opposed to what lay *beyond* it. My curiosity piqued, I waved for the colossal hound to proceed. "The sooner ye tell me what I want to know, the sooner ye can go chase down that second entrance."

"Very well. As far as I can tell, the Gjoll flows above a chasm, below which lies a realm filled with all manner of things. Junk, mostly. The souls who inhabit it appear to wander aimlessly, though lately I have begun to notice a pattern. Oh, and they speak."

"What do they say?"

"They tempt with knowledge they should not have, trying to lure in anyone who might be listening. They promise impossible things which can never be, and sometimes they even show visions of these things...no matter how cruel those images might be."

"Are you saying they tried to take you away from me?" Hel asked, sounding distraught.

"And failed," Garmr replied, lowering his head until his mistress could reach up and scratch the ridge of skin just past his nose.

I, meanwhile, was busy reflecting on what Garmr had said, trying to decide if his description gelled with my understanding of Atlantis as a whole; the beguiling spirits sounded a lot like those Helen had mentioned, whereas the junk and the wandering souls coincided with what Circe had told me. Obviously, I had to admit it was at least possible this underwater realm was the Atlantis I'd heard so much about, which also meant Ryan may very well have arrived at his intended destination. Though, if what Hel said was true about the river stripping people of their regrets, it was also possible he'd lost something in the exchange. The question I had to ask myself was whether it was worth the risk to follow after him.

"Besides, that was a long time ago," Garmr added, cutting short my mental dilemma. "Ever since I started getting treats, I no longer hear their voices."

"Oh your treats! I almost forgot. Here, take this" Hel insisted, passing me a black velvet bag full of what felt like blocks of cheese. "Toss him one of those."

I opened the pouch, examined the contents, and retrieved what looked like a pastry filled with golden nectar that was far fresher than it had any right to be given where Hel had produced it from. Struck by a nagging sense of familiarity, I held the treat aloft only to find Garmr staring so intently at my hand that even *I* thought I looked tasty; within seconds, his jowls were coated in a fresh deluge of slobber. So, rather than risk him getting impatient and taking half my arm along with it, I chucked the treat as high into the air as I could. Garmr lunged, snatching the pastry up in his jaws so swiftly that I got clipped by a sudden gust of wind—not unlike when a semi-truck blows past you on the highway.

Within a matter of seconds, the hound began to glow, the veins beneath his fur pulsing with golden light the way mine occasionally flashed emerald.

"Ambrosia biscuits," Hel explained, pointing to the bag. "Made from Idunn's apples, which keep the gods young and powerful. Another gift from my father. He saved Idunn once, you know, from Thiazi. I mean, my father was the one who abducted her on Thiazi's behalf in the first place...but in the end he saved her."

"I didn't know that," I admitted, trying to sound both nonchalant and interested at the same time while the chest on my hip pulsed, vibrating like an antiquated beeper at the mention of its owner's name. "So, uh, what do the biscuits do, exactly?"

"Toss him another one," Hel suggested, giggling. "Then you shall see."

I did as Hel asked and threw a second biscuit. This time when Garmr moved, it was like watching an ambush predator strike; he sprung into the air with enough force to create a wind tunnel that whipped my hair across my face and forced Mabel to huddle further into her cloak. By the time he landed some two hundred feet away, Garmr had become even larger than he'd been a moment before, his muscles throbbing with pent up power, his fur bathed in golden light.

And then he began to chase his own tail.

"So, they're like steroids, huh?" I eyed the bag warily. "They make him stronger? Faster? Dumber?"

Hel was nodding animatedly.

"How many d'ye give him in one go?"

"Oh, no more than two. Otherwise he would break everything, or get fat. Either way, we would never get to play any of our games. That's what we do after I give him the treats. The treats make them so much more fun."

"Ah." I glanced back at the city sprawled out behind us with its bells and arches and thatched roofs, marveling at the fact that any of it still stood. "And...where d'ye two play, exactly?"

"My room, usually. We play fetch out here, of course."

"Of course," I replied, refusing to let my mind fixate on the physics involved in what she was describing; I had enough metaphysical mysteries in my life without the added headache of how a dog the size of a warehouse could play fetch—or what could possibly be big enough to throw without incidentally leveling all of Helheim.

"Anyway, you should take a couple with you in case you see my brother after you leave. I am sure he would love some..." Hel hesitated, catching my expression. "You *were* planning to leave, right?"

"I am, but—"

"Because you would be more than welcome to stay! Garmr and I would love it, if you could. We get lonely, and the spirits never say anything new after a while."

"No, I'm sorry, but I do have to leave. I was just tryin' to decide where to go next, that's all. And ye should know I'm not likely to run into Fenrir, no matter what I decide. I have a feelin' your brother won't be stickin' around much longer. Not once the Valkyries come and Odin finds out where he's been."

"Oh, right, I forgot." Hel hung her head again, her dark hair falling over her face like a shroud. "Odin is such a jerk! He's always sticking his eye where it does not belong. I wish my brother would just eat him, already. It would serve him right."

For a second, I considered countering with the fact that Odin's death would mean a full unleashing of all things Ragnarök—and was therefore *bad*

—but then thought better of it; the end of times probably appealed a hell of a lot more to her than it would to me.

Pun intended.

"I wouldn't worry about Odin right now," I said, instead. "Fenrir has managed to stay a step ahead of him so far. I'm sure he'll be fine."

With your father's help, I added, mentally.

"I am sure you are right!" Hel agreed, grinning so widely that the frozen half of her face seemed almost alive. "Well, you should keep the biscuits, anyway. As a gift from me to you. Maybe they will prove useful to you, one day."

"I...alright, if ye say so." I tied the pouch to my hip, securing it alongside the chest containing the heart of a jötunn whom Loki had once tricked, vaguely aware of the odd sense of symmetry involved. "I appreciate it, Hel."

"I do hope you can come back and visit sometime. This place can be *so* boring, you have no idea."

"Maybe one day," I replied, refusing to be baited into a commitment to return; I'd given my fair share of those in the past and had learned to regret it. "Tell Garmr I said goodbye once he's...back to normal."

"I will! But remember, your friend made a deal. Do not be long saying goodbye, or Garmr will have to come back and collect you, himself. And you would not like that." Hel giggled and danced away, her cloak trailing behind her like some noxious cloud, leaving Mabel and me to stand alone by the gates.

"You're going to go after Ryan, aren't you?"

"That is why I came," I admitted, trying not to show how exhausted I felt by the prospect. "Besides, what sort of friend would I be if I left him down there to rot for eternity when I knew I could save him?"

"Except you don't know that," Mable shot back. "You don't even know if jumping into the river will work, or what the water might do to you if it does."

Both were valid points.

"And what's it matter to ye, anyway?"

"It doesn't," she snapped. "You do what you want."

"Hopin' to tag along, is that it?"

"Of course not! The last time I chased after Ryan, *this* happened." Mabel flashed me, exposing the battered body beneath like one might reveal a grisly crime scene photo. "Besides, he never cared about me. I saw how he looked at that nymph, Calypso. He was ready to throw it all away, after all his talk of finding justice for what was done to our people, and for what? For her. For her! But not me. Why not *me*?"

"Have ye considered it's because you're a psychotic bitch?"

"You know," Mabel replied, snatching her cloak closed once more, "I used to hate you because I thought you meant something to Ryan. That you were special to him. I looked at you and saw an obstacle standing in my way. Now I realize you're nothing but a fool. Ryan would never have come down here to save you, you have to know that. Which means you're the one obsessed with *him*. The one who won't let *him* go. Your problem is that you can't get it through your thick head that Ryan doesn't give a shit about you."

"Ye may be right," I admitted. "But, when it comes right down to it, this isn't about Ryan, anymore. It's about me. It's about walkin' out of here knowin' I tried everythin' I could to bring him back...or why bother walkin' out at all? If ye can't be there for your loved ones when they need ye the most, then what's the point of bein' alive to begin with?"

"You seriously believe that?"

"I do."

"You do realize that's not the way life works, right?"

"Look, I never expected ye to understand."

"Well, I think you're insane for trying," Mabel replied, though her tone suggested the opposite. "Ryan sealed his fate a long time ago. We all did. If he rots, that's because he made his choice."

"And ye? What are ye plannin' to do?"

"I'm going to show the dog where we got in, and then I'm going back to Fae."

"Plannin' to look up the Winter Queen and beg for sanctuary?" I asked, reminded of Mabel's previous associations with the Faeling royal, which included a plot to abduct me at the Winter Queen's behest. "See if fate will give ye a second chance?"

"Don't be stupid. The Winter Queen would want to put me to work, to use me the way she uses everyone else. And that's never going to happen. I won't let anyone take advantage of me, ever again. No one."

I noted the heat in Mabel's gaze—the determined thrust of her chin—with interest. Perhaps she would indeed make it out of Helheim and return to Fae. Something told me not to discount the possibility, no matter how remote; the scum of the earth have always been the best survivors.

"Ye know, in another afterlife," I mused, "we might have been friends. Assumin' ye had no reason to hate me and I didn't despise everythin' ye stand for. Oh, and all those times ye tried murder me, let's not forget that."

"Yeah, well, I'd say that's for the best," Mabel declared as she shuffled off in the direction of Garmr's glow, nestled into her cloak. "Not all of us want to be saved."

Staring down at the churning waters of the Gjoll, its currents roaring louder in my ears than any river I'd ever heard, I had to wonder how much of what I'd told Mabel was true. In the moment, I'd meant every word. But that's the funny thing about moments—they come and go. Was I really prepared to risk my life to save Ryan knowing how slim the odds actually were of succeeding? The answer, of course, was yes. Whether I'd failed him along the way or not, this was it—the last shot either of us would have at redemption.

But that didn't mean I had a death wish.

Mabel had been right about that part; this trial by river had "bad investment" written all over it. Unfortunately, it was also the only game in town. All signs pointed to Ryan having done what I was preparing to do now, which meant my chances of ending up where he had were astronomically better than what they would be if I tried to find some other, potentially safer, way. Not that I had that kind of time; I could feel Circe's potion wearing off with every passing moment, not unlike those first few hours of the flu when your body twinges and aches for no reason. Basically, if I was going to go after Ryan, that meant it was literally now, or never.

I closed my eyes, wishing I'd thought to ask Freya the sign for "wet suit," and cannonballed off the bank before I could second guess myself.

The water was absolutely fucking freezing. Like Jack Dawson going blue while floating on his quarter of Rose's massive door *freezing*. I came up for air planning to shriek but couldn't; my lungs had shriveled up to wrinkly, three-day-old party balloons. Instead, I got swept up by an undercurrent that yanked me beneath the seething waters so violently I must have looked like a *Jaws* victim. I tried to fight it, to kick back up to the surface, but there was no use.

The Gjoll had me.

Once I was fully submerged, however, the bone-aching chill began to dissipate, replaced by a warmth that spread from my chest to the rest of my limbs in a slow, pleasurable crawl. I found I didn't need air—not so long as this thawing heat remained. All I needed was to stay right where I was, and everything would sort itself out.

That's when the voices started.

At first, all I could hear was the faint rush of water overhead, like a fan left on in the other room. But then, in the slightest of increments, that dim buzz coalesced into words, then phrases.

Home.

Love.

Join us, and be free.

Eventually, they became something else altogether, something far more complex: emotions. I floated, pulled along in the river's wake, and felt things I couldn't describe in mere words. Fleeting, raw feelings so powerful that they produced random flashes of insight into bitter memories I had either forgotten or repressed. The jab of self-condemnation as I cradled Jimmy's limp body, for example, or how I'd lashed out when he pulled away from me afterwards—even the ache of watching him leave for good. These were followed by numerous instances in which I'd avoided Dez out of self-ishness or spite, chased by the heart-wrenching moment I saw what she had done to my room, the day I came back from Fae, to make it feel more like home.

And then, of course, there was Ryan.

Guilt washed over me as I pictured the Faeling's face on the day he left Boston, the day he found out his father had died. Why hadn't I reached for him, comforted him the way a true friend would have? My aversion to touch, I reminded myself, coupled with my insane desire to keep everyone at arm's length. The same reason I'd been so dismissive of him when we met again in Fae, so eager to forge a new path and leave the old me behind even at the expense of a steadfast friend. Even then, I'd seen the pain lurking behind his eyes, the rage he kept bottled up inside, but I'd considered him too weak to be a threat. And I'd been wrong. But then, rather than try to help him, to walk him away from the edge of the precipice, I pushed him over it—worried more about my well-being than his.

For what felt like hours but could only have been seconds, a barrage of similarly haunting memories came and went, each saddling me with a deluge of emotional baggage until it felt appropriate that I end up sinking to the bottom of the river, that I be swallowed up by forces outside my control. The weight of my regrets were like chains, dragging me down link by link, forged by all the choices I should have made but hadn't, all the people I could have saved but didn't. Such, I thought to myself as I sunk deeper and deeper, was life.

Perhaps death would be better.

Of course, there was only one way to know for sure.

4 2

I sat cross-legged on a marble floor staring at a painting propped up against a pile of discarded memorabilia, fascinated by its expression of vibrant color. The painting depicted a dark vase brimming with bright yellow poppy flowers, hemmed on one side by three scarlet blooms. Not extraordinary as subjects went, but all the more impressive for being so eye-catching. I reached out, brushing my fingers along the canvas, and tried to imagine what hand had produced such evocative, masterful strokes.

"Oh, you found another one."

I didn't have to look over my shoulder to know who spoke; the man with the blue skin was always on the lookout for beautiful things among the detritus that flooded into the city. Which was how he claimed to have found me. At the time I was wandering among the outskirts, addled the way so many of us are when we first arrive, unable to remember much of anything —especially about myself. Later, when I'd asked him why he was scouring the outskirts in the first place, he admitted he had no idea. Only that he'd felt the urge to go there that day. Back then, it had seemed strange, even improbable.

Now, I understood exactly what he meant; I woke every day with odd compulsions, drawn to this or that part of the city. More often than not, those impulses led to jaw-dropping finds like this one.

"You should bring that back with you, this time," the man insisted. "If you don't, you know what will happen."

It would get swallowed up again, I thought to myself. Lost for all eternity, or at least until someone else uncovered it. I hunched forward, tucked the painting into a recess provided between a photo album and a gym bag, and clambered awkwardly to my feet, the armor I'd been wearing upon arrival clinking and clanking with every little movement.

"Why must you always do that?"

The man's voice was chiding but unsurprisingly tinged with amusement. This was the game he and I so often played, after all—him tempting me to collect what I found for posterity's sake, and me, refusing to be tempted. Not because I found fault in his desire to hoard beauty, but because I thought beauty ought to be sought after, that it should be earned. It was a philosophical difference of opinion, I supposed, and one we kept coming back to despite the fact that neither of us even knew our own names.

"Let's go home, Blue."

I reached for the man's hand and clasped it in my own, only dimly aware of the glove that separated his flesh from mine. That was another topic of conversation which occurred often between us: why I'd never tried on anything else in all the time I'd been here. Unfortunately, that I couldn't explain as easily; the thought of removing my armor simply never crossed my mind. It felt as much a part of me as my arms and legs.

"Say, Red," the man began as we started meandering in the general direction of the makeshift shacks we called home, "let's take a detour on our way back. There's something I'd like you to see."

I shrugged in tacit agreement, not daring to get my hopes up; Blue had shown me many things, but very few had appealed as much to me as they had to him. Lately, I was beginning to think he did it to impress me, or perhaps to show how highly he regarded my eye for treasures. Either way, though, it wasn't like we were pressed for time.

We walked in silence the rest of the way, passing the occasional person going about his or her business without so much as a hello. Not out of rudeness, but simply because that's how it was, here. Words were understood by all to be inadequate things—a form of intimacy rife with pitfalls. And so it was best, by far, to remain silent.

Unless you were Blue, of course.

"Come on, it's just over that hill and up those stairs," he urged. "You won't believe the view from the top, or what I found."

My companion's excitement, as it so often did when he got like this, soon proved infectious. I began to walk faster, marching up the hill with him at my side, dodging the occasional landslide of debris as leftover junk fell from the rivers that swirled across the sky. Fortunately, the downpour here was less intense than most, mainly unmatched socks and the occasional wallet. There were some parts of the city where you could only survive by finding shelter from the hail of car keys and cell phones and other such misplaced objects—a fact which I'd had to learn the hard way.

The stairs were larger and thicker than they needed to be, extending high enough into the sky that by the time we reached the top step, I was winded and ready to lie down. Blue, of course, was not; between his odd skin tone and his boundless energy, I suspected the two of us were not of the same species. Not that it mattered.

"It's only a little further, I swear. Come on, once we hop over, you can rest."

I set my hands on my hips, ignored the faint stitch in my side, and straightened, seeing immediately what had drawn him back to this place; from this height, the stairway offered a nearly unobstructed view of the entire city. There were the great mounds and their raging storms to the east, our tenements to the west. To the south lay the endless outskirts. The vista directly in front of us, however, was obstructed by what appeared to be some sort of mausoleum which seemed to have been connected to the stairs, once upon a time. Now, a vast chasm separated the two.

"You won't even be able to wrap your head around what's inside there, seriously," Blue insisted, measuring the distance with his hands as though it mattered to him. "So, do you want me to throw you, or catch you? It's your call."

I eyed the gap, apprehensively. We'd already discovered I could jump nearly as far as Blue could, but I'd never tried from this high up before.

"Throw me," I replied. "But try not to overdo it. I barely survived last time."

"You got it."

Blue took hold of my waist with both hands and launched me into the air in one smooth, regularly practiced movement. My landing, however, was not as graceful; I rolled as I hit the ground but still managed to jar my shoulder and lose feeling temporarily in both my legs. Thankfully, Blue was beside me a second later, half-escorting, half-carrying me through the gaping doorway of the mausoleum.

"It's dark," I noted, unable to see my hand in front of my face, let alone whatever fantastical sight Blue had intended.

"Yeah, I covered the hole in the roof before I left. Didn't want anything disturbing this place except us. Are you good to stand on your own? Alright, good. Stay here, and I'll take care of it. Keep your eyes peeled."

When the light finally spilled into the cavernous room, my eyes had already adjusted, forcing me to look away rather than stare. And yet, despite only having the briefest glimpse of the mausoleum's contents, I had to admit Blue was right to have insisted I come here.

"Aren't they something?"

No, I thought, they were *incredible*.

Lining the circumference of the room were a cache of weapons unlike any I'd ever seen or heard of. Swords and shields, spears and axes, even pistols and the occasional rifle...you name it, and this place had it. But it was the jaw-dropping *quality* of the weapons which astounded me; each tool of war had obviously been meticulously crafted to the point that even the least ostentatious among them would have been worth a veritable fortune.

Blue settled in beside me with a manic grin splashed across his face, practically radiating with pride. I couldn't fault him for it, though; he'd stumbled across a true treasure trove in a city overflowing with trash—not exactly an easy feat.

"They're beautiful," I admitted.

"Right?" Blue clapped his hands together. "Now it's time for us to pick one to take back with us.

I began to shake my head, but Blue was already guiding me towards the nearest stash, gesturing to one weapon after another with a haphazard description for each. I stopped him with a raised hand after he referred to what was clearly a mace as a "popsicle with spikes."

"Why don't ye pick yours, first?" I suggested. "In the meantime, I'll look around."

"Alright, but I mean it this time. You have to take something, or next time I find something like this, I won't tell you."

"I will."

"You promise?"

The request sat heavy in the air between us. Frankly, I was too shocked to respond one way or the other, at first. In this city, words might lead to disappointment, but promises? They were made to be broken, and everyone knew that.

Even Blue.

"Alright," I said at last, against my better judgment, "I promise."

43

ogether, we weaved between dwellings created from discarded materials, the vast majority of which resembled pitched tents at best. But then the goal here wasn't aesthetics so much as it was functionality; this side of the city was known to be mercifully light on falling debris, but all it took was a single pool ball to come plummeting from the sky to cave in your head and ruin your day. Thankfully, Blue had chipped in when designing mine, which meant a reinforced roof and at least a modicum of privacy.

As we got closer, it became obvious our arrival had caused a stir; dozens of eyes tracked our every move and what few conversations there were tended to die in our wake. Of course, we often drew stares whether we liked it or not, what with me wearing armor from head to toe and Blue being...well, blue. This level of scrutiny, on the other hand, was typically reserved for something out of the ordinary. Like, for example, the conspicuous hardware we were carrying.

"I have to get something from my place," Blue said, waving hard enough that the ornate blade sheathed at his hip jiggled, slapping against his thigh. "But then I'll be right over."

I waited for my companion to vanish behind another hut fashioned almost exclusively out of oversized dress shoes before I ducked through my own doorway, wary of the weapon bound to my back and making sure it didn't clip anything. Once inside, I took quick stock of my surroundings, making certain all my personal effects remained untouched, though I knew I needn't have bothered. Theft was a foreign concept in this city; everything anyone could ever need or want ended up here, eventually.

There were a few items, however, I kept hidden just to be safe. Each had been on my person when I first arrived, though none had offered any insight into who I was or how I'd come to be here. After checking to make sure Blue wasn't yet on his way back, I dragged a crate full of odds and ends across the floor, revealing the hole I'd dug to keep them hidden. Then it was simply a matter of cataloguing them. First, the chest with its mysterious jewel. Next, the sack full of bland, off-putting bread. And, finally, the glass shooter with its amber contents.

Reassured to find all three items exactly where I'd left them, I dumped the contents of the crate in a corner of the room, flipped the box over, and replaced it over the hole. Then, I undid the strap I'd used to tie my weapon to my back and laid my chosen instrument horizontally across the top of the box where I could admire it. It really was lovely—in the wicked, lethal sort of way all implements of war tend to be. In the end, I was so distracted I didn't even notice Blue had arrived until he spoke.

"So, are you happy with what you chose?" he asked, standing on his tiptoes to look over the curved pauldrons covering my shoulders.

I wasn't sure how to respond to that, especially considering I hadn't really chosen it at all. If anything, the weapon had picked me. Indeed, it was as if I could still hear it calling to me from amidst the hoard—a much more potent version of the urges which had provoked my daily excursions. Finding it from there had been no big feat; the instant I laid eyes on the weapon, I knew it belonged to me. Somehow, I even knew its name: Areadbhar.

Slaughterer.

Even now, the dory epitomized deadly intent—the foot-long Damascus steel blade sat affixed to a cornel wood shaft capped by what appeared to be a sauroter fashioned from alexandrite. And yet, despite its elegance, there was one flaw I couldn't account for. I reached down and flipped the spear to reveal a crater sitting squarely in the heart of the blade.

"What does that look like to ye?" I asked, pointing.

"Oh, that's interesting! So, yours has one, too."

Blue hoisted his sword, still in its sheath, and angled it so I could see the pommel. Glittering gold bands wound the hilt, only to unfold at the base as though meant to curl around an object that wasn't there. The flaw was glaring, the effect unfinished. And yet, after a moment's study, I realized I was looking at the same thing in both instances: a socket.

"That's why I chose this sword," Blue admitted, tapping the aperture for good measure.

I shot him a quizzical glance, but the man was too busy fetching something from a pouch around his neck to notice. Before I could ask him what he meant, however, he began adjusting the gold prongs—forcing them wide enough to accomodate the stunning blue jewel he held in his other hand. I felt a shiver of nagging familiarity at the sight of it, reminded instantly of my own precious stone.

"The moment of truth," Blue intoned. He held his jewel out over the pommel, graced me with a conspiratorial smile, and thrust it into the opening. I gasped as the gold prongs closed over the precious stone like fingers curling to make a fist, then covered my eyes as the sword began to glow white hot in Blue's hand, the blade thrumming with what sounded like a cry of abject joy. Through the gaps between the arms I'd thrown up to block the glare, I could make out shapes gathering outside my doorway—a growing crowd of onlookers unable to hide their curiosity.

Suddenly, the blue jewel flared, shining so brightly I had to pinch my eyes shut.

Someone laughed.

And then, almost as abruptly as it all had begun, the noise died and the light vanished, leaving me to blink away spots in my vision. When at last I could finally see, I found Blue sneering at the naked blade in his hand. He then began swishing it about as the crowd—sensing the show was over, perhaps, or simply preferring not to be involved—dispersed. Blue's blade hummed a different note with every sweep and strike, cleaving the air like someone singing a hymn. Seemingly unimpressed, however, the man balanced the blade across his hands and tilted it back and forth, watching with mild disdain as the hilt changed colors with every rocking motion.

"Well, it certainly took him long enough," Blue said, putting on an odd accent for what I assumed was comedic effect. "And he went for Charlegmagne's sword, no less. What a fool you can be, Herr Frost. Still, I suppose it will have to do."

"Blue?" I waved a hand in front of the man's face to get his attention.

"Are ye alright?"

Blue flinched at the sound of my voice, turned, and settled a gaze upon me so full of loathing it made my skin crawl. I took a step back, then another, unable to control my racing pulse as the man I thought I knew faced me with a naked blade in his hand.

"Did you truly believe you would be rid of me so easily, *fräulein?*" Blue asked in that stranger's voice. "That Maximilliano's parlor tricks would be enough to silence the legend of Doctor Frankenstein for good?" Blue edged forward, the tip of his sword dragging across the ground and creating a molten furrow in its wake. "Although I must confess, having to throw myself into the devourer so prematurely was not what I had in mind. I had originally hoped to remain sequestered in Helheim until the appropriate moment."

"I have no idea what you're talkin' about," I said, shrinking beneath this madman's gaze, my eyes averted so as not to encourage the bloodlust I sensed emanating from him. "Blue, this really isn't like ye."

"Of course it isn't. Herr Frost is gone. And for that you have my condolences, *fräulein*. You know, I must say I found it quite strange that you two should find each other down here. If I were not already using this body, I would very much like to have studied you both. It would have been fascinating to test the nature of your bond. Nothing so crude as what those German fascists did to all those poor twins, of course...though I suppose they had the right idea."

I slid along the wall in increments as the madman spoke, unsure how much more I could handle; not only was Blue behaving abnormally, it seemed he'd also devolved into a babbling lunatic. So, rather than continue to listen to his ravings, I resolved to make a break for it. Once outside, among the other citizens, I could at least rely on safety in numbers. Maybe even ask for help, if it came down to that.

Thinking to avoid his sword arm, I juked left, lunging for the open doorway. Unfortunately, I didn't even come close; the madman's fist struck my shoulder hard enough that my armor squealed in response to the blow and sent me careening across the room. My spear went clattering against the far wall as a result, the crate overturned. Before I could so much as groan, I found the madman's foot on my armored chest, pressing me to the floor.

"It really is a shame you do not recall any of this. I would have preferred to have seen your honest reaction when you realized Doctor Victor

Frankenstein was very much alive, when you saw me at last in the body I've been augmenting for so long. But I can see now what this place has done to your mind." The madman turned his attention to the doorway and the citizens who shuffled past. "It is quite remarkable how it forces every one of you to repress who you are, to quell the instincts which brought you here in the first place."

Remember who you are.

The voice—like my own but far less timorous—blazed inside my head with terrifying insistence. I gulped, heart pounding, desperately wishing I could do what it said. But I'd already spent so long trying to solve that mystery when I'd first arrived; I used to pull each of the objects out from their hole and handle them for hours, running my fingers along the scrollwork across the chest, fiddling with the drawstring on the pouch, and twisting the cap of the bottle.

Something to remember us by.

This time, the voice was different—slithery, somehow, like dry autumn leaves blowing across the pavement. In my mind's eye, I saw a skeletal hand passing over a shooter filled with amber liquid, and with that vision came another phrase.

A gift. And a reminder.

Realizing how close I was, and prompted almost solely by subconscious instinct, I slid my hand into the hole while the madman was distracted, rummaging about as I tried to locate the bottle by touch alone. I heard something clink and worked my hand in that direction.

"Oh, please do stop squirming," the madman said as he turned his attention back to me. "It will not save you. Besides, if you stay quite still I can end this with one blow. Wouldn't you prefer that to the messier alternative?"

At last, I felt something brush against my fingertips; I snatched up the bottle and—with a violent rocking motion—rolled out from beneath my assailant's heel before he could raise his sword to strike. Then, without quite knowing why, or how it would help, I tore off the cap and downed the bottle's contents.

For a moment, nothing happened.

Then, as though I'd been struck by lightning—or at least hit with the prongs of a potent stun gun—I began to seize, my body writhing even as my mind swarmed with disjointed memories that arrived in no particular order, assaulting me with their vibrancy. One moment I was six years old on the playground with the taste of blood in my mouth, my lip swollen to the touch, my knuckles burning. The next I was seventeen, my back pressed up against a bear of a human being whose hands, like mine, were raised in a salute to the rock gods we'd come to worship. I was three, tottering towards a table with Dez's hands hovering lest I tumble and fall. Twenty-two, in the hospital with a shattered patella and first degree burns, ignoring the cops who'd come to find out why a young woman had leapt from a burning apartment owned by a reputed drug dealer. These and so many more came and went—including memories which had originally belonged to my disparate selves—the result flooding me with more emotions than I'd experienced in years.

When at last my body stilled, I lay staring up at a ceiling made of sheet metal.

"Forgive me for asking such an impertinent question, but are you dead, *fräulein?*"

Honestly, I wasn't sure how to answer Frankenstein's question. I mean, my life *had* just literally flashed before my very eyes. But I didn't feel dead. Merely tired, with the same sort of headache Charon's beers had left me with—a dull throbbing right between the ears. Fortunately, a surge of adrenaline hit the moment I realized both where I was and who I was with, chasing away my fatigue.

"Oh, you'll wish I was," I wheezed, glaring up at the miserable son of a bitch, wishing I'd treated Mabel's warnings more seriously—not that it would have made any difference, as far as I could tell. I sat up, listing to my left somewhat, pretending to be more hurt than I was so I could reach back into the hole without the doctor noticing.

"Oh, it's *you!*" Frankenstein exclaimed. "How remarkable! Tell me, what was in that concoction you consumed? You must understand, chemistry is one of my greatest passions."

"Parsley, sage, rosemary, and thyme," I intoned as I gathered myself to stand, hyper aware of the wonderfully gilded sword the doctor appeared to be using as a cane. "I got it from Mrs. Robinson at the Scarborough Fair."

"Ah. A shame I won't be able to visit Frau Robinson, myself. Perhaps I could send someone...no, that could prove troublesome."

With Frankenstein distracted by Simon and Garfunkel lyrics, I dove to the other side of the room and collected the spear. I brandished it at the body-swapper, daring him to come closer. But instead, he took one look at me and laughed. Like, *really* laughed; tears welled up in his eyes even as he waved me off.

"Oh, *fräulein*, please do not be insulted. I do not expect you to understand, but without a devourer to charge that weapon you hold, this is like having a child threaten me with a stick."

"Like one of these, ye mean?"

I held up Thiazi's light-sucking jewel of a heart I'd fetched from the chest and watched the color drain from Frankenstein's stolen face. His mouth gaped open as I pressed the devourer Skadi had gifted me into the socket of my spear, at a complete loss for words for the first time since I'd met him. Unfortunately, that could never have lasted long—especially once he realized the jewel and the weapon remained unbonded.

"Of course!" Frankenstein exclaimed, clutching at his chest in relief. "I must admit you have surprised me twice, *fräulein*. First, you managed to awaken your mind, and now I learn you are in possession of a devourer! I am afraid this is where the surprises must end, however. It seems you lack the power required to wield such a destructive tool. But do not be ashamed, we cannot all call ourselves Masters."

"I don't give a shit what ye call me, ye demented fuck. But this 'tool' has a name."

Governed by a primal urge, I pricked my finger on the tip of the spear. A single drop of blood ran down the length of the blade like an errant raindrop—enough to incite the ravenous hunger I'd sensed lurking within from the moment I'd pulled it from the pile—only to sizzle and evaporate a moment later. The shaft began to burn feverishly beneath my hand, hot enough I could feel it through my glove, but I refused to let go. Instead, I pressed my wounded digit to the surface of Thiazi's pulsing heart and drew a rune in blood.

Gar.

Spear.

"What are you doing? Stop that!"

"It's time to wake up, Areadbhar," I whispered, ignoring the doctor, my breath fogging the steel patina along the blade. The effect was as immediate as if I'd shoved a key in a lock and turned it; the spear bucked wildly as the devourer settled into place, trying to break free of my hold so she could—presumably—slaughter everyone in sight. Not because I willed her to, but because that was what Areadbhar had been created to do. Indeed, what had made her so fearsome a weapon that the noblest of the Tuatha De Danann, Lugh, had refused to wield her in battle—allowing her instead to wreak endless havoc among his enemies, ungoverned by nuances like mercy or surrender.

But then, I wasn't Lugh.

And I was never going to let that happen.

I'd already offered her my blood and the heart of a giant, which meant there was only one step left if I wanted to assert my dominance: I had to let her taste my power. But for that, I would need help from someone who refused to acknowledge my existence, from a deity whose abilities dwarfed my own immeasurably, from a being who could not be bothered to save me from the surgical incisions of a lunatic no matter how hard I'd prayed for her intercession.

Which is why, this time, I wasn't asking.

Operating purely on instinct, I closed my eyes, reached deep down within my consciousness, and—without so much as a hello exchanged— scooped up a steaming pile of stolen power. Thanks to Charon's concoction and the subsequent memories I'd been hit with, I'd learned where my inner goddess kept it hidden. How to use it the way she had, on the other hand...well, that was an experiment for a different time.

Right now I had other priorities.

I opened my eyes to find Frankenstein staring down at the veins in my arms in complete shock, the entire room bathed in their emerald glow. Areadbhar stilled under my hand, her speartip swirling with the faintest of green flames, the devourer in her center sucking the light from the air like a black hole. When she finally submitted to me, however, it felt like a hammer blow to my chest.

A reminder, perhaps, that control was as much a burden as a boon.

"This, this is not possible," Frankenstein stammered, pointing at me with the tip of his sword. "This has to be the same trick you pulled before in the Titan Realm. You *cannot* be a god. They have all been accounted for, I checked. We know the whereabouts of every single one."

"Well then, it sounds like ye all might need to do another census." I rolled my shoulders and cracked my neck, limbering up for the fight I suspected was coming. "Now, I'll only say this once, so pay attention...get the hell out of me friend, Frankenfucker, or I swear I'm goin' to finish what Max started."

As I'd assumed he would, Frankenstein declined my invitation—vehemently. In fact, his retort came in the form of a physical assault that left half the neighborhood on fire and the other half blasted into the sky. Not that I mourned the loss of my ramshackle abode and its notable lack of flair; apparently my repressed self was both a reserved conversationalist *and* a minimalist. Which—especially if you were an advocate for nurture as opposed to nature—meant my role models had a *lot* to answer for.

Because I was neither of those things.

"Is that all you've got, ye bastard?" I yelled above the din of Frankenstein's singing sword, batting away his strikes with an epic spear that also happened to be touted as one of the Four Treasures of the Tuatha De Danann.

Case in point.

"You must realize I will not fall here no matter what you do," Frankenstein insisted, swinging the blade with more skill than I'd have given him credit for. Thus far, it appeared the doctor was eerily talented, remarkably fast, and considerably stronger than I was even with the power I'd stolen from my other half. Besides which, he had a tactical advantage I found difficult to overcome: he wore Ryan's face.

"If you damage this body," the doctor continued, "I will repair it. And even if you somehow manage to destroy it, I will return with another. So you see? This ill-fated battle of yours is futile. Now that I know how to reach this place, time is the only thing I require."

"Too bad time isn't on your side," I said offhandedly as I probed for an opening, mimicking the defeatist tone Hemingway and Freya had hit me with when delivering the same quote—albeit under very different circumstances.

"Oh, but he is."

I frowned at the response, wondering if he'd misheard me; his sword was crooning awfully loud, going on runs that could have put a gospel choir to shame. Before I could puzzle out what Frankenstein might have meant, however, the doctor raised his blade to deliver a chopping blow from overhead—continuing his strategy of bashing away at my defenses with his overwhelming strength. As battle tactics went, it was a good one; everyone tires eventually, but it's usually the individual with the larger, more cumbersome weapon who suffers the most, especially the longer a battle drags on. In this case, that person should have been me.

Areadbhar, though modeled after the lighter spears used by the Greeks and Romans long before suits of armor became so highly prized, stood two feet taller than I did from end to end and required constant motion to keep Frankenstein's blade at bay. But I'd spent months, perhaps even years depending how one measured time in another world, learning how to fight with a spear against all manner of opponents wielding all sorts of weapons —and I'd done it without the paragon of all polearms, the protection of mythical armor, and the thrumming power of a god coursing through my veins. Basically, if Frankenstein thought he could outlast *me*, he was in for a rude awakening.

Besides, he'd already screwed up.

He simply didn't know it yet.

I planted Areadbhar's buttspike into the ground as his sword came whistling—literally, whistling—towards my head, then executed a move I'd been taught by Lady Aife herself; I leapt to my right, tucking my body into the tightest ball possible as Frankenstein's sword bit deep into the dirt where I'd stood only a moment before, creating a molten chasm that extended some ten feet and sent those few fools who'd decided to wait us out, running for their spiritual lives. Then, after reversing my momentum by using the spear shaft as a fulcrum, I launched myself feet first at the doctor—essentially dropkicking the bastard with all the kinetic force of a pole vaulter.

My boots slammed into the bastard's chest with an ear-popping thwack and sent him skipping towards the horizon like a well-chucked stone. Fortunately, debris exploded into the air with each bounce, which both allowed me to track his progress even as his body disappeared from view and reminded me of fireworks. I hefted my spear, letting her rest in the nook of my shoulder while I debated whether to find Frankenstein and beat his ass again, or wait for him to come back for more.

Given that the bastard had hijacked Ryan's body, it wasn't a tough decision.

I'd only made it perhaps twenty feet or so, however, when something out of the ordinary caught my attention. I hesitated, craning my ears to make sure I wasn't crazy, but there they were again. Whispers—murmurs so soft and sibilant they could have been the wind if not for their haphazard, back-and-forth nature. Clearly a conversation, at first I figured the voices had to belong to a couple of unfortunate Atlantians hoping to weather the storm. But I quickly realized that wasn't possible; there was nowhere for anyone to hide, not after all the damage we'd done to the residential area. So where could they be coming from?

Before I could answer that question, however, the whispers ceased.

And, almost as if on cue, Frankenstein came hurtling towards me from high overhead, poised to drive his yodeling sword into my chest with a two-handed grip. For a moment, I simply stood there watching him, my mouth agape at the realization that he'd managed to close that absurd distance between us with a single *jump*. Then—because I wasn't a freaking idiot—I got the hell out of the way.

Which worked, sort of.

Rather than impale me like I was sure Frankenstein intended, his sword sunk into the ground to the hilt, creating a massive fissure that spread across the entire landscape, widening incrementally at first, then with increasing momentum as the weight of the top layer caved in on itself. Of course, by then Frankenstein had already withdrawn his blade and danced to the far side of the chasm, leaving me to scramble to find safe footing on the other side.

By the time the fissure finally stopped growing, Frankenstein and I were staring at each other from perhaps a hundred feet apart. From that distance, the blue bastard looked a lot like a pixie—not that I would ever have lumped him in with those reprobates...they didn't deserve that sort of slander. Realizing he was delaying, I brandished my spear and waited for him to jump the gap, eager to continue the fight now that I'd established the ground rules.

You see, Frankenstein had slipped up big time the second he admitted he'd repair any damage done to his host body—a theory I'd literally crash tested when I booted his ass halfway across the city. And, now that I knew he meant what he'd said, I had absolutely no reason to hold back. Besides, the way I saw it, I had only one option left that didn't include letting myself be murdered by a psychopath: I had to incentivize Frankenstein to abandon Ryan's body and seek out greener pastures elsewhere.

And nothing makes a bully rethink their life choices more than when they get picked on by someone stronger than they are.

"What's wrong, Frankenbitch?" I called when the doctor didn't immediately leap across the fissure to take me on, even going so far as to throw my arms out wide in invitation—letting him see how little he terrified me, how little I thought of his martial prowess.

"It's Frankenstein! Frankenstein, *verdammt!*"

Despite the distance between us and the fact that he wore my friend's face, the doctor's agitation was painfully obvious. Indeed, Frankenstein seemed plagued by the same frantic madness which I'd encountered outside the walls of the Laestrygonian capitol. Gone was the facade of the posh, well-spoken scientist. Indeed, it had been supplanted by what I believed was his true face: the mad genius who'd gotten cocky and overplayed his hand.

"Sorry, d'ye say 'Frankenshit?' I can't hear ye from over here!"

Frankenstein truly lost it, then; the doctor began tearing whole clumps of hair from his host's head with the hand not blue-knuckling the sword, spouting what I assumed were German obscenities. Then, as though unable to resist the urge any longer, he launched himself at me, lunging across the divide as though the rules of gravity no longer applied to him. To his credit, the strike was so blazingly fast that—even though I'd baited him into it—the best I could manage was a parry and an amateurish counterattack; I swatted the blow wide and extended my leg, tripping the doctor so that he sprawled face first into the dirt. The maneuver may have won me style points, but I knew it wouldn't be enough. What I needed was to land the sort of blows Frankenstein would have no choice but to recover from, to drain every last bit of patience and reason from the demented monster until he essentially rage quit.

Except it seemed Frankenstein had other plans.

Rather than resume our fight, the doctor—in a fit of anger and impotence—climbed to his feet, screamed wordlessly until spittle flew from his mouth, and chucked his sword at me like a child having a tantrum.

Unfortunately, of all the retaliations I'd anticipated, having a freaking *sword* thrown at me was not one of them; I thought to dodge, but the blade was coming at me too fast to deflect it, let alone dive out of the way. At this point, the question wasn't whether the singing sword was going to hit me, but rather how much damage would it do when it did.

Which is a shitty question to have to ask yourself, in case you're wondering.

Before I could answer that question, however, I felt Areadbhan jerk out of my hand and hurl herself into the path of the spinning blade with far greater speed and accuracy than I could have achieved had I tried to throw her. I'd hardly opened my mouth to tell her to come back when the two weapons collided, showering the sky with light and exploding in a burst of power that sent me soaring backwards.

Towards the chasm.

I skidded across the ground, clearing the edge of the crevice, my arm flung out like a prayer. Fortunately, it seemed someone was listening; I caught the lip of the chasm on the way down, able to stop myself from plummeting into the dark pit below. Sensing I had to hurry unless I wanted to play out a *Looney Tunes* skit with Frankenstein peeling away my fingers one at a time, I strained to get my second hand over the edge.

And that's when the whispers started up again—much louder this time. More insistent.

Sadly, I didn't have the time or mental wherewithal to decipher what they were saying. Instead, I took hold of the lip with both hands and swung, using my momentum to get a single leg and at least half my body over. From there, I could make out Frankenstein kneeling over the steaming remains of our two weapons; the doctor cradled his stomach, his expression horrifically pained. Which, frankly, was great news.

Because if he thought he was hurting now, then he had another think coming.

With a grunt, I swung my other half over and rolled away from the crevice to stare up at a improbable sky dominated by surging rivers which seemed somehow closer than they had before. I took a deep breath, embracing what it meant to be alive, and clambered to my feet only to realize the adrenaline rush of being blasted off a cliff had considerably masked the damage done to my body by the sudden backlash of power; it hurt to put weight on my left leg, I had trouble raising my right arm above my shoulder, and the rest of me simply *ached*. Worse still, I could tell immediately there was something wrong with Areadbhan because the spear lay still in the dirt, wisps of green smoke rising from her blade. Frankenstein's sword, on the other hand, was a mangled mess from the hilt down—including, I noted with a glimmer of satisfaction—at least a half dozen azure shards which had once combined to form a devourer.

"Looks like it's the end of the line for ye, Frankendick," I said as I approached, doing my utmost to betray as little pain as possible in the hopes that the doctor would finally see this as a lost cause and retreat. If not, things were going to get ugly, fast.

When at last he took notice of me and looked up, however, I knew instantly that it wasn't Frankenstein who held my gaze.

It was Ryan.

"Quinn," he groaned, still clutching at his stomach. "Please, you have to kill me."

I collapsed to my knees beside my smoldering spear and cradled Ryan's face in my hands, suddenly overwhelmed by the memories he and I shared together in this strange place. Blue...that was what I'd called him. Not because of his skin tone, but because of the electric shade that rimmed his pupils. And he, in turn, had dubbed me Red for the color I turned whenever he teased me about going along with one of his schemes. Blue had been admittedly different than my Ryan—less self-conscious, more fun-loving. The sort of person I imagined he might have been if left solely to his own devices, allowed to make his own life choices.

And now he wanted to die.

"What the hell are ye talkin' about, ye idget?"

"He's still...inside me," Ryan replied through gritted teeth, a teardrop rolling down his cheek only to freeze before it could get past his chin.

"Who? Ye mean Frankenstein? But how?"

"The devourer..."

Ryan gestured to the broken jewel by way of explanation, and I began to piece together what must have happened. Apparently, Frankenstein had swapped his spirit for Ryan's back in my hut, forcing the Faeling's soul into the devourer. Which meant—once it shattered—Ryan had returned to his body only to find it a hostile battleground. The question was, who had what it took to win the war?

As if answering my question, a series of dueling expressions began rippling across Ryan's face, each belonging to one of the two inhabitants. In Ryan's case, all were variations on a theme which could only be described as intense suffering. In Frankenstein's, however, I saw madness, and madness alone.

"Quinn...you have to...do it," Ryan urged. "Please, I can't...hold him...for long."

Alarmed to discover Frankenstein could potentially resume control at any moment, I glanced down at my own damaged weapon, disturbed to find a sizable crack splintered across the surface of Thiazi's heart, spewing light and obscuring the rune I'd inscribed. Indeed, from where I knelt, the jewel looked battered beyond repair—the damage clearly more than Areadbhar could sustain and still function. At this point, even picking her up was a risk, let alone using her to defend myself should Ryan fail.

"Can ye not chase him out?" I asked, my mind whirling with fragmented possibilities. "Wait, I know, maybe we could threaten him into leavin'? I could stab ye a couple times, nowhere fatal obviously, and tell him to get out unless he wants to bleed out?"

Ryan made a series of choked sounds in the back of his throat, shaking his head, and I realized he was laughing.

At me.

"What's so funny?" I demanded, suddenly cross.

"Same...old Quinn," he croaked. "No...half measures."

"Look, I didn't come all the way down here to see ye roll over for some psychotic, body-swappin' boogeyman with a God complex, ye hear me?" I gripped both of his arms, marveling at how cold they felt despite the protection of my gloves even as I willed him to shake off the doctor's spirit. "Ye have to get rid of him. Then we can go home, Ryan. Don't ye want to go home?"

"Can't."

"Of course ye can," I snapped, my skin flushed. "Listen, I know ye did t'ings ye regret. T'ings ye may even believe ye deserve to pay for. But this isn't the way. Ye have to move on, and evolve, and ye can't do that if ye dwell on the past."

But Ryan clearly didn't agree; the Faeling was shaking his head so violently by the time I finished that his whole body rocked back and forth from the effort. He unfolded his arms and gripped my shoulders, forcing me to look into his eyes.

"Can't." Ryan shook me as if willing me to understand, swallowed, and tried again. "Can't...let him...go."

And that's when it hit me.

Ryan wasn't asking me to kill *him*.

He was asking me to kill *them*.

"No way!" I shrugged off the Faeling's hold and turned away, unable to hold his gaze. "I didn't come here to kill that sick bastard, Ryan O'Rye. I came here to find ye, and to take ye home so ye can be surrounded by people who care and remember what that's like."

"I...remember." I felt Ryan's palm brush my cheek, then pat it hard enough to sting. "Red."

"Oy, that hurt—"

"You...remember," Ryan interjected, grabbing my hand and pressing it against his chest, his whole body vibrating with tension. "Blue."

Who I really am, I could have sworn I heard him add, though of course I knew he hadn't.

But that wasn't fair. It wasn't *enough*. After everything I'd gone through to find him, after all this time, we deserved to make *new* memories—to fix everything we'd broken...including each other. Hell, our tenure in Atlantis had only made that more apparent; we belonged together. Not as lovers, or even as friends, but as soulmates destined to spend our final moments toasting the inevitable heat death of the universe. The evidence was irrefutable: free of our hangups and our poor decisions and our bitterness— in a realm full of other candidates—we had not only found each other, we'd been practically inseparable.

Why? Because at his best, Ryan was supportive, caring, and decent. And because, without him, I'd never be at my best.

He was my person.

And, cruelest of all, I hadn't realized that until now.

"Dammit, Ryan, I need ye!" I pounded my fist weakly against his chest, fighting back the storm of sobs that threatened to break the moment I stopped to really think about what he was asking me to do. "I *need* ye. We have to find another way. There has to *be* another way."

But there wasn't another way, and we both knew it. For Frankenstein to die—truly die—it was clear he had to go down with the proverbial ship. If he managed to jump overboard, even at the last moment, he'd do exactly what he said he would and return to Atlantis in someone else's body to complete whatever task he'd assigned himself. But who was to say that was all he'd do? What was to stop him from terrorizing Ryan and me, or from hurting the people we cared about to get to us? Ryan was right: Frankenstein couldn't be allowed to survive this.

"Use...the spear..."

Ryan gestured for me to retrieve Areadbhar and reached up to bare his chest, exposing a patchwork of hideous scars and—in the space where his heart should have been—a shimmering globe implant that I recognized as the core piece of Polyphemus' mechanical eye.

"Oh, Ryan," I whispered, my stomach churning at the notion of what had been done to his body. "Jesus, I'm so sorry."

"Don't be such...a girl...about it."

"I always know when you're tryin' to rile me up, Ryan O'Rye," I said, fighting back the urge to slug him on principle. Though of course that would have been a lot easier to do if I weren't constantly having to wipe at my cheeks. Still, I managed to pick up my spear without having to be asked twice—even if it did tremble in my hands. "And I want ye to know...it's not goin' to work. Because I love ye, ye idget, and I can't stay mad at...someone...I love."

"You...too."

"And ye better not go wanderin' too far after this, alright?" I swallowed hard past the lump in my throat, wishing I had sleeves to wipe my face with. "I tracked ye down in the afterlife once already. When the time comes, I'll do it again."

The faintest smile flickered across Ryan's face as he guided the tip of my spear to the hollow of his throat.

"I'll be...closer...than you think."

Then, before I could say anything else, Ryan thrust himself forward. I managed to shut my eyes just before the blade buried itself in his neck, then braced myself for sounds of pain, for the inevitable spasms, for the gruesome realities of dying. But none of those occurred; instead, there was light.

I opened my eyes to find the devourer glowing, its cracked surface mending itself even as Ryan's blood spilled down his chest and pooled into his shirt and trousers. I felt Areadbhar twitch, saw the green flames ripple along her blade until they reached the Faeling's mortally wounded throat.

Within seconds, Ryan went up like a match soaked in lighter fluid; his skin seemed to curl and wizen before my very eyes, caving in on itself as though what had remained after his passing was more shell than person. The heat soon became unbearable, and I had to step clear of his body lest I, too, get burned.

When it was finally over, there was little left of Ryan to mourn but ash and dust. And yet, I said nothing over his remains, mainly because I had nothing left to say.

To anyone.

46

I'd been sitting—staring at the gilded gravemarker I'd created by plunging the blade of Charlemagne's singing sword into the ground next to the chest which had once held Thiazi's heart but now represented mine—for so long I completely lost all sense of time, when the ground started to shake. The tremors were slight at first—hardly enough to rattle the ribcage. But, as the quakes continued to occur, I began to notice panicked Atlantians gathering what they could from what was left of their homes before fleeing towards the great mounds. They looked terrified—more so even than when they'd stumbled upon me squatting amidst the wreckage I'd helped create. The correlation between the two suggested that the quakes, like me, were not indigenous to Atlantis.

And they were getting worse.

Due to a lack of alternatives—and because I trusted their judgment more than my own—I decided to follow the natives and find out whether they had access to shelter. But first, I rolled gingerly to my feet and patted myself down to make sure I had everything I'd come with, including the sack of god biscuits and the empty bottle which had contained Charon's concoction. Once satisfied I wasn't leaving anything except my aching heart behind, I started limping across the landscape, conspicuously trailed by a floating Areadbhar. The mythical spear appeared to have made a full recovery, though I still wasn't entirely certain how that had come to pass—nor was I eager to dwell on it, just yet.

My trek became more arduous by the moment, however, as the tremors increased in both duration and severity. I began skipping between aftershocks to keep from putting too much pressure on my bum leg, genuinely concerned for the integrity of this realm; whatever was happening below the surface, it was bound to be causing seismic damage the likes of which Atlantis had never seen.

By the time I reached the great mounds, the Atlantians I'd followed were nowhere in sight. Overhead, the branching rivers churned and surged, both larger and closer than I'd ever seen them. And yet, there were no storms in sight—no debris raining down from the heavens. Prompted by a sudden desire to reach the top of the nearest mound and look out across the horizon, I began hiking up the side using an overqualified Areadbhar as a walking stick, stopping only when another quake threatened to send me tumbling to the bottom beneath an avalanche of lost items.

When I finally reached the summit, I was panting and as exhausted as I could ever remember being, which was why it took me a moment before I turned to find all of Atlantis spread out before me, the view even more stupendous than the one Ryan and I had shared from the stairway outside the mausoleum. Or it would have been, were it not for the dozens of fissures spread across the landscape, scarring the entire terrain. As I watched, another appeared, branching from the nearest crevice with an audible cracking sound.

Within seconds, I felt the resulting shockwave.

Larger even than the last, I had a moment to wonder if I wouldn't be joining Ryan sooner rather than later before I teetered and ended up staggering along the edge. In an effort to keep my balance, I began pinwheeling my arms, only to clip something withered and dry. I glanced up in surprise to find a dessicated arm reaching for me from the other side of the frothing river overhead, its skeletal hand beckoning.

A hand I definitely recognized.

With no other alternatives besides falling to my presumable death, I snatched hold of the offered metacarpus mere moments before the mound beneath my feet started caving in, swallowed by an ever-widening crevasse. Dangling in mid-air, I stared into that gaping hole, wondering what could possibly have triggered destruction on such a massive scale. Could

Frankenstein really have caused some sort of chain reaction, earlier? I shook my head as the hand gripping my wrist began towing me skyward, realizing I was ascribing natural phenomenon to an unnatural place; seismic activity in Atlantis was far more likely to be caused by a stomping giant than it was by tectonic shifts.

Then, just as my arm slid into the frigid river waters, I caught a glimpse of something emerging from the gaping hole as what looked like a single, solitary finger—easily taller and wider than any skyscraper I'd ever seen—rose up from the depths before curling onto the earth with a colossal, dirt-spewing boom.

I opened my mouth to say something, perhaps even to scream, only to find it full of brackish, unbearably spicy river water as the hand yanked me through to the surface. I came up spluttering, my tongue swollen as though stung by a dozen fire ants at once, my exposed skin scalded and raw as what little glow had remained in my veins after my battle with Frankenstein sputtered and died. A second skeletal hand snatched me by the pauldron and pulled me onboard a familiar riverboat, then handed me an ice cold beer.

"I sure hope you didn't swallow any of that swill," Charon said, his voice slithering across my mind, tilting his head in the general direction of the river even as he fetched a second brew for himself. "Go on, drink up."

"Will it help?" I asked, though out loud it sounded a lot more pathetic, not unlike that moronic kid's in *A Christmas Story* who got his tongue stuck to a frozen pole.

"No idea." Charon toasted me. "But it won't hurt."

47

I nursed the beer between my throbbing hands, taking judicious sips, wary of whatever hellish homebrew Charon had given me this time. Fortunately, the beer embodied the bland, nigh flavorless quality I'd come to expect from your everyday dimestore brand. The boatman must have realized I was pathetic enough as it was without getting me white girl wasted on fermented river juice.

"So, how d'ye find me?" I asked, glad to be able to use my tongue again.

"Had a hunch you'd end up down there before it was all said and done," Charon replied, shrugging his bony shoulders as he worked the oar. "You had that lost feel about you. That's why I gave you that shot."

"Oh, right!" I retrieved the empty bottle and passed it over. "What the hell was in that, by the way?"

"A little Lethe cocktail I put together a while back. Does wonders for the memory, but it's got a real kick." Charon palmed the shooter, oblivious to my gaping stare. "Anyway, once I saw what was going on down there, I thought you could use a hand."

"What *was* goin' on down there?"

"Foundation trouble, by the looks of it," Charon replied, matter-of-factly. "That sort of thing happens here a lot more than you'd think. Break-outs. Break-ins. Whole wings that weren't there before going up where old annexes used to be. You get used to it."

"Sounds awful, if ye ask me."

"But I didn't."

Charon reached down, took hold of the beer he'd sat on the lip of the boat, and took a long swig as though he could care less what I thought about his workplace. Then again, if I were him, I supposed I'd have gotten all that out of my system centuries ago; there was no use complaining about a situation you could never hope to escape from. Besides, who was I to judge?

"Where are ye takin' me, by the way?" I asked after several minutes of silence passed, realizing he hadn't yet revealed our intended destination—though I assumed there was only one place left for a wandering spirit like me to go now that my time in the afterlife was at an end. "Me body is in the Titan Realm, by the way, if you're lookin' to drop me off."

"Actually, we're headed the opposite way," Charon replied. "The boss said you had a message to deliver, and that you'd know what it was."

I frowned, the gears in my head revolving so slowly that I couldn't for the life of me puzzle out what Charon was talking about. The fact was I was a shell of my former self; emotionally eviscerated, physically battered, and mentally exhausted, I found the mere *concept* of speech draining, let alone the act itself. I'd come to save Max and confront Ryan and—within those limited parameters—gone two for two. And yet, it felt like I'd failed.

Ryan, it turned out, was right.

I really wasn't fond of half measures.

"Give me a hint," I urged as I held out my hand for Areadbhar, then cradled her across my chest like a security blanket. "And don't be your usual, cryptic self, please? I've had a long day. Or days. Weeks? Jesus, how long have I been here?"

"Yeah, things don't work like that, here. Once you cross over, night and day are mostly tied to geography. If there's a moon where you are, it's night. If there's a sun, it's day. If you're somewhere with a lot of fire, it's a bad day."

"Very funny," I drawled, though I quickly realized Charon's offhand explanation largely accounted for my goddess' dormancy. After all, the only moon I'd seen during my entire stint had hung in the sky above Valhalla. The other realms I'd visited—including Niflheim, Helheim, and even Atlantis—had all been suffused with at least some form of natural light.

Of course, he hadn't exactly answered my question.

"Charon, how long has passed in the Titan Realm since I got here?"

"Couldn't say. Time can be fickle down..." Charon drifted off, cocking his head as a sound drifted out over the water that didn't belong to the frothing waters we sailed upon. "They must be doing construction again. Anyway, it looks like we made it."

Intrigued, I draped myself over the side of the boat, craning my neck as we rounded the bend to the rhythmic tune of dozens of hammers striking steel and at least as many saws cutting through wood. Of course, nothing could have prepared me for what I saw when at last we turned the corner; I leered, struggling to process what I was seeing, though under normal circumstances I'd have sworn I was looking at a colony of some kind.

Except these weren't normal circumstances.

And this was Hell.

"Uh, Charon," I said, alarm propelling my voice an octave higher than usual. "When ye say we made it...*where*, exactly, are we?"

"The warden calls it Cell Block F. But everyone else calls it Temple Island."

48

*C*haron left me stranded on the riverbank only after I'd extracted a promise from him that he'd return to collect me once I'd spoken with Calvin and Makayla Temple—a condition I'd insisted upon after learning Hades seriously expected me to pass along his stupid message after he'd done exactly jack squat to bring Max and I together. In hindsight, I was pretty sure Charon couldn't have given a shit about my grievance one way or the other; he'd simply wanted me off his damned boat. As insurance, however, I'd left Areadbhar behind with instructions to keep the boatman honest.

After all, nothing incentivizes quite like the threat of violence and mayhem.

I spun and marched farther inland, initially determined to deliver my message and be done with it. But, as I passed the first half dozen or so mangled spirits bustling about the barren crag with their rusted metal beams and charred wood planks, I began to rethink that policy. After all, the Temples knew things other people didn't—truths about me, about my parents, and about my destiny—which only they could reveal. Not that I felt I could trust them; they'd kept secrets from their own son, for crying out loud. Big, hefty secrets—the kind with literally world-shattering ramifications.

Of course, first I had to find them.

I stopped a spirit dragging a sack full of rocks across the ground, though I found it hard to maintain eye contact; half his face was caved in as though he'd been stepped on by a horse as a child. His good eye locked onto my waving hand like it was some sort of majestic bird until he realized it belonged to a person.

"Hello," I said, uncertain of the social protocols involved in addressing a ghost. "Can ye tell me where to find the Temples?"

"You must be new," he replied, patting my arm reassuringly. "Look for the biggest house in town. And don't worry, they'll get you sorted. Back when I was alive, they used to say 'the devil always gets his due.' Well, the devil never had to collect from the Temples, I can tell you that much!"

The spirit chortled at his own joke, flashed me a lopsided smile, and went on about his business, chugging right along as though lugging rocks from one place to another was a perfectly acceptable way to occupy one's time.

"Uh, t'anks," I mumbled after him, unsure what to make of his anecdote. Had the Temples really set up their own little colony in Hell? And, if so, who had authorized it? For some reason, I couldn't see Hades letting anyone do *anything* that wasn't strictly by the book. Plus, Hades had sent me to deliver his message, as opposed to one of his phantom emissaries. Which meant the Temples must have struck a deal with someone powerful enough to make the god of the dead think twice before interfering in their affairs.

Good to know their reputations weren't exaggerated, I supposed.

I found the house the spirit mentioned not long after walking into the heart of the dilapidated village the colonists had fashioned for themselves. Not that it was hard; the three-story monstrosity rose like a castle fort above the rest of the buildings, its facade made entirely of soot-stained chrome and shaped like a leering skull with windows where the eyes should be. Frankly, it should have looked like a gimmicky Halloween house—the sort of place that would make toddlers cry and have teenagers rolling their eyes in disdain. But it didn't; it looked fucking *scary*. And, somehow, expensive.

Of *freaking* course these were Nate's parents, I thought as I banged on the front door, my every knock reverberating along the skeletal face like the clanging of a gong. After only a few seconds, the skull's two front teeth were thrown wide to reveal a plush red carpet snaking into a dim, candlelit room.

The effect was both ostentatious and eerie, meant to simultaneously entice and repulse.

"Oy!" I yelled, eager to dispense with the pageantry. "Get your dead asses out here, I have a message from Hades!"

Two startled people popped up out of the gloom as if by magic, looking remarkably as though they'd been lying in wait for someone. They took their time stepping into the light, which gave me the opportunity I needed to study their faces without being too obvious about it; I'd seen the Temples before from afar, but had subsequently hoped for a closer look. Calvin's, I noticed, hadn't changed much at all—as stately and shrewd as I remembered, his bolder features were drawn fine and thin so as not to offend, his hair dusted grey but still luxuriously full. On the other hand, Makayla's— though it bore more significant signs of aging—remained the more conventionally attractive of the two, her eyes large and faintly doll-like, with the sort of brilliant, effervescent smile that so often propels a woman from leading lady to starlet.

"Sorry!" Makayla said, hitting me with that megawatt smile as she ushered me inside. "We thought you were someone else."

"Someone ye planned to invite to dinner and then eat?" I ventured, eyebrow cocked at the room's decidedly Gothic ambiance.

"Of course not!" Makayla laughed and waved that away. "Can I get you something to drink? And Calvin, would you mind grabbing a couple chairs from the foyer? Or the sunroom, whichever works. But not the patio! You know how they get when it acid rains."

"Yes, dear." Calvin leaned over to lay a peck on his wife's forehead, stepped through a doorway brimming with infernal light, and reappeared moments later carrying two robust armchairs that could have gone for a couple grand at auction. Once he'd arranged them, the middle-aged wizard began patting his forehead with a handkerchief retrieved from his breast pocket. "My apologies for the delay. So, young lady, you said you came here with a message? Who was it from, again?"

"Calvin, at least let the girl sit down," Makayla mumbled playfully under her breath. She slipped into one of the chairs and took her husband's hand so that he stood looming over her shoulder, the two looking remarkably as though they were posing for a portrait to hang on their mantle. "Please, sit and rest. So long as you're in our home, you're our guest."

"My wife is right, as usual," Calvin acquiesced, patting her hand. "Forgive me. I did not mean to rush you."

Although feeling a tad like a guest star in a family sitcom, I took the Temples up on their offer; my poor leg was still killing me, and the chairs looked supremely comfortable. Once settled, however, I decided it best to delay my delivery. Instead, I folded my arms across my stomach and studied the pair. Now that I knew what to look for, I realized I could see fragments of Nate in both their faces—the line of Calvin's nose, the square thrust of Makayla's chin. The mere resemblance made me want to like them instinctively, the way you might feel about a dog on the street that was the spitting image of your childhood pet. Except it wasn't your dog, and you risked losing a finger if you chose to forget that fact.

"Do either of ye recognize me?" I asked, breaking the silence with a question that had been burning inside me from the moment I stepped through the door.

The Temples exchanged puzzled glances.

"I am sorry to have to ask," Calvin replied, "but should we?"

"Maybe. Ye knew me ma, back in the day. People tell me I look like her, though what they mean is I looked like her in photographs. She died when I was born, ye see...but then I expect ye already knew that bit. Under the circumstances, it'd be odd if ye didn't."

I heard the wood under Makayla's hand creak a moment before she abandoned her chair and closed the distance between us, her face hovering perhaps a foot from mine, searching it like a sculptor preparing to chisel off some excess stone. Then, just as abruptly, Nate's mother stepped back and resumed her seat wearing a troubled expression, her skin suddenly as pale as mine.

I, meanwhile, fought the urge to clear my suddenly dry throat as the precise nature of my current situation became painfully clear: assuming myself safe, I'd inadvertently put myself at the mercy of two notorious schemers who I knew for sure had conspired to create me, though for what purpose I could only speculate. I'd come looking for answers, but what if they refused? Or, worse, what if they took issue with the questions?

"Calvin, this is Morrigan's daughter," Makayla said, the forced cheer she'd expressed earlier replaced by something far more genuine, if a bit less welcome—sympathy.

"Yes, dear. I can see that now."

"Would you mind getting it, then? It should be upstairs, in the chest with the…" Makayla glanced at me as if afraid to say more in mixed company. "Well, you know what to look for."

"Of course."

Calvin disappeared for a second time before I could wrap my head around the Temples' bizarre reactions and stilted conversation. By the time he'd returned, however, I'd already demanded a dozen explanations from his wife. Her response, of course, had varied in its arrangement, but never its message, which ultimately boiled down to "please be patient."

"Listen, I'm not a patient person by nature," I growled as Calvin resumed his station at her back, holding something cupped in his hands the way you might a baby bird or a cricket—any creature, really, that you were afraid might get away. "I want to know everythin' ye know. I want to know why ye stole what ye stole in Fae. Why ye picked me parents. Why ye started all of this. Begin at the beginnin' and I'll let ye know when to stop."

The Temples locked eyes again.

"We knew you'd come, one day."

"Your mother told us," Makayla added, smiling as if to soften the blow of what they had to say. "She was particularly gifted, in that way. Most seers can predict only one future at a time, you know. Only she could see more. Dozens, sometimes hundreds. There are critical points. Blind spots. Divergences…"

"Could you tell us," Calvin interjected as his wife fell inexplicably silent, "whether you've met our son, yet?"

"Ye mean Nate? Aye, of course I have. Why, was I not supposed to?"

"There is no such thing as 'supposed to,'" Calvin replied, firmly. "No future is exact, just as no two people are alike. Predictions are like children. No matter how diligently they are nurtured, you can never be entirely certain how they'll turn out."

"D'ye say 'nurtured' or 'tortured'? I'm only clarifyin' because I've seen the aftermath of your child rearin' skills."

"Does that mean you and Nate are—" Makayla began, then immediately covered her mouth as though afraid to utter the second half of her question.

"What, enemies?" I waved that away. "Listen, far be it from me to pass judgment, but the world, make that *all* the worlds, would be a lot safer if he weren't so damned insecure. And that shit starts at home."

"We gave Nate everything we could," Calvin insisted. "We gave him everything we knew he'd *need*."

"Except faith," I countered. "In people. In his friends. Dammit, the man has *trust issues*. From bein' lied to his entire life. Which, more often than not, makes him behave like a dick. An admittedly funny, but routinely frustrating *dick*."

"So, you and Nate..." Makayla said, clearly not willing to let this go until I clarified my relationship with her son. "Are..."

"We're friends," I deadpanned, sighing.

Inexplicably, a wave of relief spread across both their faces. Makayla actually sniffled and dabbed at her eyes. Clearly, I was missing something—some integral detail that explained why Nate's parents cared so much about where Nate and I stood. Unfortunately, I hadn't the first clue as to what that could be; Nate had plenty of friends already, not to mention a few low-key incredible women I knew personally who were looking to upgrade.

"Why the hell d'ye both look so pleased?"

"No future is exact," Calvin repeated, cryptically. "And some are worse than others."

"Jesus, ye sound like a depressin' fortune cookie. Why won't either of ye give me a straight answer? Nate was right, it's like pullin' teeth with ye people."

"You're right, young lady, of course you're right," Makayla replied, nodding. "But things are often more complicated than they seem. Some truths open doors that are better left closed. Which is why, before we go any further, I am afraid you have a choice to make. One that will determine how much, or how little, we can tell you."

"Oh? And who made up that garbage rule?"

"Your mother, actually." Makayla grinned wryly. "She wasn't a patient person, either, you know. She made us swear that—when the time came and you finally found us—we would offer you two choices. Two directions, really. She also assured us that, depending which path you were on, you'd have no difficulty deciding."

I bit back my reply, choosing to fume in silence. What was it with interfering parents, today? First the Temples, and now my own mother—a woman I knew only through the spirit she'd left behind to guide me. Who, by the way, hadn't exactly done a bang up job. Still, if playing along meant getting straight answers, then there was really only one response.

"Fine. I'm listenin'."

"The first option represents truth," Calvin said, his voice taking on a melodious, storytelling quality that added weight to every word out of his mouth. "If you choose this path, we will be bound to answer any of your questions, free to tell you everything you wish to know and more. But, if you linger here with us, your body will die and you will have no choice but to watch from the wings as all who can no longer step foot on stage must."

"The second path represents the unknown," Makayla continued, picking up right where her husband left off. "If this is your choice, we must tell you nothing. You will have no choice but to rejoin the other players, to return with our blessing and nothing else."

"Wait, that's it? *Those* are me choices?" I asked, flabbergasted. "Are ye sure ye didn't leave anythin' out? Like maybe I can ask a half dozen questions or so and then catch the first boat out of here?"

The Temples remained still as statues, clearly awaiting my decision.

I sat back and replayed the Temple's disparate options in my head, weighing them against one another. At their core, they boiled down to a choice between—not so much truth and the unknown—but the past and the future. If I chose the former, I could uncover all manner of secrets, including answers to questions that had plagued me my whole life. Questions that still ate at me, chipping away at my relationships and my self-esteem. But then, what could I *do* with those answers? Even assuming they were the ones I so desperately wanted to hear, I'd be too dead to care. Choosing the latter, on the other hand, objectively netted me nothing. And yet, at least the future held possibility. By now, I'd seen my fair share of the afterlife and knew what it had to offer. I'd weighed its broken spirits, measured its shattered souls...and had found it wanting.

So, in the end, I supposed my mother had been right, after all.

If my choices were to live in the past, despairing over what I couldn't change, or to live for the future, hoping for the best...

Then there wasn't much of a choice, was there?

"I'll go with the unknown."

"We had hoped you would," Calvin confessed, as he came around from his side of the chair. He extended his hands as if presenting me with whatever he'd been holding this entire time—which I had, admittedly, forgotten all about until that moment. "Our blessing, as promised. Now, please take it and go."

"Oh, and if you happen to see our son," Makayla added, sounding a bit choked up as she took my hand and shepherded me towards the door, "please, give him our love."

I sat in Charon's boat, scrutinising the "blessing" I'd been gifted by the Temples for refusing to die in their living room. I held the mysterious, oddly shaped device overhead, trying to make out the strange sigil inscribed across the bottom, but either the light in this stretch of tunnel was too dim, or my eyes were beginning to go, because I couldn't decipher a single word. Once I was back on top, I decided, I'd take another look. Knowing the two who'd given it to me—even if only by reputation—I had to assume whatever it was would no doubt prove useful at some point in the future.

"How much farther?" I asked, forced to slip the miniature pyramid in with the Ambrosia biscuits for lack of pockets; aside from removing my helmet, I wasn't in the mood to fuss with my armor any more than I had to. Frankly, I wasn't in the mood to move, at all.

"That depends," Charon replied.

"On what?"

"On how many more times you plan on asking that question."

"So sensitive…" I mumbled before turning my head to watch the water rush past, lulled by the dim shapes moving beneath the surface. I slid into a more comfortable position and began to drift a little, my mind still for the first time in what felt like ages. I hardly noticed when my eyes closed on their own, or when my chin dipped towards my chest, or when I slumped against the boat's starboard side.

What I *did* notice, however, was Charon's oar when he jabbed me with it.

"Oy!" I said, with a start. "What was that for?"

"I asked you a question," he said. "But you were too busy dying to answer."

"I was not!" I sat up, my heart pounding with the realization that Charon could be right; I had exactly zero energy left. Unless we reached the other side, and soon, I was literally dying on borrowed time. Unfortunately, all I could do—aside from getting the hell out of Hell—was keep myself awake and distracted. "What was your question, anyway?"

"I asked you what the message was."

"What message?"

"The message Hades gave you to pass along to the Temples. What was it?"

"Shit!" I swung my head around as though I might find Temple Island right behind us, but of course we were miles and miles downriver by now. I palmed my forehead, grinding it between my brows. "He told me to tell 'em somethin' about their 'machinations' causin' problems, and that they needed to 'reveal their'...plan? Hand? It was somethin' like that. But I forgot to tell 'em!"

Charon was uncharacteristically silent, and suddenly it was as if I could feel his judgment like a physical weight crushing me to the floor of the boat. Dear Lord, I thought, what if he demanded we turn back around? I doubted I'd survive another trip, or that I could convince him to take me anywhere else for free. With a knot already forming in the pit of my stomach, I lowered my hand, prepared to meet the boatman's eyes.

Except he wasn't looking at me, at all.

He was shielding his face from a bright light at the end of the tunnel.

"Well, looks like you made it in time," Charon said as he used his oar to swing the boat horizontally and pin us in place. "Last stop. Or first stop, I guess, depending how you look at it."

"Ye aren't upset?" I asked before I could help myself. "About me not passin' along the message, I mean."

"Not my department. Besides, there'd be paperwork, and I avoid that like the plague."

I sighed with relief as I took hold of Areadbhar and climbed unsteadily to my feet, the ball of tension in my guts easing with every passing second. Stepping lightly so as not to rock the boat, I made my way to Charon's side, eyeing the bright white light with no small degree of amusement.

Of course it would be on this side.

"So, do I just jump through, or what?"

"Your guess is as good as mine." Charon shrugged before gesturing to my spear, then my armor. "You do know you can't take that with you where you're going, right? Any of that stuff."

"Nice try," I said, smirking.

But Charon wasn't joking.

"That's all considered contraband," the boatman explained, his voice—even in my own head—dripping with sincerity. "Spirits aren't allowed to carry items back and forth from one realm to the other, not anymore. We eased the restrictions a bit, several centuries back, and you wouldn't believe the complaints. So many hangings."

"Can't ye make an exception?"

"No, not unless you have permission."

"Permission from whom?"

"Depends what you're carrying, really. But any one of the gods could do it."

"Seriously? I got this armor from Freya. This devourer from Skadi. I mean come on, I even have Scooby Snacks from Hel. You're really tellin' me none of 'em can get through security?"

"Unless one of them shows up to wave you through, that's exactly what I'm saying." Charon kicked open his cooler, fetched a beer, and cracked it. "Want one for the road? If the beer's inside you when you leave, I don't think it counts."

I ignored the boatman's offer and groaned in frustration, struggling to understand how all the gods and goddesses I'd crossed paths with in the afterlife had forgotten to mention this glaringly significant detail. Of course, Skadi and Hel's contributions had both been gifts, so I couldn't exactly hold them accountable. But Freya? How in the Nine Realms could the Vanir possibly ask me to track down Hilde and then forget to sign off on me taking the armor I'd been promised? Unless, of course, she hadn't forgotten. What if that had been her plan all along? The reason she'd taught me so little about how to use Brynhildr's armor, about what it could and couldn't do? From her perspective, this was a win-win; either I succeeded and brought Hilde to her in exchange for a suit of armor I no longer possessed, or I failed and—a month and a day after I returned to the mortal realm—I became a Valkyrie whether I liked it or not.

There was no way I could let that happen.

Besides, it wasn't just about the stuff. There were *memories* associated with the things I'd collected here—trials I'd had to go through, horrors I'd had to survive. My armor didn't symbolize my contract with Freya, it symbolized security. Without it, I'd likely have died for real a dozen times over. Similarly, both Thiazi's heart and Hel's biscuits represented selfless acts of friendship that I refused to belittle. And then there was Areadbhar, the spear which would be indelibly connected to Ryan for reasons both bitter and sweet.

Leaving her behind, I realized, would be like cutting off my own arm.

"Oy! Charon..." I called, an idea forming in the back of my mind. It would be tricky, I decided, especially considering my solution included a few unknown variables, but I knew it was lucrative enough to get the boat-man's attention. "What if we made a deal?"

"A deal?" The boatman echoed, his chin and cowl covered in suds and stains. He crushed his now empty beer can between his hands. "Do I look like I can be bribed?"

"D'ye really want me to answer that?" I asked, eyeing his cooler full of imported beers for emphasis. "Come on, at least let me tell ye what I have in mind."

"And what could you possibly offer me that I don't already have?" Charon drawled, his sarcasm thick enough to walk on.

"How about a magic boat that propels itself?"

50

*A*ccording to Circe, I'd been in what amounted to a coma for exactly three weeks to the day when I finally woke. Fatigued both mentally and physically, I'd apparently needed near constant supervision over the next several days; my memories of that time were hazy, at best, and recovery was slow—made more difficult of course by the fact that the witch had to corral my inner goddess every night lest she go galavanting across the Eighth Seas and leave poor underweight, malnourished me to foot the bill come morning.

What I did remember, however, was immediately asking after the conspicuously absent Neverlanders; once I heard how long I'd been under, it was their fates that had concerned me most. At first, Circe had been reassuring, telling me half-truths like "the last time I saw them they were stable" or "once you're better, I'm sure you can see them." Then, right around the time I actually *was* en route to a full recovery, she told me the truth.

In her defense, I couldn't blame the witch for keeping it to herself for as long as she did.

Because some shit just sounds crazy no matter how you say it.

Apparently, not two days after I'd taken the potion she'd prescribed, Circe's island paradise had welcomed a visitor to its airspace—a flying, sentient island who called herself NeverEden. How said island had passed from Fae to the Titan Realm remained a mystery even to Circe, but the why

239

had been remarkably straightforward: she'd come to collect her ailing citizens. Following a brief negotiation between James and a giant talking hound who'd served as the island's emissary, all three had agreed to return home—especially once it became clear that NeverEden's mere presence was enough to reverse the effects of the illness which plagued Tinkerbell and Tiger Lily. James had thought to bargain on my behalf, as well, but—between needing Circe's care to stay alive and NeverEden's declaration that I had other duties to fulfill—he'd been overruled.

They'd left shortly thereafter, though to where was anyone's guess.

Ironically, Circe had been more shocked by my immediate acceptance of the whole affair than she was by the affair itself—no doubt afraid it would be one of those "you had to be there" moments that would leave me feeling either lied to or bitter. On the contrary, however, I'd been overjoyed by the news; knowing NeverEden was out there somewhere—not to mention the fact that Cathal would be looking after James and the other Neverlanders—was a great relief. One day soon, I swore, I'd track her down and reunite with them all.

But first, I had to go home.

I owed it to my friends, of course, but also to myself; Boston was the place I'd grown up, and no amount of travel—no matter how foreign—could hold a candle next to it in my heart. Now that Ryan was gone, I realized I needed to cherish the things I already had more, and that the people I cared about needed to know just how much I'd missed them. Christoff and his kids, the ever-dependable Othello, broody Scathach, loyal Robin, and Max...perhaps especially Max.

Of course, getting there would be the tricky part. Fortunately, I'd planned ahead by booking a river cruise with a certain boatman on his newly procured Phantom Ship—courtesy of Circe, who'd both retrieved and bespelled it to follow touch commands—in exchange for the ride and the bevy of goods I'd left in his safekeeping with a promise to see them returned as soon as goddessly possible.

Afterwards, of course, I'd focus on tying up some loose ends—like completing my end of the raw deal Freya had saddled me with, or tracking down someone who could help me litigate the territorial dispute between me and my nocturnal neighbor, or perhaps finally taking that trip to St. Louis I'd been putting off for ages. Depending, of course, on whether a certain wizard was *free* to show me around town...or to sneak me into a certain Fight Club. The future was rife with possibilities.

Regardless, if I'd learned anything from my tenure beyond death's door, it was that life—provided you did it right—would *always* be too short, because you could never have enough of something so damned valuable.

Which was why, from now on, I was going to make the most of mine.

Quinn MacKenna returns in 2020...

Turn the page to read a sample of **OBSIDIAN SON** *- Nate Temple Book 1 - or* **BUY ONLINE (It's FREE with a Kindle Unlimited subscription)**. *Nate Temple is a billionaire wizard from St. Louis. He rides a bloodthirsty unicorn and drinks with the Four Horsemen. He even cow-tipped the Minotaur. Once...*

TRY: OBSIDIAN SON (NATE TEMPLE #1)

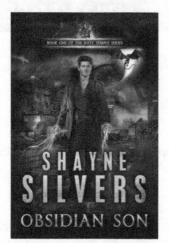

There was no room for emotion in a hate crime. I had to be cold. Heartless. This was just another victim. Nothing more. No face, no name.

Frosted blades of grass crunched under my feet, sounding to my ears like the symbolic glass that one would shatter under a napkin at a Jewish wedding. The noise would have threatened to give away my stealthy advance as I stalked through the moonlit field, but I was no novice and had planned accordingly. Being a wizard, I was able to muffle all sensory evidence with a fine cloud of magic—no sounds, and no smells. Nifty. But if I made the spell much stronger, the anomaly would be too obvious to my prey.

I knew the consequences for my dark deed tonight. If caught, jail time or possibly even a gruesome, painful death. But if I succeeded, the look of fear and surprise in my victim's eyes before his world collapsed around him, it was well worth the risk. I simply couldn't help myself; I had to take him down.

I knew the cops had been keeping tabs on my car, but I was confident that they hadn't followed me. I hadn't seen a tail on my way here but seeing as how they frowned on this kind of thing, I had taken a circuitous route just in case. I was safe. I hoped.

Then my phone chirped at me as I received a text.

I practically jumped out of my skin, hissing instinctively. "Motherf—" I cut off abruptly, remembering the whole stealth aspect of my mission. I was off to a stellar start. I had forgotten to silence the damned phone. *Stupid, stupid, stupid!*

My heart felt like it was on the verge of exploding inside my chest with such thunderous violence that I briefly envisioned a mystifying Rorschach blood-blot that would have made coroners and psychologists drool.

My body remained tense as I swept my gaze over the field, fearing that I had been made. Precious seconds ticked by without any change in my surroundings, and my breathing finally began to slow as my pulse returned to normal. Hopefully, my magic had muted the phone and my resulting outburst. I glanced down at the phone to scan the text and then typed back a quick and angry response before I switched the cursed device to vibrate.

Now, where were we?

I continued on, the lining of my coat constricting my breathing. Or maybe it was because I was leaning forward in anticipation. *Breathe*, I chided myself. *He doesn't know you're here.* All this risk for a book. It had better be worth it.

I'm taller than most, and not abnormally handsome, but I knew how to play the genetic cards I had been dealt. I had shaggy, dirty blonde hair—leaning more towards brown with each passing year—and my frame was thick with well-earned muscle, yet I was still lean. I had once been told that my eyes were like twin emeralds pitted against the golden-brown tufts of my hair—a face like a jewelry box. Of course, that was two bottles of wine into a date, so I could have been a little foggy on her quote. Still, I liked to imagine that was how everyone saw me.

But tonight, all that was masked by magic.

I grinned broadly as the outline of the hairy hulk finally came into view. He was blessedly alone—no nearby sentries to give me away. That was always a risk when performing this ancient rite-of-passage. I tried to keep the grin on my face from dissolving into a maniacal cackle.

My skin danced with energy, both natural and unnatural, as I manipulated the threads of magic floating all around me. My victim stood just ahead, oblivious to the world of hurt that I was about to unleash. Even with his millennia of experience, he didn't stand a chance. I had done this so many times that the routine of it was my only enemy. I lost count of how many times I had been told not to do it again; those who knew declared it *cruel, evil, and sadistic*. But what fun wasn't? Regardless, that wasn't enough to stop me from doing it again. And again. And again.

It was an addiction.

The pungent smell of manure filled the air, latching onto my nostril hairs. I took another step, trying to calm my racing pulse. A glint of gold reflected in the silver moonlight, but my victim remained motionless, hopefully unaware or all was lost. I wouldn't make it out alive if he knew I was here. Timing was everything.

I carefully took the last two steps, a lifetime between each, watching the legendary monster's ears, anxious and terrified that I would catch even so much as a twitch in my direction. Seeing nothing, a fierce grin split my unshaven cheeks. My spell had worked! I raised my palms an inch away from their target, firmly planted my feet, and squared my shoulders. I took one silent, calming breath, and then heaved forward with every ounce of physical strength I could muster. As well as a teensy-weensy boost of magic. Enough to goose him good.

"*MOOO!!!*" The sound tore through the cool October night like an unstoppable freight train. *Thud-splat!* The beast collapsed sideways onto the frosted grass; straight into a steaming patty of cow shit, cow dung, or, if you really wanted to church it up, a Meadow Muffin. But to me, shit is, and always will be, shit.

Cow tipping. It doesn't get any better than that in Missouri.

Especially when you're tipping the *Minotaur*. Capital M. I'd tipped plenty of ordinary cows before, but never the legendary variety.

Razor-blade hooves tore at the frozen earth as the beast struggled to stand, his grunts of rage vibrating the air. I raised my arms triumphantly. "Boo-yah! Temple 1, Minotaur 0!" I crowed. Then I very bravely prepared to protect myself. Some people just couldn't take a joke. *Cruel, evil,* and *sadistic* cow tipping may be, but by hell, it was a *rush.* The legendary beast turned his gaze on me after gaining his feet, eyes ablaze as his body...*shifted* from his bull disguise into his notorious, well-known bipedal form. He unfolded to his full height on two tree trunk-thick legs, his hooves having magically transformed into heavily booted feet. The thick, gold ring dangling from his snotty snout quivered as the Minotaur panted, and his dense, corded muscles contracted over his now human-like chest. As I stared up into those brown eyes, I actually felt sorry...for, well, myself.

"I have killed greater men than you for lesser offense," he growled.

His voice sounded like an angry James Earl Jones—like Mufasa talking to Scar.

"You have shit on your shoulder, Asterion." I ignited a roiling ball of fire in my palm in order to see his eyes more clearly. By no means was it a defensive gesture on my part. It was just dark. Under the weight of his glare, I somehow managed to keep my face composed, even though my fraudulent, self-denial had curled up into the fetal position and started whimpering. I hoped using a form of his ancient name would give me brownie points. Or maybe just not-worthy-of-killing points.

The beast grunted, eyes tightening, and I sensed the barest hesitation. "Nate Temple...your name would look splendid on my already long list of slain idiots." Asterion took a threatening step forward, and I thrust out my palm in warning, my roiling flame blue now.

"You lost fair and square, Asterion. Yield or perish." The beast's shoulders sagged slightly. Then he finally nodded to himself in resignation, appraising me with the scrutiny of a worthy adversary. "Your time comes, Temple, but I will grant you this. You've got a pair of stones on you to rival Hercules."

I reflexively glanced in the direction of the myth's own crown jewels before jerking my gaze away. Some things you simply couldn't un-see. "Well, I won't be needing a wheelbarrow any time soon, but overcompensating today keeps future lower-back pain away."

The Minotaur blinked once, and then he bellowed out a deep, contagious, snorting laughter. Realizing I wasn't about to become a murder statistic, I couldn't help but join in. It felt good. It had been a while since I had allowed myself to experience genuine laughter.

In the harsh moonlight, his bulk was even more intimidating as he towered head and shoulders above me. This was the beast that had fed upon human sacrifices for countless years while imprisoned in Daedalus' Labyrinth in Greece. And all that protein had not gone to waste, forming a heavily woven musculature over the beast's body that made even Mr. Olympia look puny.

From the neck up, he was now entirely bull, but the rest of his body more closely resembled a thickly furred man. But, as shown moments ago, he could adapt his form to his environment, never appearing fully human, but able to make his entire form appear as a bull when necessary. For instance, how he had looked just before I tipped him. Maybe he had been scouting the field for heifers before I had so efficiently killed the mood.

His bull face was also covered in thick, coarse hair—he even sported a long, wavy beard of sorts, and his eyes were the deepest brown I had ever seen. Cow-shit brown. His snout jutted out, emphasizing the golden ring dangling from his glistening nostrils, and both glinted in the luminous glow of the moon. The metal was at least an inch thick and etched with runes of a language long forgotten. Wide, aged ivory horns sprouted from each temple, long enough to skewer a wizard with little effort. He was nude except for a massive beaded necklace and a pair of worn leather boots that were big enough to stomp a size twenty-five imprint in my face if he felt so inclined.

I hoped our blossoming friendship wouldn't end that way. I really did.

Because friends didn't let friends wear boots naked…

Get your copy of OBSIDIAN SON online today!
http://www.shaynesilvers.com/l/38474

If you enjoyed the BLADE or UNDERWORLD movies, turn the page to read a

*sample of **DEVIL'S DREAM**—the first book in the new **SHADE OF DEVIL** series by Shayne Silvers.*
Or get the book ONLINE! http://www.shaynesilvers.com/l/738833

Before the now-infamous Count Dracula ever tasted his first drop of blood, Sorin Ambrogio owned the night. Humanity fearfully called him the Devil...

TRY: DEVIL'S DREAM (SHADE OF DEVIL #1)

God damned me.

He—in his infinite, omnipotent wisdom—declared for all to hear…

Let there be pain…

In the exact center of this poor bastard's soul.

And that merciless smiting woke me from a dead sleep and thrust me into a body devoid of every sensation but blinding agony.

I tried to scream but my throat felt as dry as dust, only permitting me to emit a rasping, whistling hiss that brought on yet *more* pain. My skin burned and throbbed while my bones creaked and groaned with each full-body tremor. My claws sunk into a hard surface beneath me and I was distantly surprised they hadn't simply shattered upon contact.

My memory was an immolated ruin—each fragment of thought merely an elusive fleck of ash or ember that danced through my fog of despair as I struggled to catch one and hold onto it long enough to recall what had brought me to this bleak existence. How I had become this poor, wretched, shell of a man. I couldn't even remember my own *name*; it was all I could do to simply survive this profound horror.

After what seemed an eternity, the initial pain began to slowly ebb, but I quickly realized that it had only triggered a cascade of smaller, more numerous tortures—like ripples caused by a boulder thrown into a pond.

I couldn't find the strength to even attempt to open my crusted eyes, and my abdomen was a solid knot of gnawing hunger so overwhelming that I felt like I was being pulled down into the earth by a lead weight. My fingers tingled and burned so fiercely that I wondered if the skin had been peeled away while I slept. Since they were twitching involuntarily, at least I knew that the muscles and tendons were still attached.

I held onto that sliver of joy, that beacon of hope.

I stubbornly gritted my teeth, but even that slight movement made the skin over my face stretch tight enough to almost tear. I willed myself to relax as I tried to process *why* I was in so much pain, where I was, how I had gotten here, and...*who* I even was? A singular thought finally struck me like an echo of the faintest of whispers, giving me something to latch onto.

Hunger.

I let out a crackling gasp of relief at finally grasping an independent answer of some kind, but I was unable to draw enough moisture onto my tongue to properly swallow. Understanding that I was hungry had seemed to alleviate a fraction of my pain. The answer to at least one question distracted me long enough to allow me to think. And despite my hunger, I felt something tantalizingly delicious slowly coursing down my throat, desperately attempting to alleviate my starvation.

Even though my memory was still enshrouded in fog, I was entirely certain that it was incredibly dangerous for me to feel this hungry.

This...*thirsty*. Dangerous for both myself and anyone nearby. I tried to remember why it was so dangerous but the reason eluded me. Instead, an answer to a different question emerged from my mind like a specter from the mist—and I felt myself begin to smile as a modicum of strength slowly took root deep within me.

"Sorin..." I croaked. My voice echoed, letting me know that I was in an enclosed space of some kind. "My name is Sorin Ambrogio. And I need..." I trailed off uncertainly, unable to finish my own thought.

"Blood," a man's deep voice answered from only a few paces away. "You need more blood."

I hissed instinctively, snapping my eyes open for the first time since waking. I had completely forgotten to check my surroundings, too consumed with my own pain to bother with my other senses. I had been asleep so long that even the air seemed to burn my eyes like smoke, forcing me to blink rapidly. No, the air *was* filled with pungent, aromatic smoke, but not like the smoke from the fires in my—

I shuddered involuntarily, blocking out the thought for some unknown reason.

Beneath the pungent smoke, the air was musty and damp. Through it all, I smelled the delicious, coppery scent of hot, powerful blood.

I had been resting atop a raised stone plinth—almost like a table—in a depthless, shadowy cavern. I appreciated the darkness because any light would have likely blinded me in my current state. I couldn't see the man who had spoken, but the area was filled with silhouettes of what appeared to be tables, crates, and other shapes that could easily conceal him. I focused on my hearing and almost instantly noticed a seductively familiar, *beating* sound.

A noise as delightful as a child's first belly-laugh...

A beautiful woman's sigh as she locked eyes with you for the first time.

The gentle crackling of a fireplace on a brisk, snowy night.

Thump-thump.

Thump-thump.

Thump-thump.

The sound became *everything* and my vision slowly began to sharpen, the room brightening into shades of gray. My pain didn't disappear, but it was swiftly muted as I tracked the sound.

I inhaled deeply, my eyes riveting on a far wall as my nostrils flared, pinpointing the source of the savory perfume and the seductive beating sound. I didn't recall sitting up, but I realized that I was suddenly leaning forward and that the room was continuing to brighten into paler shades of gray, burning away the last of the remaining shadows—despite the fact that there was no actual light. And it grew clearer as I focused on the seductive sound.

Until I finally spotted a man leaning against the far wall. *Thump-thump. Thump-thump. Thump-thump...* I licked my lips ravenously, setting my hands on the cool stone table as I prepared to set my feet on the ground.

Food...

The man calmly lifted his hand and a sharp *clicking* sound suddenly echoed from the walls. The room abruptly flooded with light so bright and unexpected that it felt like my eyes had exploded. Worse, what seemed like a trio of radiant stars was not more than a span from my face—so close that I could feel the direct heat from their flare. I recoiled with a snarl, momentarily forgetting all about food as I shielded my eyes with a hand and prepared to defend myself. I leaned away from the bright lights, wondering why I couldn't smell smoke from the flickering flames. I squinted, watching the man's feet for any indication of movement.

Half a minute went by as my vision slowly began to adjust, and the man didn't even shift his weight—almost as if he was granting me time enough to grow accustomed to the sudden light. Which...didn't make any sense. Hadn't it been an attack? I hesitantly lowered my hand from my face, reassessing the situation and my surroundings.

I stared in wonder as I realized that the orbs were not made of flame, but rather what seemed to be pure light affixed to polished metal stands. Looking directly at them hurt, so I studied them sidelong, making sure to also keep the man in my peripheral vision. He had to be a sorcerer of some kind. Who else could wield pure light without fire?

"Easy, Sorin," the man murmured in a calming baritone. "I can't see as well as you in the dark, but it looked like you were about to do something unnecessarily stupid. Let me turn them down a little."

He didn't wait for my reply, but the room slowly dimmed after another clicking sound.

I tried to get a better look at the stranger—wondering where he had come from, where he had taken me, and who he was. One thing was obvious—he knew magic. "Where did you learn this sorcery?" I rasped, gesturing at the orbs of light.

"Um. Hobby Lobby."

"I've never heard of him," I hissed, coughing as a result of my parched throat.

"I'm not even remotely surprised by that," he said dryly. He extended his other hand and I gasped to see an impossibility—a transparent bag as clear as new glass. And it was *flexible*, swinging back and forth like a bulging coin purse or a clear water-skin. My momentary wonder at the magical material evaporated as I recognized the crimson liquid *inside* the bag.

Blood.

He lobbed it at me underhanded without a word of warning. I hissed as I desperately—and with exceeding caution—caught it from the air lest it fall and break open. I gasped as the clear bag of blood settled into my palms and, before I consciously realized it, I tore off the corner with my fangs, pressed it to my lips, and squeezed the bag in one explosive, violent gesture. The ruby fluid gushed into my mouth and over my face, dousing my almost forgotten pain as swiftly as a bucket of water thrown on hot coals.

I felt my eyes roll back into my skull and my body shuddered as I lost my balance and fell from the stone table. I landed on my back but I was too overwhelmed to care as I stretched out my arms and legs. I groaned in rapture, licking at my lips like a wild animal. The ruby nectar was a living serpent of molten oil as it slithered down into my stomach, nurturing and healing me almost instantly. It was the most wonderful sensation I could imagine—almost enough to make me weep.

Like a desert rain, my parched tongue and throat absorbed the blood so quickly and completely that I couldn't even savor the heady flavor. This wasn't a joyful feast; this was survival, a necessity. My body guzzled it, instantly using the liquid to repair the damage, pain, and the cloud of fog that had enshrouded me.

I realized that I was laughing. The sound echoed into the vast stone space like rolling thunder.

Because I had remembered something else.

The world's First Vampire was *back*.

And he was still *very* hungry.

Get the full book ONLINE! http://www.shaynesilvers.com/l/738833

Check out Shayne's other books. He's written a few without Cameron helping him.
Some of them are marginally decent—easily a 4 out of 10.

MAKE A DIFFERENCE

Reviews are the most powerful tools in our arsenal when it comes to getting attention for our books. Much as we'd like to, we don't have the financial muscle of a New York publisher.

But we do have something much more powerful and effective than that, and it's something that those publishers would kill to get their hands on.

A committed and loyal bunch of readers.

Honest reviews of our books help bring them to the attention of other readers.

If you've enjoyed this book, we would be very grateful if you could spend just five minutes leaving a review on our book's Amazon page.

Thank you very much in advance.

ACKNOWLEDGMENTS

From Cameron:

I'd like to thank Shayne, for paving the way in style. Kori, for an introduction that would change my life. My three wonderful sisters, for showing me what a strong, independent woman looks and sounds like. And, above all, my parents, for—literally—everything.

From Shayne (the self-proclaimed prettiest one):

Team Temple and the Den of Freaks on Facebook have become family to me. I couldn't do it without die-hard readers like them.

I would also like to thank you, the reader. I hope you enjoyed reading *BRIMSTONE KISSS* as much as we enjoyed writing it. Be sure to check out the two crossover series in the TempleVerse: **The Nate Temple Series** and the **Feathers and Fire Series**.

And last, but definitely not least, I thank my wife, Lexy. Without your support, none of this would have been possible.

ABOUT CAMERON O'CONNELL

Cameron O'Connell is a Jack-of-All-Trades and Master of Some.

He writes The Phantom Queen Diaries, a series in The TempleVerse, about Quinn MacKenna, a mouthy black magic arms dealer trading favors in Boston. All she wants? A round-trip ticket to the Fae realm...and maybe a drink on the house.

A former member of the United States military, a professional model, and English teacher, Cameron finds time to write in the mornings after his first cup of coffee...and in the evenings after his thirty-seventh. Follow him, and the TempleVerse founder, Shayne Silvers, online for all sorts of insider tips, giveaways, and new release updates!

Get Down with Cameron Online

facebook.com/Cameron-OConnell-788806397985289

amazon.com/author/cameronoconnell

bookbub.com/authors/cameron-o-connell

twitter.com/thecamoconnell

instagram.com/camoconnellauthor

goodreads.com/cameronoconnell

ABOUT SHAYNE SILVERS

Shayne is a man of mystery and power, whose power is exceeded only by his mystery...

He currently writes the Amazon Bestselling **Nate Temple** Series, which features a foul-mouthed wizard from St. Louis. He rides a bloodthirsty unicorn, drinks with Achilles, and is pals with the Four Horsemen.

He also writes the Amazon Bestselling **Feathers and Fire** Series—a second series in the TempleVerse. The story follows a rookie spell-slinger named Callie Penrose who works for the Vatican in Kansas City. Her problem? Hell seems to know more about her past than she does.

He coauthors **The Phantom Queen Diaries**—a third series set in The TempleVerse—with Cameron O'Connell. The story follows Quinn MacKenna, a mouthy black magic arms dealer in Boston. All she wants? A round-trip ticket to the Fae realm...and maybe a drink on the house.

He also writes the **Shade of Devil Series**, which tells the story of Sorin Ambrogio—the world's FIRST vampire. He was put into a magical slumber by a Native American Medicine Man when the Americas were first discovered by Europeans. Sorin wakes up after five-hundred years to learn that his protege, Dracula, stole his reputation and that no one has ever even heard of Sorin Ambrogio. The streets of New York City will run with blood as Sorin reclaims his legend.

Shayne holds two high-ranking black belts, and can be found writing in a coffee shop, cackling madly into his computer screen while pounding shots of espresso. He's hard at work on the newest books in the TempleVerse—You can find updates on new releases or chronological reading order on the next page, his website, or any of his social media accounts. **Follow him online for all sorts of groovy goodies, giveaways, and new release updates:**

Get Down with Shayne Online
www.shaynesilvers.com
info@shaynesilvers.com

f facebook.com/shaynesilversfanpage
a amazon.com/author/shaynesilvers
BB bookbub.com/profile/shayne-silvers
O instagram.com/shaynesilversofficial
Y twitter.com/shaynesilvers
g goodreads.com/ShayneSilvers

BOOKS BY THE AUTHORS

CHRONOLOGY: All stories in the TempleVerse are shown in chronological order on the following page

PHANTOM QUEEN DIARIES

(Set in the TempleVerse)

by Cameron O'Connell & Shayne Silvers

COLLINS (Prequel novella #0 in the 'LAST CALL' anthology)

WHISKEY GINGER

COSMOPOLITAN

OLD FASHIONED

MOTHERLUCKER (Novella #3.5 in the 'LAST CALL' anthology)

DARK AND STORMY

MOSCOW MULE

WITCHES BREW

SALTY DOG

SEA BREEZE

HURRICANE

BRIMSTONE KISS

NATE TEMPLE SERIES

(Main series in the TempleVerse)

by Shayne Silvers

FAIRY TALE - FREE prequel novella #0 for my subscribers

OBSIDIAN SON

BLOOD DEBTS

GRIMM

SILVER TONGUE

BEAST MASTER

BEERLYMPIAN (Novella #5.5 in the 'LAST CALL' anthology)

TINY GODS

DADDY DUTY (Novella #6.5)

WILD SIDE

WAR HAMMER

NINE SOULS

HORSEMAN

LEGEND

KNIGHTMARE

ASCENSION

CARNAGE

FEATHERS AND FIRE SERIES

(Also set in the TempleVerse)

by Shayne Silvers

UNCHAINED

RAGE

WHISPERS

ANGEL'S ROAR

MOTHERLUCKER (Novella #4.5 in the 'LAST CALL' anthology)

SINNER

BLACK SHEEP

GODLESS

ANGHELLIC

CHRONOLOGICAL ORDER: TEMPLEVERSE

FAIRY TALE (TEMPLE PREQUEL)

OBSIDIAN SON (TEMPLE 1)

BLOOD DEBTS (TEMPLE 2)

GRIMM (TEMPLE 3)

SILVER TONGUE (TEMPLE 4)

ANGHELLIC (FEATHERS...8)

Made in United States
North Haven, CT
23 July 2023

39411662R00168